Apprehension Began to Worm in Alf's Belly. . . .

"Perhaps the Rainbow Serpent is an intelligent computer," the Russian general said quietly, "perfectly preserved until now by the Vault's force fields."

"We don't know for sure that they all died on Selene Alpha," the astronaut replied. "They could have fled to the safety of suspended animation. NASA is working on it. We know they're from the stars—artificial hibernation is almost a prerequisite. Believe me, Alf, it's feasible that one or more of the aliens have returned to consciousness in the Vault and are simply gathering strength and information before they choose to emerge."

"To conquer the world?" Alf asked ironically. But his mind presented the loathsome image of a giant snake coiled on a throne—an image from childhood—gorged on human meat, red eyes gleaming in the dark with dreadful intelligence. . . .

Damien Broderick

A Time Opera

PUBLISHED BY POCKET BOOKS NEW YORK

Another *Original* publication of POCKET BOOKS

POCKET BOOKS, a Simon & Schuster division of
GULF & WESTERN CORPORATION
1230 Avenue of the Americas, New York, N.Y. 10020

ISBN: 0-671-83150-X

First Pocket Books printing November, 1980

10 9 8 7 6 5 4 3 2 1

Interior design by Cathy Carucci.

Printed in the U.S.A.

FOR
THE RABBIT

The melodramatic imagination is, then, perhaps a way of perceiving and imagining the spiritual in a world where there is no longer any clear idea of the sacred, no generally accepted societal moral imperatives, where the body of the ethical has become a sort of *deus absconditus* which must be sought for, posited, brought into man's existence through exercise of the spiritualist imagination. . . . The melodramatic mode of utterance is a victory over the repression and censorship of the social reality principle, a release of psychic energy by the articulation of the unsayable. One might say that the gothic quest for renewed contact with the numinous, the supernatural, the occult forces in the universe, leads into the moral self.

—PETER BROOKS

Contents

ONE:

THE CYCLONE'S EDGE

jumble of stone and boulders reached forty meters into the bright sky. If you looked too intently at it, it seemed to shudder.

Alf shifted his itching arm, opened and closed one hand on the bouncing vehicle's steering wheel, tugged at his singlet where it stuck to chest and back in a damp relief-map of the Burrkan initiation scars festooning his upper body. "Christ, it's *bloody* hot," he grumbled. Even the conditioned air was tepid. The temperature gauge flickered over again into the red. Inside the wounded radiator, with its poached-egg sealant, the water was boiling.

He glanced again at the immobile boy. With sudden peevishness he thought: Why don't I save my breath? The child was like some eldritch radio telescope, attuned only to messages from the empyrean, broadcasting nothing but an empty carrier signal.

At once he experienced a rush of remorse. It was hardly the child's fault. Besides, his analogy was faulty. Something moved in the boy's curious brain. Perhaps Mouse gamboled there in an interior landscape of vivid flowers, drifting on his toes like the fey autistic children of his special school.

There were no flowers in the Tanami desert. With the minimal exception of a few hardy, stunted saltbushes, some patches of lichen clinging to the rock, no living thing was visible. It was plain why white men had not bothered combing the place. The Land Rover's sturdy wheels thrummed and thumped on broken stone. Alf let The Beast roll back a few meters to a level stretch of rock and cut the ignition.

For a moment he closed his eyes, pressing forward on the steering wheel. His irritation with the boy, he knew, was a bid to deny his own central emotion. Up there, in that grotesque pile of ancient rubbish, was a dinosaur fossil. If his luck held. Alf Dean felt a tremor in his muscles: dread, intoxication. You're waiting for me, Kung-manggur, he thought. He was close to a state of superstitious invocation, like a particle physicist calling up the spirit of a favorite hypothesis in the gigavolt cracking of a nuclear proton. Be there, you son-of-a-bitch. The Road-maker, one of his filthy old teachers had named it. They had crouched in the dust, and the man had doodled symbols old before Sumer. The Rainbow Serpent, the BabyMaker. Alf raised his dark head and stared into the explosive light. You bastard, he thought, quivering. I'll nail you to the wall.

He climbed out of the vehicle and stretched his cramped limbs. From every side heat thrashed him, bright from myriad fragments of rock crystal. Even through his heavy boots the scorched earth burned at his flesh. Hastily, he reached back inside for his bushman's hat, for the protection of a shirt.

Abraded desolation. In the early Cretaceous, a hundred million years before, all this pitiless waste was sunk beneath vast seas. How astounding. And long before that, during the Lower Ordovician. Half a billion years. Yet the land endured, Alf thought. It persisted to be bleached and scarified, not once, but many times. The time before the Dreaming.

"Poor black bastards," he muttered. His mouth quirked at the unconscious posture of ironic objectivity. His own broad nostrils, thick chiseled lips, wavy hair were pure Australian Aborigine. Sometimes he thought he detected a trace of the Buramoingu dialect in the crisp phonemes of his bourgeoise accent. Unhealthy fantasy. He swiped uselessly at the blowflies blustering at his eyes. Even here. God*damn* it! he thought. You'd imagine science could do something definitive about the great Australian pest, and bugger the ecological ramifications, if there are any.

"It really is the arse-hole of the universe," he said aloud. After a moment the boy turned in his seat and smiled his shy, winning smile. He hears us, Alf thought. Dr. Fish is right; Mouse responds. In ways we cannot comprehend, true, but he feels the love, the giving we offer him. Even without Fish's pompous apologetic jargon of "socializing facilitation," I'd talk to him, he thought. He opened the boy's door and squeezed his shoulder.

Mouse scrambled out beside him and peered in dazzlement at the cliff face, the shadowed caverns. "Caves," he said with excitement. "Bunyip."

"You bet." Alf grinned. "But we probably won't find anything much today. Like to help me get out the rucksacks?" Today, tomorrow. How utterly meaningless such terms must be for the child. One of the deficits of his condition, as Fish had been at pains to stress, was a failure to "bind time," to perceive sequences of cause and effect. Still, the boy seemed genuinely to be anticipating the prospect of the caves. Carefully, Alf rechecked the contents of his rucksack, examined the first-aid kit, tried the flashlight batteries. He locked The Beast and hoisted the rucksack on his back.

They stood for a moment gazing up at the ancient cliff. The vaguest hiss of dry wind from the desert. Slight movements at the edge of audibility, as stone expanded and shifted under the sun's baking onslaught. Yet that nearly total silence was itself a kind of sound: a vast distant hum which filled the head without touching the ear. It was a presence of solitude more profound than Alf Dean had ever known, even in the open country to the north. Strangeness touched his spirit; he understood why even the nomads who had dwelled in this desert had found the place sacred and terrible—as sacred, perhaps, as Uluru, the prodigious stone monolith which Alf's adopted white culture called Ayers Rock, six hundred kilometers to the south. There, the rains of the Cretaceous had returned. Ayers Rock was drowning in a freak of storm weather which cynics attributed to the supposed presence of an experimental military base. Once again, the blacks had been hounded away heedlessly from their cathedrals. Alf grunted with sympathetic, impotent anger.

And yet . . . that was exactly what he proposed to do himself. Tear at the abandoned buttresses of a faith which had been stable for tens of millennia and now was all but dead in any case. He would not merely denounce the mystery of the Rainbow Serpent, but would prove it no more than a misconception of savages, a sacred delusion built on the ossified bones of an extinct reptile, a dinosaur from the age of floods. But nothing was ever that transparent. Neither the wellsprings of the numinous, nor the impulse of a man's motives.

Alf Dean felt his obsession coil and tighten in his belly. The Ngularrnga tribe, from which his natural mother had been abducted to the racist compounds of the Darwin Mission, called the BabyMaker Wedarragama. Yet neither the Ngularrnga, nor the Murinbata of the Daly River reserve where Alf had done his graduate work, nor any other of the hundreds of linguistically and culturally discrete tribes possessed rites exclusively honoring the Rainbow Serpent. The Earth Mother had the grandeur of Kunapipi, a corroboree cycle steeped in cosmic and mundane significance, a liturgy patterning six months of each year in its ornate embrace. But not Wedarragama.

Merely his face and his name, inscribed on stone and bark and men's memories. . . .

Here, though, in this small section of the Tanami desert, there had been Serpent rites. The tribe was gone, smashed by disease, drunkenness, and the theft of dignity, and their singular rite had vanished into extinction with them.

He moved suddenly, clapping the boy on the back. "Come on, kid, let's go. Before we spook each other."

Mouse uttered a little cry of delight and bounded ahead to clamber up the dusty slope. Seeing his agile grace, Alf remembered the group of damaged children at the Monash center, bouncing like spider monkeys on trampolines, wholly in the dimensions of tactual and haptic space.

The first four shallow openings they found led nowhere. Wind had scoured indentations, and shifting pressures had split stone—even in this most stable region of a stable continent—but there were no promising caves. The hints Alf had compiled in field work and archival research suggested a series of deep caverns, cutting far into the cliff. He halted briefly to catch his breath, sipping sparingly from the water container.

The boy looked back piercingly. "Tired old man," he said without scorn or impudence. He skidded down the incline, dust and pebbles tumbling ahead of him. Alf allowed him a modest drink. Mouse sighed with pleasure and sat on a rock, leaning his head against his uncle's knee.

How normal he looks, Alf thought. Healthy, even strong for his age. The ruin was hidden inside the boy's curly head: neural nets incomplete, transmitter proteins deranged and malformed. If Fish was right.

Alf spied a series of almost invisible gouges in the sandstone. "See these marks, Mouse?" The boy's fingers drifted across the impressions. "I'm almost certain they're the remnants of a religious design. Must be immensely old. Maybe we're on the right track." He had seen just such marks in the Ngama and Lukiri caves. By custom, ceremonial insignia were located out of view of the uninitiated. He peered at them searchingly. Nothing remotely like the Rainbow Serpent motif.

But he's up there somewhere, Alf told himself. His huge palpable bones are locked into stone, even if his acolytes are dispersed and lost.

They resumed their climb. Dust caked in messy paste

on sweating skin. Mouse began to forge ahead again. Once, the boy jumped back in alarm from a flash of blue-gray scales. It was only a lizard, startled from its nest into the sun.

Because he was above and ahead, it was Mouse who found the entrance.

The cavern's jaws were partially hidden by two great slabs of rock, positioned with enormous effort hundreds or even thousands of years earlier to forbid entry. Time had allowed one of the slabs to slip grindingly aside. Alf saw the boy wriggle through the narrow gap.

"Goddamn it, get back here!"

Convulsively, he propelled himself to the entrance and stared into void, jamming his sunglasses into a pocket of his shirt. Mouse stood motionless just inside the opening, head cocked to one side as though listening; the flashlight was clutched against his chest. Alf seized it, thumbed on the beam. "Christ knows what's in there, Mouse."

The black place was a horizontal cone, extending wider and deeper the farther back it went. Where the pale electric beam splashed the far wall, it made the ancient drawings dance: red, white, smoky yellow.

"Paintings," Mouse stated confidently, and started toward them with the stride of a statesman. In furious alarm Alf caught him, spun him around.

"Bloody stay *put!*" The boy flinched. "Look, you know I don't like shouting at you. We'll both view the nice pictures *after* I've checked."

It was impossible to know if the boy understood, but he stayed where he was, with that indefinable quivering in his tense body, while Alf moved away. Testing his footing with each step, the anthropologist sent the circle of light darting from wall to floor to roof, probing for fractures which might be triggered by some minor unwary movement. He returned to the mote-dancing blur of the entrance.

"Okay, kid."

The paintings were a sour anticlimax. Alf studied them closely for several minutes, checking absently to ensure that Mouse did not damage them with his floating fingers. He unsnapped his Leica, took a series of flashlit exposures.

"Bad luck," he said. "Couple of centuries old at most, very similar to other recent work." They were undeniably of sacred ceremonial significance, but he failed to detect any reference to the Rainbow Serpent. "I don't see why they went to the trouble of blocking up the cave." Raspingly, he rubbed at his jaw.

Mouse gazed at his uncle's face in the wan light of the flashlight. His arm wafted up in the direction of the entrance. "Old," he said. "Old." His high voice reverberated.

"Yeah. Old's right. Maybe a later bunch did all this. Let's see if there's any more to this place."

Slowly they paced the cavern's chipped perimeter, beam cavorting ahead. The curved wall was marred by splits and vertical crevices. Mouse pressed at the raddled surfaces with spread hands, as though his dreaming mind expected a secret door to open, admit them to some world more clarified and radiant than he'd ever known. Sorry, kid, Alf thought. We never got around to inventing the hinged door.

Mouse gave a little shriek.

"Moved," he said.

Alf was instantly beside him. One of the great splits in the rockwall trembled ever so slightly at the boy's touch. Alf brought his flashlight close to the vertical fault line. Carefully, he pressed against the edge. For a brief moment it felt as if a great portal had begun to open. He chided himself for his fantasy, but steadily increased his pressure. This is ridiculous, he told himself. I'm responding to the suggestion of an imbecile.

And the solid stone swung into deeper blackness, pivoted at top and base, swung with massive noiseless force until it stood at right angles to the rockwall proper.

"Jesus!" The anthropologist leaped back, dragging the child with him. He stared incredulously at the new opening. A door, he thought, astounded. The slab was perfectly balanced. Hewn with flint tools. The human effort contained in the concealed entrance staggered him.

He shined his flashlight along the rock tunnel. Mouse crouched next to him for a better view. Unlike the pivoted door, the tunnel was plainly a natural formation. Like the cavern, it was evidently of the variety created by abrasion rather than solution; it possessed none of the outlandish lime carbonate deposits, the icy crystal stalactites of the notable tourist attractions on the distant Australian east coast. It sloped gently upward, continuing back into the stony hill until the flashlight beam was lost. Apparently there had been no subsidence, no crash of rock from above to block the tunnel. The air was dry and choking.

"By God," Alf said softly, "I do believe we've found it."

Several meters in from the entrance the rock was vivid with inlaid, engraved patterns. Alf knew them at once, though they differed in detail from the Murinbata diagrams he was most familiar with. Here were "X-ray" portraits of black hunters, bones and principal organs sketched with conventional abstraction within the outlines of their flesh. Here were kangaroos, perentie goannas, lily roots—the Lesser Dreamings, the totems. And here, in its bold, blatant glory, was the Rainbow Serpent himself, the old BabyMaker, the FireStealer, the Whirlwind Man, his great eyes huge as an owl's, his skull radiant with spokes of light flamboyant as any Amerind chieftain's feathered headdress, the sinuous double outline of his body with its tiny vestigial limbs, its bifurcate tail. . . .

"It's a warning," Alf said at last. "Initiates Only. Do Not Pass Go. Here—"—he laughed foolishly, the tension of discovery gusting from him—"—Be Dragons! The dinosaur fossil must be embedded farther up the tunnel."

Mouse smiled angelically, and tugged at his sleeve. "See the bunyip."

Alf sobered. "Not just yet, old son. I don't trust that—"

But Mouse had darted past, dashed several meters up the tunnel. The boy stopped dead, waiting placidly.

"Fuck it, Mouse!" Fists clenched in a spasm of dread, Alf stepped in after him. "You haven't got the sense of a mouse. Get back here."

Somehow the boy had been slipping into the absolute blackness as Alf advanced with the skittering light. As the anthropologist lunged, he jumped away and began to run on his toes.

Alf hurled himself in pursuit, shouting with useless anger. The light swerved like some mad white moth. Their footsteps clattered and crashed. Stale musty air stung Alf's throat.

The boy kept running, knocking against rough stone outcroppings. The tunnel turned abruptly, diverted by a seam of harder stone. Alf smashed bruisingly, careened off, and the flashlight spun to the ground. Raging, he retrieved it, blundered on. Mouse loomed. His hand came down with harsh force on the boy's shoulder.

"Can't I trust you for a moment?" The child's blue eyes, struck by flashlight, filled his gaze like the sparks of glimmering stars. "Haven't you learned anything at that place? How—"

And he stared over the boy's muscular shoulder, releasing his shirt. Phosphor glow had entered the darkness. Head ringing with confusion, Alf was captivated and aghast. A great rectangular metal frame stood at the tunnel's sealed end. Soft violet light pulsed like a living membrane within the burnished metal bars.

Vaguely he heard Mouse say, without resentment, "Nice. Pretty, Alf."

Violet intensified, fled through dazzling blue, green, brilliant yellow. It could not be there. They were hundreds of meters into a sun-scorched hill in northern Australia, scores of kilometers from the nearest human beings, many hundreds from industrial civilization. It's a movie set, he thought, absurdly. The base of the thing was embedded in thick dust. It's *old,* he told himself.

He stared back to Mouse and the shock became too much to sustain. He began to laugh, great yells and howls of mirth; the boy joined him with high, beautiful peals; they leaned against one another, pounding ineffectually with loose fists, and Alf's laughter became shrill. Mouse stopped laughing, withdrew himself delicately, and tugged at Alf's arm until they both sat, legs sprawled in front of them, on the cold dusty ground. Alf leaned against rock, wiped his streaming eyes, gasped for breath.

"Sorry," Mouse said.

"Yeah." Alf blew his nose noisily; he was trembling. "I'll bet you are, you willful little bastard. But tell me, great explorer—what the fuck *is* it?"

They stared in silence at the pulsing golden light. After a moment Mouse said, "Bunyip?"

"Bunyip's right. Jesus." He climbed to his feet but maintained a decent distance from the impossible, extraordinarily lovely object. One thing was patent: if any Australian Aboriginal tribe had built the thing, Alf might as well tear up his doctorate and start from scratch, along with the whole Anthropology Department.

This is the Rainbow Serpent, he told himself incredulously. Origin of a myth so old that it has no living relevance, if you judge relevance by continuing ritual. Back to the archaic Dreaming. The source and ground of reality. His thoughts skidded sideways. The tribes employ the English word "dreaming" for *ngakumal* and *ngoiguminggi,* their totems and totem-sites, but that's an adaptation to the language of their conquerors. They never use *nin,* the word for true dreaming sleep. Yet the borrowed elision was superbly deft. The dream-experience, after all, is recognized by them as part of the continuum of authentic reality. Agentive and prophetic, he thought, recalling Professor Stanner's monograph. An ontological embodiment of the entire totemic universe. The Dreaming. The wily old phenomenologists, he thought admiringly.

Fear started to break in again through his barriers of abstraction. This brilliantly illuminated frame before him was a machine, he knew. A device planted by visitors from the stars, presumably, Christ knew how many thousands of years earlier. It's homeostatic, he thought. We triggered it by coming in here. But what does it *do?* His vanished cousins had placed signs of prohibition at the entrance to the doubly sealed tunnel. Skull and bones on a bottle of lethal poison.

Silently, yellow radiance rippled in hypnotic moiré. Abruptly the field of color turned pure dazzling white. The light vanished. And they were looking *through* the grid at a flight of steps which started at a slightly lower elevation than the cavern floor and extended up out of sight.

Alf walked forward a meter, stopped, shook his head. He moved right, left. He lit a cigarette.

"This is fantastic," he mumbled. "Three-dimensional display. A hologram. You can actually see into the picture. Why would it show us *steps,* for Christ's sake?"

With great assurance Mouse said, "For climbing." Alf grinned at him. A breeze ruffled the boy's light, fine hair. "Wind."

Skin crawled on the anthropologist's scarred back. "It's just blowing in from outside. Up the tunnel."

Blue eyes gazed at him. Mouse twinkled his fingers. "Smoke."

Oh, my God, Alf thought. He's right. The streamer of smoke from his cigarette was blowing into the grid. No, he told himself. It's an optical effect. Just what you'd expect with holograms. But he trod slowly to within a meter of the grid, watched the smoke drift gently between the metal bars. Dry-mouthed, he took a match from the box and threw it toward the grid.

The match sailed through the bars, fell on the third step, bounced, lay there.

Wiping his sweating face, Alf backed carefully away from the device and squatted before it. "We're in this up to our necks, kiddo," he said. "It's an interstellar artifact. Or maybe it's the remnant of some primeval human civilization, so old there's no other trace left of it. No, that's nonsense. Mr. von Daniken will be pleased. No wonder the locals were scared shitless of the place."

Teleportation, he thought. This is Captain Cook, or was it Kook? Kirk? Beam me up to the Transporter Room. Aye, aye, Captain.

Maybe the stairs were not even on Earth. In for a penny, he told himself, in for a pound. But the logic fell apart on that. Presumably the air was identical on both sides, though the pressure over there must be slightly lower. Even so, there'd be some diffusion. And we'd be choking on methane, he concluded, or whatever vile gas they breathed. The odds against the atmosphere of another world matching ours were overwhelming. So it's probably somewhere else on this planet. Where? Tibet? Why hasn't it been found?

Alf knew suddenly that he was going to climb through it. All caution was lost in the unarguable necessity of seeing at once where the steps led. He turned to his charge.

"Mouse, I want you to listen very carefully. You're going to do exactly what I say. Right?" The boy gazed back gravely. Oh, Jesus, this is shameful, Alf thought. "Now I want you to sit right here without a squeak. I'll go as far as the top of the stairs. Then I'm coming straight down and we'll head for home. The experts can do all the dirty work on your little discovery. We'll watch the explorations on TV, from the comfort of our living room. Okay? Not one step, or you'll never come with me on another trip."

The boy nodded compliantly. Alf slipped the straps of his rucksack from his shoulders, handed Mouse the flashlight for its emblematic comfort, and strode back to the grid. I must be insane, he thought. Sweat covered his body. Very cautiously, he stepped across the bar buried in the rock floor, moved into the other place, and looked to either side. He glanced back, grinned at Mouse, and began to mount the steps.

Like a broken bottle in the guts, then, ripping up mercilessly into his sternum, the pain opened his mouth in a bellow of uncontrollable terror.

2. Central Australia

The defective child sees his uncle step across the grid's bar, glance from side to side, and mount the stairs. Something strange occurs. The sound of his footsteps is gone. He watches as Alf turns with a look of startled horror and throws his arms wide with a terrible silent scream. The sunglasses fly from Alf's shirt pocket, clatter noiselessly on the lowest step.

Clutching his chest, his face, the man falls to his knees like a puppet with its strings cut, thuds sideways down the steps. He lies motionless at the bottom, breathing with great silent gasps.

The boy blinks, drops the flashlight in fright, hesitates, and runs forward, skidding on the dusty rock floor, bursts between the bars of the grid and drops to his knees beside his uncle. In the instant he passes the gate's invisible barrier, Alf's harsh, ragged gasps become audible. The air is fine; it has a crisp tang.

"Oh. Oh. Oh," says the boy. He heaves at the man's bulk, tries to lever one of Alf's limp arms across his shoulder, drags him toward the gate. Behind a grid of metal bars embedded, on this side, in a huge blank wall of mottled marble, he sees the cavern. Staggering, he hoists Alf up and virtually hurls them both at the gap.

His nose and forehead impact, ringingly, on nothingness. A savage jolt bruises the arm trapped between Alf's sliding body and the steel-hard transparent barrier.

Mouse lets his uncle drop again on the lowest step, turns, and smashes at the resilient air with his fists. A meter away, the rucksack leans in the dust, a length of rope spilling from it. Something prevents him from reaching it. He abandons the attempt.

Alf, when he turns back to him, is unconscious and choking, wheezing horribly. Mouse sobs, and shakes him. "Wake up. Bad boy." But Alf lies bent, his black skin bloodless.

Mouse stands. He cannot return to the cavern; there is another direction. He sprints to the top of the steps.

A vast, dimly lit space extends before him at the top. It is like the interior of a gigantic box. The chamber seems quite empty except for the white sphere positioned in the center of the enormous floor.

Nothing moves. The place is absolutely quiet. He glances back down at his uncle. Alf's breathing has eased, but he lies motionless at the foot of the steps, face contorted.

A faint, distant scraping echoes from the shadowed depths of the chamber. Poised on his toes, Mouse searches the gloom. Still there is nothing but the white sphere, an enormous billiard ball, perfect and unmarked. Its bulk hides much of the farther wall.

Mouse takes one slow step, and then another, into the immense space. He begins to walk more briskly toward the sphere. His lips part, and he sings a song that Dr. Fish has taught him:

"I had a little froggy—"

The sound of his voice is lost in the huge silence.

A wave of dizziness sweeps through him. He stops, clutching his head. The moment he is still, the vertigo is gone. He takes another step, and the chamber spins.

Behind the sphere's hypnotic bulk, voices sound faintly. Mouse retreats, cupping his hands around his mouth and yelling at the top of his voice into the emptiness: "Help! Alf sick!"

Echoes boomed in the huge stillness. Crouching slightly, the boy waits. He hears a babble of male voices, a distant clatter of running feet.

A deep, harsh voice demands: "Who's there? Come out from behind there with your hands up. We have the zone covered with a machinegun."

"Sick!" he yells back, staring at the great white egg. He stays where he is.

"Shit, it's a kid!" someone says in astonishment. There is a gabble of argument farther off, and the first voice yells, "I know it's impossible, Sarge, but I tell you it's a kid, and he's right in there in the middle of the fucking lethal zone! Hey, son," the man shouts, "stick close to the wall and make your way around to us! Whatever you do, keep away from that white globe in the middle of the floor."

Mouse runs back to the smooth, mottled-marble wall of the chamber, cutting across at an angle, and begins to circle toward the voices. His dizziness is gone; there is in its place a kind of hum, a deep vibration singing in his bones, a sense of awesome power which could tear him to ribbons if he makes the wrong move.

Past the point where the bulge of the sphere has obscured his view of the men, he sees them standing framed in a great jagged opening which has been blasted from the other side through the wall of the chamber. They stay well back from the edge; nobody comes forward to help him. He reaches one corner of the chamber, runs the hundred-meter width of the huge box, starts along the wall to the pile of rubble lying at the base of the hole. The air begins to stink now of grease, sweaty human bodies, strange chemicals.

Mouse reaches the heap of broken stone, breathing hard, and looks up at the three men in gray uniforms who loom above him. One holds a sub-machinegun; it is pointed at his chest. The boy cringes, and his hands move jerkily in the air.

"For Christ's sake, Corporal!" says a tall crewcut man with three stripes on his arm. "Put the gun down. You're terrifying the boy." He swings back to Mouse. "Relax, son, we're not going to hurt you. It's just that we weren't expecting you." The third man sniggers nervously. The first ignores him and adds, mildly, "We're rather interested in finding out how you got here."

He is unfolding a rope ladder as he speaks, and he drops one end over the edge. "Come on up; we'll fix you a cup of coffee. There'll be a few questions, but you don't have anything to fear."

The boy clambers up over lumps of chipped marble, dust puffing at his feet, making him cough. He seizes the ladder and climbs nimbly the remaining meters to the edge of the hole. The crewcut man helps him into a broad tunnel that extends back from the opening.

"Alf," Mouse says urgently. His eyes dart in distress. "Sick." Abruptly, he bursts into tears and tugs at the man's arm, attempting to draw him back over the edge.

"Jesus," one of them says, "it's a fucking dummy."

The sergeant rounds on him furiously. "Shut up! He's scared piss-less. Another word from you, Private, and you'll be spending your next rest break down here." He turns back to Mouse. "Who's Alf?" he asks, acutely. "Are you saying there's someone else in there, someone who's hurt?"

Tears running unheeded down his cheeks, the boy nods. "Help," he says imploringly.

The sergeant regards him uncomfortably. "I'm sorry, son, there's no way we can help him. Fact is, you're the only person who's ever been in the Sphere zone without collapsing inside thirty seconds. There's something about the place—a defensive field, the scientists call it. The only way to help Alf is to come with us and tell us how you got in there."

"You're wasting your time, Sarge," says the one with the machinegun. "It's like Steinmetz says—the kid's a moron. Let's get him back to base. This place gives me the creeps."

Blindly, Mouse spins and runs to the edge of the man-made opening. The sergeant darts forward to stop him, but the boy is too agile. He slides over the edge, clings for a moment, drops into the mound of dust and rock. A sharp fragment of stone slices into his leg as he rolls, and gravel skins his hands and knees. On his feet again, he skids down the pile of rubble to the surface, gazes briefly back up at the cursing soldier.

He starts his run across the chamber. The voice of the crewcut man rings after him. "Come back, you crazy kid! The second time in *kills* you!"

Again a wave of vertigo strikes him. He staggers. He begins running parallel to the wall, retracing the path he'd followed to the opening.

Alf still lies sprawled at the foot of the steps. Mouse hurls himself at the grid, beating at the invisible barrier with his bleeding fists. It remains as unyielding as metal. He goes back to his uncle, grasps him under the arms, and starts tugging him up the steps.

The boy is physically healthy and strong for his age, but he has to proceed in stages, each step a new burst of energy and effort that leaves him gasping. Dizziness comes and goes in waves; streamers of fire are lancing in his head. Alf groans, but remains torpid. The man's back thuds against the steps bruisingly with each heave upward.

They reach the top. Mouse sits down for a moment, the muscles in his arms trembling, his breath coming in great gulps. Beyond, the Sphere sucks at his eyes. It is huge, solitary, vibrant with some immense leashed power. With an effort he turns away, looks at Alf, places his grazed palms on the man's face. Sick and choking, lips tinged with blue, Alf screams horrendously at the touch without awakening, without opening his eyes. The boy jerks away, keening and rocking.

After a time he stands, hoists the man against him, and starts the long, aching trek to the tunnel. Streamers of light cascade in his head. He is no longer moving. His body is gone, muffled in darkness, patterns of touch thuttering against his being. His name, he realizes, is Helen Keller; vibrations go outward from him, into a sparking void, rebound, return altered. With wondrous, kindly warmth she enfolds him; they fuse. He tumbles in these new places, and she takes his hand as Annie had taken hers, gently, firmly, sweetly. He recalls, dimly, the glorious beam of sunlight shining, through the window on her mother's face, he runs on Helen's pudgy baby's legs to it, arms outstretched, and it is whipped away in the shrieking pain of her fever, her loss, the closing in of her reality to heartbeat and hunger, the textures which flutter at the skin, rich fragrances and the heavy thuds under her feet, wind ripe and afterward chill against her face; he falls with her into an oblivion of meaningless fogs. He is the Phantom in a No-World.

And here is the patterning in her cupped hand, repeated, insistently, changing and recurring, the furry small shape and the slithery tiny ones, the inexorable return on her palm's flesh of those dancing touches; he rages with her as the tang of food is withheld, as the hateful cold instruments are pressed into her hand; he softens and weeps for the love he knows in his utter isolation, caressing him.

Then the crash of thunderous understanding, as the spark leaps from palm to brain with the gush of cold water on the wrist, the patterned dance which names it: "water." All through her body rings the shock. The repeated motions on her skin, stored without meaning, clash into place, fierce, hard-edged, separate, yet linking in chains of wonderful connection: the names, the names.

Mouse crouches with her by the scent of something small and struggling, reaches for the new tiny shapes, a wiggling slithery form for each of her fingers. The connections coruscate with incredulous joy: mother, the old dog, the baby, five babies—and the new word jumps upon her cupped hand: "puppy." They squirm to the mother, and she feels them sucking at the gorged teats; they are smaller than small. Eagerly, frowning, she seeks the refinement she needs. It comes: "very small." The squeal in her throat thrills her as she laughs with pleasure. The puppies are very small!

Mouse stands with Helen in the No-World which has exploded into richness, into expression. Annie is there with them, poor Annie with her sore, weak eyes, dutiful and loving, stern and accepting. The memories which are not his rush like a cascade of cold water in his strange brain, seeding there, taking root where they can. He remembers the discovery of writing, the embossed letters which made up the words, the Braille dots, the exuberant discovery of script. It is too much; his brain cannot cope with this partial interface, this inundation of brilliance, this other life entire. There is more, hammering into echoes, soul upon soul standing behind Helen, connections buzzing into dreadful confusion. The vista explodes outward. Helen has not departed, but he sees the great concourse of general notions which this multitude shares, the inexhaustible well at which they drink. There is a gate through which he has never been able to pass, though he has hammered at it with his fists. It opens and he slips through; he is buoyant, aloft in realms of connection and generation. He sees that his heart is slowing, that the blood fails in his brain as he is trapped here in the vortex of power. Alf is sagging against him, dying. He knows bitterly, now, that he cannot stay. A visitor, he must go back. But the gate has opened once; when it swings closed, it will remain ajar. His wings close; he plummets. Helen is gone. Yet she has left as legacy a kinesthetic memory. His fingers twitch, tracing out that century-old dialogue:

What is my soul?

No one knows what the soul is like, Annie tells them, her eyes brimming with tears, *but we know it is not the body, and it is that part of us which thinks and loves and hopes, and which Christian people believe will live on after the body is dead. No one can see the soul. It is invisible.*

But if I write what my soul thinks, then it will be visible, and my words will be its body!

The sergeant's voice, amplified by a loudspeaker, rings out: "Leave the sick man where he is for the moment, son, and come back to the tunnel. We have a doctor standing by, and we've brought down a stretcher so you can wheel him here. The doctor says it's very important to get him on the stretcher. Dragging him along the ground makes it more difficult for him to breathe, and that's very bad for him in the condition he's in. Do you understand?"

Mouse straightens up. "Yes!" he yells back.

He sprints along the base of the wall. The soldiers have lowered a long stretcher on a wide wheelbase. A worried-looking man in a white coat stands with them; he reminds Mouse of Dr. Fish. Several uniformed officers have joined the original three men. The boy reaches the mound at the foot of the opening, drags the stretcher down the last few centimeters, unties the ropes they've lowered it with.

He waits, then, and searches for the gate. Like the egg Alf cracked into the damaged radiator, floating down in the turbulent, hissing water, coagulating, drifting to the splintered hole, streamers of albumin and whirling yolk hardening, crisping, burning, blocking the damage, something moves into his ruined brain.

"It is Alfred Dean who is injured," he says clearly. "He is mother's brother to this person Hieronymus Dean, or Mouse. His condition resembles emphysema, coupled with an acute psychotic break. He shall be fetched immediately."

The doctor stares at him. "You're a brave boy. Your mother's—your uncle is going to be just fine if we hurry." He glances away and swallows with difficulty. "I thought you said he was retarded," he tells the crewcut sergeant indignantly. He bites his lip and looks fearfully over the edge. "I want you to listen carefully, son, while I describe the best way to lift him on to the stretcher."

Everything is blurred, double-images receding to infinity. Shaking with fatigue, Mouse pushes the light stretcher back to Alf, squirts medication from a spray pack into the anthropologist's nostrils, clamps an oxygen mask across his face, wheels him back to the opening. There he ties the man firmly to the stretcher, positioning the broad elastic straps in such a way that they do not further constrict the laboring chest and diaphragm. Carefully, he attaches the ropes to the corners of the stretcher. His fingers are clumsy with exhaustion, with fine manipulation of a degree they have never before attained. Several times he fumbles the knots.

"Take it slowly," the doctor says soothingly. "He's going

to be all right; you've done a wonderful job. You'll both be safe and in the best possible care in a few moments. Just take it nice and easy."

The words glide over the surface of his jumbled mind. Then the soldiers are hauling Alf up over the rubble. The vast chamber clangs with hollow metallic echoes as the stretcher scrapes and bumps up the wall. Mouse follows it, grasping the swinging wooden rungs of the rope ladder with numb fingers, forcing his body over the edge.

The sergeant catches him as he slumps, hoists him on brawny shoulders, and carries him along the tunnel in the wake of the stretcher. A wave of tiredness sweeps over him; the blur of activity, within and without, becomes a whistling grayness. He passes almost instantly into unconsciousness.

3. The Vault

At one level there was pain, and the chatter of voices.

For a time it had been excruciating, truly intolerable. Alf knew that he was going to die. Agony so piercing could not be borne. The torment in his lacerated viscera, his compressed skull, his racked, torn limbs smashed everything from his awareness but the single shrieking desire for an end to it. And finally he realized that he had not literally been maimed, that his pain was a kind of metaphor for psychic trauma. It eased, diminished, blurred into a generalized bruise spiked with knives: suffocation pressing his face, and the equally terrible and alternating anguish of breathing.

A voice said, "Cheyne-Stokes respiration. He's terminal, I'm afraid."

Another voice said angrily, "You have to pull him out of coma. We *must* learn how he got into the Vault. The child can't tell us—he's a hopeless retard."

"So, for God's sake, get them both up to the surface.

We need electronic equipment—EEG, EKG, a Birds respirator."

"You know we can't do that."

At the first level, the level of pain, Alf Dean also heard his own whimpering gasps for life. Through the anxious and choleric voices, he listened to his own damaged flesh. Faint sighs of breath, and the dull pressure between them. The sighs increasing in volume, shuddering inspirations of air, and the knives, the knives. Silence, and paralysis. Choking, unable to speak, move, force the rusted lock on the cage of his chest. And then, again, the first faint hush of a new cycle . . .

"I've given him two hundred fifty milligrams of aminophylline, intravenously. That'll firm up the periodic respiration, General Sawyer, but he doesn't stand a chance."

"Major, I don't like to hear that kind of defeatist talk around here."

"Don't worry, sir, he's in deep coma. He can't hear us."

"Irrelevant, soldier. *I* don't want negative thinking. Get the bastard conscious."

On a second level, Alf Dean spun like a charged particle along the weft and warp of a stupefying matrix of facts he had never learned and relationships between them which he never could have conceived. The military physician who hovered over his laboring, supine body had injected him, Alf knew, with a soluble derivative of theophylline, a bronchodilator of the xanthine diuretic group. The pharmacology of the caffeine-like drug traced itself in his awareness like an illuminated map of the serial moves in a chess game. Despite this vast, dazed access of knowledge, he realized that he had never heard of aminophylline before in his life. That paradox should have filled him with alarm, driven him scrambling up through nightmare to consciousness and light, but the cycle of his harrowed breath beat through its imprisoned rhythm, and his terror was isolated by rapture.

For at a third level, Alf Dean Djanyagirnji was ravished by timeless splendor. Hands and feet gestured, stamped: in ritual he partook of the totem corroboree of Dreaming. Kangaroo bounded, great tail slapping the red dust. Emu ran, a massive matted flightless mop on cruel feet, eyes darting in malicious glee. Goanna scurried, frightened, into shade, emerged again to bask in delightful warmth. Firehawk lofted on streams of cool fast sky, glowing fragments of campfire embers in his beak. Barramundi in the colder stream of bubbling river flashed brilliance from scales, fins, flicking like a dream. The cycle of Alf's trapped breath was here a greater rhythm: life, passage, corruption, hunger, sateity. The stinging chill of rain, and the humid gusts of its rising from the renewed soil.

A dragon named Sri Ramakrishna said to him: I have shared your condition often during my life. The limitless, shining ocean of consciousness, of spirit. Billows rushing from all sides so that I panted for breath and fell senseless, caught up in the folds and banners of sheer light. . . . The dead Serpent regarded him kindly, holding out its hands. Each hand had two thumbs. Alf recoiled, spun back into the matrix of facts and facts, the drumming of black feet in the earth, the whirl of gorgeous light. . . .

On that pathway, weaving and shuttling amid the bright sparks of reality endlessly arrayed, Alf slipped into hallucination. Or was it memory? Dream? By the white man's reckoning, it was 1942. At piccaninny dawn, the sky paling and the grass cool under his hard soles, in the Turtle Egg Season, he crept with hunter's stealth toward the Strange Thing which the men of that calendar had dropped out of the night. All his wary silence was in vain. Swollen by their child, his wife Wanntukgara crashed behind him with the grace of a maimed wallaby. She had no right to be here. Tracking was man's work. With a brutal gesture, without turning his head, he instructed her to remain where she was. He watched the birds, scanned the ground for the spoor of frightened, fleeing animals. The Strange Thing lay ahead, very close now. A giggle at his shoulder. He turned, scowling. Wanntukgara, her faded green cotton smock torn, printed yellow daisies dirty, grinned at him, on hands and knees. These women had no respect. Yet he lowered his hand without striking her. Her brown affectionate gaze held no mockery, nothing to diminish him. Still, the racket she made! He smiled back at her. Who was here to observe their presence? The aircraft which had hurled the Strange Thing on to the Mission station had been alone, possibly lost. All the white men's hard, thin beams of light were miles away, to the West, concentrated around Darwin. Each night for a week, he had heard, the beams had slashed the sky like the threads of gigantic spiders caught in moonlight. Sometimes they crossed the path of an intruding aircraft, and hammering broke the night: yellow spears, fading to red, split the stars. The battles of whites were horrible, gross, bereft of dignity or courage. When he had been under the Buka taboo, after circumcision, his grandfather had said to him: "Puyungarla, the white men are ignorant of balance and honor. They seize our women and sacred land itself, and they kill without counting the death. Do not be like them. They will seduce you with tobacco and alcohol, and threaten you with guns and whips. But you are a man now, Puyungarla. One day you will be the father of men, if that poor little cut thing of yours ever heals and stands up straight. Do not betray your manhood by abandoning your heritage out of greed or fear."

In hallucinated psuedo-memory, Alf smiled. It had stood up, too right. His fine brown gin, his woman, his wife, Wanntukgara, had crept upon his thighs in the night, as the old women crouched at the edge of the fire to lend her comfort in their nearness and call their shrill advice, and she had slid down wonderfully to envelop his sturdy spear, and the fire of it had rushed into her, into that secret pouch of her body which had been made ready by the Rainbow Serpent, and their seeds had joined, had quickened with the infusing spirit of the new child's Totem . . .

. . . and she felt the child beat at her belly even now, as she stepped lightly behind her fine husband. On the horizon the sun trembled, fat and crimson. She followed Puyungarla closely, knowing that it would irritate his pride, but wanting to be with him when he found the Strange Thing and made it his own: a sorcerer's thing, egg from a metal bird, magic thing. It would surely give them power and force among the white men.

Alf moaned, an added timbre to the hoarse grunt of his terrible breathing. The transition in dream from male role to female had not bothered him. Something dreadful, though, was about to occur, something he remembered in every cell and organ, something—

"Sorry, did you say something, Major?"

"Hmm? No."

"It must have been— Jesus, look at his face!"

She stepped forward and stared at the squat, heavy object half-buried in the soil. Her heart pounded. The child sensed her emotion and kicked against her distended belly. Go back, her husband told her. She lingered, on her haunches in the grass. Puyungarla moved toward the Strange Thing with brief, bird-like steps. The Firehawk was his Totem. How appropriate that he should claim a marvel fallen from the skies, dropped from the beak of a metal bird. Delicately, he touched its surface. She watched him study it, his young face hard and deliberate. He was beautiful and strong, and their child would be a son, surely, for the women had prophesied it, a son who would be a hunter and roam naked and free when the white men had done with killing one another, killing as beasts and true men never killed, killing unrestrained by the Law, killing until all their numbers were reduced in mutual slaughter to nothing. Puyungarla put his wiry black arms around the stout waist of the object and heaved. It teetered fractionally in its pit. A faint sound came from it, a click and an echo, like a tin can dropped on dry grass, and monstrous flame smacked gushed rolled thunder cried whirlwind plucked her husband into the air with his body shattered and pink blood hazing the icy sky metal shrieking and biting her like huge flies her arms wrapped in terror about her tearing belly and the child—

"Christ, did you see that? His whole body *spasmed.* He's torn the goddamn glucose drip out of his arm. I thought you said this guy was terminal comatose."

"Shit! He's ripped the vein. I think the endotracheal emplacement is still okay. Get me a— No, we can't use any sedation; his heart wouldn't take it. Hold his legs. If this doesn't finish him, we might have a live one."

Alf fled from nightmare to nightmare. I'm sorry, the dragon told him. We should have kept that mnemonic pathway closed and guarded. Fortunately, you won't remember it. Relax, son, you're very ill. We need you healthy and sane for what is to come.

That was my father! Alf cried. Horror and grief filled his soul. The connection between mind and body had been temporarily severed, or he would have wept.

Yes, said the dragon named Puyungarla. And your mother. And you, Alf Djanyagirnji. And you.

It was too much to cope with. Alf cringed away from the phantom and drew knees to chin, clutching forearms tight against chest. In the same instant, with trepidation, he knew that his paralyzed body had failed to move a single voluntary muscle. Convulsively, he drove his legs down again, thrusting against bonds he could not see, and something truly terrible occurred. Like a straining limb withdrawn from a sucking, adhesive mass of contracting plaster, Alf pulled away from his own laboring flesh. He rose above his body, rolling slightly, and floated toward the low ceiling. All his senses were blurred. Vision held no focus, edges shimmered with the spectrum of light swirling on oil slick. Several men—two, three?—bent over his comatose torso, fiddling with tubes that branched, multiplied, coalesced.

The register of his emotions was curiously muted. A faint, azure sphere of light, he hung over his body and struggled for clarity. Voices echoed and clattered. He was no longer cold. And still, at some level of identity beyond both matter and mind, he danced timelessly the Dreaming, the totems, swept by streamers of auroral light and the warm welcoming song of the dragons all around him.

"Fuck it, he's arrested," one of the voices said.

"What?"

"His heart has stopped, General. Get me a— Oh, Christ! Orderly!"

Another shadowy figure burst into the room.

"Ten cc epinephrine, 1:1,000, in a cardiac syringe. Stat, man. Christ, this is barbaric. General, if I save this man, I'm moving him straight upstairs if I have to haul him there on my back. God damn your security clearances."

With extraordinary detachment, Alf hovered above his dying body and watched the needle push into his dark breast. Blood rose into the barrel of the syringe. Remotely, he found the sight distasteful. He turned away, moved through the wall, and discovered that he was staring down at Mouse.

Shame made him cringe: the first strong emotion he had experienced since leaving his body. Oh, Mouse, he thought, what are you doing here? I told you to stay put.

The boy raised his head and seemed to look directly at Alf, at the softly radiant sphere which Alf had become. A hard blue shell of light shone around the child's skull. Mouse smiled, his perfect teeth dazzling like an advertisement for municipal fluoride. Hello, Alf, he said. I think you'd better go back now. Don't worry, we'll be okay. Hey, one thing—get them to bring delFord here.

Alf said: Who?

They'll know, Mouse told him.

Absolved, dizzy with astonishment, Alf allowed himself

to drift back through the wall. His body was breathing by itself, and greasy perspiration covered its face. There was a stubble of beard on its dark cheeks and neck. A tube protruded from its crusted mouth, held in place by a semi-rigid plug. That lump is not me, Alf thought with revulsion. It drew him, though, summoned him, denied him the pleasure of weightless drifting. He fell like a leaf toward the draped body on the bed. His telepathic conversation with Mouse receded into deep unconsciousness.

In darkness, he was jostled. Now the voices seemed too distant for interpretation. The immense mass of the earth pressed him. A whine, a clatter, jolting, endless journey from hell to—

—a moment of consciousness: pounding rain, a sky roiling with heavy charcoal clouds, feet running, a cold sheet of streaked plastic lifted past his face and held above him to warm off the rain by two swearing orderlies while a third tugged his stretcher, the chill suddenly elevating the hairs on his skin, pain in his throat, chest, piercing shocking hurt in the depths of his brain—

He came half-awake with a spotlight glaring on his face. Several voices were engaged in laconic, droning dialogue. A high-pitched electronic beeping punctuated their words; it yelped to the beat of his heart. As his eyes opened a fraction, another voice called out excitedly. Alf let his lids close. Red haze, a cavorting strip of afterimage. He could not understand what the men were saying. Straining for meaning, he realized that they spoke in a language unfamiliar to him. It sounded like . . . what? Stage Russian? No, by God, it sounded like the authentic article. Which was absolutely ridiculous, in the middle of an Australian desert, just he and Mouse and the scrubby spinifex . . . Alf giggled vaguely, and his teeth grated on something jammed into his mouth. It was too much effort. He relapsed into unconsciousness.

When he awoke again he panicked. A clinical odor filled his nostrils. Male voices were talking, talking. Keeping his eyes closed, Alf told himself: There's been an accident. I'm in the hospital. Prickling at fingers and toes. He could not recall the accident. With increasing alarm, he found that he could not remember anything at all since . . . yes, there *had* been an accident—a stone had been thrown up by The Beast's front wheel and gone straight through the radiator. He'd had to stand out in the roasting sun for fifteen minutes trying to heal the damned thing and finally broke an egg into the boiling water. Good old bush expedient, floats to the hole and cooks, sealing it like regrown skin. Yet a mishap like that could scarcely put you into the hospital. There seemed to be spiders perched all over his scalp. Wires. Hell, he was in an intensive-care ward, wired for EEG.

One of the voices said, "Theta's dropping out. I'm getting stronger beta. He's coming round."

"Right. Page Security."

Somebody had kicked him in the throat. He swallowed and it hurt. In a dry, croaking voice, Alf said: *"Cooma el ngruwar, ngruwar el cooma, illa booka mer ley urrie."*

"He's awake." A man in white was craning past a pole topped by a bottle of pale liquid. "What did you say?" With a practiced movement, the man pulled up Alf's right eyelid and speared a penlight beam into the center of his brain. Alf blinked and jerked back his head. "Good, full pupillary contraction. Let's just try the other one."

"Throat." The anthropologist tried to lift his arm, to massage the afflicted region. An I.V. tube snagged on its support.

"Yeah, it'll rasp for a while. We've been breathing for you. What language were you speaking just now?"

Another voice laughed raucously. "Physician, heal thy self-image. I never knew you hankered to be an intelligence agent, Irwin."

"Aboriginal rite," Alf told the first man. "Traditional saying." After they'd kicked him in the throat, they had obviously pulled a bike chain through his gullet. He forced himself to finish his answer. "It means: 'One is all, all is one, the soul will not die.' "

"Wow," said the second voice, still scornful. "The reincarnation of the Three Musketeers." A door banged, and a number of additional men came into the room, crowding around the bed.

"Shut your mouth, Casey," one of them said. "You were given strict instructions not to talk to the patient. Has he said anything, Joinville?"

"Very little, sir." The first medical man repeated Alf's translation word for word. "He won't be able to handle too much stress right now; he's just woken up. And his larynx will still be sore from the endotrach."

"I'll bear that in mind, Doctor," the sharp baritone said.

"Okay buddy, let's hear your tale. We'll start at the start. How did you and the kid get into the Vault zone without being observed?"

Appalled, Alf pushed himself up from the sweaty sheets. "Mouse?" he cried. "Oh, Jesus, I saw Mouse in there. Is he—?" Confused, then, he sagged back. "No. No. Nightmare. Mouse stayed in the cavern." Again his muscles spasmed. "God Almighty, how long have I been here? You've got to get Mouse out of that place." He began to cry. "The poor little bastard . . ."

"Easy, Mr. Dean." A note of concern softened the baritone. "That is your name? Alfred Dean? And the child's name is. . . ?"

"Mouse," Alf said, choking on the taste of warm salt. His emotions were out of control. Nothing made any sense. "Hieronymus, actually. His mother had no brains. It must be hereditary." He shook his head. "You found him? He's not hurt?"

"We have him right here with us, just down the hall," the man said soothingly. He wore a military uniform, gray and punctiliously pressed. His eyes were a surprisingly soft green, and his cheeks were pitted very faintly with the acne scars of adolescence. Far from being a sinister touch, the dusting of scars was rather disarming. "Mouse is fine. All we want to know, Mr. Dean, is how you both got down there."

With labile irritation, Alf said, "Doctor."

"I'm not a doctor; I'm a United States Army intelligence officer. Surely you grasp by now that—"

Disregarding the I.V. channel, Alf heaved himself to a sitting position. "I don't give a pig's fart in hell about your credentials, sport. *I'm* a doctor." He tried to get out of bed. "Where's Mouse? I want to see him."

Instantly, one of the medics was restraining him, pressing him back onto the bed. It was hardly an equal match. "Dr. Dean, control yourself. You've only been out of the coma for two days. Your PVC's—"

"Spare me the mumbo-jumbo; I'm not that brand of doctor." Alf subsided. Mumbling, he said, "Witch doctor. I'm a Ph.D. witch doctor. His overtaxed body started to close down the blood supply to his cortex, and he fell away into gray wool swarming with vitreous humors.

They would not let him see his nephew. Were they his custodians or his jailers? He could not even estimate their provenance. Was he still in Australia? An insane question, but unavoidable. All the accents were foreign, and there was no consistency in them. Against all reason, some were American and some were . . . Russian? Eastern European, at any rate. His recovery room was makeshift modular, neat but meant to be stripped down and put up again in a hurry, after an overseas jaunt in a cargo plane. No windows. It had the look of a sickbay designed to serve a modest community, undoubtedly of military service personnel. Three other beds were currently vacant but ready for use, made up with linen and blankets.

Under the artificial lights, Alf Dean put himself back together. When the lights went off he slept, and often enough he slept when they were on. In sleep he was bombarded by disturbing images which evaporated on touch. Somehow he was aware that his interval of coma had contained long stretches of just such bizarre and fearful dreams, but he could not recall their shape. One detail alone remained to plague him: an image of himself spread on a table, dying, tubes plugged into every orifice, while simultaneously he hung above that near-corpse, hung watching it, watching and talking to . . . Whom? What? It was, of course, ludicrous even to wonder. Fantasies left over from drastic illness could hardly aid him in his present crisis.

"How did you get in there, Dr. Dean?" they were asking him again, again, again.

"In *where?*" he yelled with frustration. "I don't know where I am, you won't tell me who you are, what you represent. I've told you everything I can, and none of it pleases you. For God's sake, what more can I say?" He shook with ire. "And where the fuck is Mouse? I demand to see him!"

It did no good. The interrogations were restrained by a prudent alertness to his physical debility, but the men who questioned him told him nothing at all. The procedure was utterly ruthless. Only one fact was obvious: they believed nothing he said. Except perhaps his name. Assuming indeed that they had checked his identity with the Australian authorities, with his university, with his ex-wife for that matter, the corroboration of his statements had not persuaded them of his trustworthiness.

"Let's go over it again, Dr. Dean. You were driving

across the Tanami desert in a Land Rover, accompanied only by your nephew."

With panic which soon shifted to bile, he sketched them shaky diagrams of his route. When they brought him large-scale ordnance maps, he pinpointed the place where he had left The Beast. Their faces conveyed no trace of belief or skepticism, and so he was obliged to read their professional impassivity as hostile rejection of his truth. His anger mounted. All his life, despite his privileged circumstances, white sons-of-bitches had met his gaze with a chilly filter to mask out the spontaneous warmth they freely offered one another. This version of it was worse, but still he knew its kind of old. Trained neural receptors in his black skin were sensitive to the temperature.

"Although you are a full-blood Australian Aborigine, your nephew happens to be a white retard."

"That's right. It's a long story, and none of your business." Constricted rage throttled his larynx.

"I believe the evaluation of pertinency is our domain, Dr. Dean."

"By what right, you nosy bastard? I demand to speak to a lawyer. And what the hell is your *name?*"

"Names are unimportant. I'm sorry, but you cannot be permitted to contact an attorney at this point in time. The entire station is under the quarantine of military security."

"By whose orders?"

The man sighed. "By the orders of the Australian Government, under the auspices of the United Nations."

"Bullshit."

"Use your brain, man. You've seen American and Soviet personnel here working side by side. Doesn't that prompt some estimate of the gravity of this operation?" He caught himself, and smiled. "But, of course, you know all this, anyway. How else could you have gotten into the Vault?"

Was he locked into some farcical lunatic asylum? "I don't know what you mean by the Vault. Look, it's obvious that Mouse and I stumbled over some fucking stupendous secret research project in the desert. Holograms in the middle of ancient caves, whatever. Is it an extraterrestrial artifact? It must be. The Rainbow Serpent data goes back too far."

Dryly, the man said, "And it was the Rainbow Serpent you were looking for, of course. Not the Vault. By pure accident you crept into the middle of the most extensively guarded installation in this hemisphere. In the world, maybe."

"I don't know what you're talking about!" Alf shouted. Migraine clamped his brow, hammered down into his nasal septum. "Yes, I was looking for the Rainbow Serpent, if you wish to be simpleminded about it. Yes, I was doing so in this locality. For the love of God, I've drawn you a map—two hundred fifty kilometers west of Tennant Creek, two hundred eighty southeast of Wave Hill. Right here, you buffoon! Unless you've moved Mouse and me to one of your Omega stations while we were unconscious."

The security man considered Alf impassively. "In fact, we haven't moved you very far at all. Several klicks vertically, in essence."

Alf slapped his sheeted knee in disgust. "Do you take me for a fool? We're on the ground. I *have* traveled in a plane, you know. Don't let my skin fool you. I'm not an ignorant savage."

"Dr. Dean," the man assured him, "if I thought you were an ignorant savage, we would be conducting this interview according to rather different rules."

The door opened. The man who entered spoke with a marked Russian accent. "Search Team Four has located the vehicle, Colonel. Its position was as indicated." He handed the intelligence man a folder, saluted, and closed the door.

"Hmm." Flicking pages swiftly, the American glanced once at Alf. "Extraordinary." He rose. "Thank you for your cooperation, Dr. Dean." And he was gone, leaving Alf with an open mouth. Migraine closed on him. Brutally, he thumped the button beside his bed. An orderly appeared almost instantly. Within minutes, the anthropologist was asleep, his headache scrubbed away by the same drugs which banished anger, bafflement, and thought itself.

The pain in his throat had eased when he awoke, and he was hungry. His watch was still missing, but light came in a parallelogram slanting from his open door. A remote drumming sounded, as always, above the hush of the air conditioners. It reminded him of something commonplace, but his rational interpretive cortex blocked the association.

Vertically, the man had said. That could mean several kilometers downward, of course. And Alf's original wild speculation had been that the alien device was a teleportation portal, linking the Tanami desert tunnel with some other location on Earth. So it could have shifted him to, say, the Himalayas. Had the legend of the Yeti arisen because, over the centuries, a series of foolhardy naked black men had appeared magically, to freeze in the howling snows? But the man had also said that authorization had come from the Australian Government. There were few mountains higher than two kilometers in Australia.

Alf climbed unsteadily from the bed, shaking his head at his own bad smell. He called from the door for breakfast. The light in the corridor seemed to flicker oddly with a marginal oscillating haze.

Before he had finished digesting the food, the brass arrived. His previous interrogator was not one of their number. Indeed, Alf recognized none of them.

"The changing of the guard," he said sourly.

One of them wore stars, and looked exhausted. He extended his hand. "I'm Joe Sutton, Dr. Dean. Scientific liaison. I apologize for the peremptory treatment you've had from us in the last few days. How are you feeling?"

"Wary, General." There were sympathetic chuckles. "I want to see my nephew."

"Of course you do. We'll arrange a visit very shortly. You needn't worry; he's in good hands."

"With a tube down his throat and a drip in his arm?"

Sutton's tanned expression was horrified. "My God, no. Haven't they told you? He's fine. You're the one who's been worrying us, Alf. Can I call you Alf?"

"Call me Jackie if you feel like it. Just let me out of this bloody prison."

"Oh." The general was nonplussed. "I understood your name was—"

"My name is Alf, for Christ's sake! Why am I being detained?"

"Basically, Alf, because you've managed the equivalent of stumbling into the middle of the Manhattan Project with no security clearance and no warning given." Sutton gave a genuine grin. "For which we have to thank you. Although Victor, here, might not," he added, with an attempt at joviality. "Your arrival in the Vault caused his three best physicists to abandon Marx in favor of miracles."

"Not even my three worst physicists," objected the white-haired man at the foot of the bed, "lose sleep worrying about Marx. As for miracles, you are getting me confused with General Sawyer."

Sutton stiffened slightly. "General Sawyer's religious convictions are really none of our concern, Victor."

The Russian shrugged. To Alf he said, "Good morning, Doctor. I am Fedorenko. It is true that you have set the fox among the hens in my department." He fetched forward the burly fellow at his side. "And this is Captain Hubert Lapp, of the NASA Shuttle team. Hugh and I have some questions we would like to pose, if you feel recovered enough to help us."

Alf regarded each in turn, without warmth. "Your nameless colleague filled a tape recorder with answers. To date I haven't managed to pry the simplest item of information out of anyone. Let's see if we can start by balancing the scoreboard."

Sutton helped himself to a glass of fresh orange juice from the bedside tray. "Sure. A good beginning might be the Gate—the device you found in the Tanami desert. You must have realized by now that it wasn't built by human beings."

Literally, Alf experienced a jolt through his body. Intellectually, he had been driven to that conclusion; emotionally, he had walled off the insight, denied it, ridiculed his own imagination. Hearing the proposition endorsed by an establishment figure like Sutton was more than startling. It was physically horrendous. He sagged against his pillows, face chilled.

"Oh, my God. And I just stepped straight into it. I left Mouse there alone and walked through it."

"I assure you, Dr. Dean," Fedorenko said with concern, "the boy is perfectly safe. It was with his assistance that we got you out of the Vault. You have cause to be proud of him. And grateful." He paused, then added: "Had he not been there to get you to medical aid, you would have died, you see."

It came back: scraps of nightmare, shards of madness. Screaming pain and the breath snatched from his blazing lungs, the steps upward into strange light, falling, falling endlessly, whips of flame running back and forth into a matrix of cold clarity, infinite connection, a billion voices speaking together in a thousand tongues, the dragons—

Closing his eyes, Alf denied the memories. It had not happened that way. He had *not* left his body. . . .

Shivering, he hugged himself. "What did it do to me?" he asked in a thin voice.

"It moved you through space," said Fedorenko. "It shifted you six hundred kilometers in no time at all. It put you into a place we term the Vault."

Abruptly, a lot of the pieces slotted together. In the center of the pattern a void remained, but its periphery was whole and beyond argument. Alf Dean knew where he was. The political rumors had been correct. There *was* a covert military base in Central Australia.

He exhaled. "I see. You've known about the alien installation for years."

"Only the Vault," Sutton told him. "Not the Teleport Gate. Not until you and the child fell through it."

"You've been out to the cavern?"

"We followed your directions," Lapp said. With a grin, the astronaut said, "You might be pleased to know that we've brought your Land Rover into the station. Slung her from a chopper and lifted her in here."

That piece of news was absurdly gratifying. Alf laughed out loud. "Wonderful. I always swore The Beast could fly if you handled her right." He honked into his handkerchief, and considered them with greater cordiality. "You might ask your maintenance men to go over the radiator for me. There's a hole in it, full of boiled egg."

"We found it," Lapp said. "Delicious. Which reminds me. Anyone hungry?"

"Captain, do you think of anything but your belly?" Sutton shook his head in dismay.

Alf was galvanized with questions. "Why did it try to kill me?"

"An automatic protective system," Fedorenko said gravely. "It does not like visitors."

"But it didn't hurt Mouse?"

"Exactly. We don't know why. Perhaps it recognized that he represented no active threat."

Acutely, Alf said, "So you want to get into this . . . Vault—but it won't let you near it?"

"Just so."

"And the Tanami desert entrance has given you a way to short-circuit its defenses."

"Probably not," the general said regretfully. "Your accidental insertion shows that the protective zone extends down to the Gate. Besides, the question is academic. The Gate is now defunct."

"Huh? Then how do you know that Mouse and I really did—"

"One of our tests seems to have killed it," Hugh Lapp told him. He bowed sardonically toward Fedorenko. "The professor shot it with his ray gun."

The Russian shrugged, but he was mournful. "An unhappy by-product of our safety precautions. We could hardly risk another gauge glitch."

As forcefully as he could, Alf said, "Hang on. You've run away from me again. Ray gun?"

"Hubert's undergraduate humor," Fedorenko observed without resentment. "You must understand, firstly, that the Vault will not tolerate electromagnetic fields in its presence. Atrocious phenomena ensue. Alf, you can be thankful that you failed to take your flashlight into the Vault zone with you."

"There was enough light from the zone. I left the flashlight with Mouse."

"Evidently he dropped it when he pursued you into the Gate. We are grossly handicapped in our investigations, you see, for we are obliged to use only rudimentary instruments and methods."

"I see." Alf slipped into sarcasm, to avoid facing this latest burst of guilty retrospective terror. "Like old-fashioned pre-electronic ray guns."

Fedorenko inclined his head. "The merit of a laser beam, Dr. Dean, is that it can be transmitted quite a long way, if it is of the appropriate frequency. The pump does not need to be situated near the glitch zone. When we found the Gate you activated, it was still responsive to human proximity."

An image seared Alf's mind: a huge box-like interior of white light, a vast sphere in its center. The pseudo-memory flashed off, a neon sign extinguished. "Serpent's egg," he mumbled.

"I'm sorry?"

But the image was gone, tangled with scraps of nightmare. "Nothing," Alf said. "I've been hallucinating pretty badly. It was just—"

Lapp stared at him with interest. "I want to ask you about that, Alf. Any details?"

Beneath his black skin, blood coursed. The flush made

his face glow. "Some. Meaningless. The garbage you get in any nightmare." Deliberately, he directed his gaze to the Russian physicist. "You were talking about lasers."

Lapp nodded almost imperceptibly. The scientist went on at once. "We wished to establish if the Gate was still tuned to the Vault. Geometric constraints prevented us viewing the steps without sending someone into the defensive zone, and that would not work. Alf, you are the first adult to come out of the zone with your sanity intact. And it would have been equally pointless to send a scout through the Gate, since we had established that it is a one-way trip. So I decided to emplace mirrors along the cavern course, to direct an optical laser pulse onto the roof of the vault. There, it would be visible from our own access point."

"You bounced the beam along the tunnel? Then into the Gate, angled parallel to the steps?"

"Precisely."

"And the laser beam put the Gate out of business?"

"The Gate turned itself off. That is my estimate. Fortunately, the beam was indeed visible for several microseconds. It flashed on the roof of the Vault simultaneously with its passage through the Gate. That distance, in four-dimensional spacetime, is of the order of six hundred kilometers. Had the beam shined directly through space, such a journey would have taken one five-hundredth of a second."

Mirthlessly, Alf said, "At the speed of light."

"Quite. In reality, our calibrated instruments showed that it covered the interval instantaneously."

"You can bet your ass Victor was pleased," the astronaut said. "He's the reigning champ in faster-than-light-physics. The tachyon Czar."

Another piece jumped into place. Of course. He'd heard Fedorenko's name last year, as a hot Nobel Prize candidate.

"Unfortunately," Sutton said, with a disgruntled glance at the Russian, "that item of data cost us. The Gate went off and stayed off. We're back to square one."

No wonder the blacks had been terrified and awestruck by the Gate, Alf told himself. One-way, it was lethal. Vividly, he remembered the warning signs on the tunnel wall, the ancient Aboriginal interdictions. A dozen questions clamored for his attention. Why had the extraterrestrial engineers placed their exit at the end of a natural tube worming through an escarpment in the middle of one of the world's most inhospitable deserts? Was that location imposed on them, perhaps, by some geometric law of hyperspace? Were there, after all, authentic "places of power" which an advanced science might link together?

Or was his scale wrong? Even mountains creep and buckle and erode given sufficient time. With premonitory trepidation, he asked, "Have you established the age of the Vault?"

"Not the Vault." Fedorenko pursed his lips. "The Gate, roughly, yes. We've taken extensive mineral samples. Radiological estimates put the worked surface of the Tanami tunnel at some sixty million years B.P. Yes, Alf, I felt that way when I saw the report. It is simply beyond the imagination. But the figure is, if anything, conservative."

All the certitudes of Alf's professional life seemed to skid, to slide away. Oh, Jesus! he thought. I imagined that my hypothesis of an embedded Rhaetosaurus fossil was radical, at the boundaries of credibility. And in reality the Rainbow Serpent was a machine, for the love of God! A machine erected when this bleached heartland steamed with hot swamp, when the dinosaurs I sought were browsing like voracious tanks in the brackish seas of Central Australia.

His heart had accelerated. It smacked in the bruised cage of his chest, drove blood in painful jolts through throat, wrists, groin. He closed his eyes. For a dreadful moment he thought that once again he was on the verge of snapping free of his body, evaporating out of his damaged flesh to hover above them all in a blue sphere of light.

Desperately, he said, "The Tanami cavern might not be the only Gate exit connected with your Vault. Have you considered that?"

Lapp laughed. In a cadaverous voice, he intoned, "Beware the Bermuda Triangle." More soberly, he said, "Hey, are you okay? Maybe you've had enough for one day."

"There's a place the half-castes call the Ruined City," Alf said, clinging to the restraints of reason, to the limitations of his body. His heart gradually slowed with his slow, dogged words. "Burruinju. The Malanugga-nugga used to live in the vicinity. They've been absorbed into other tribes now, what remains of them. Blood-thirsty bastards they were, famous for raiding the women of their neighbors. We weren't all stalwart Noble Savages." His lips peeled back. "It's terrible country; I drove through it once. Worse than the Tanami, worse than Simpson's Desert. All sharp cliffs, granite, stone escarpments, wind screaming like animals. I think you might find another Gate there."

He swallowed hard. "There are documented reports. Lights. Incredibly bright, flickering on and off all across the bloody cliff face. Everything else dead-black at night, except the stars. Naturally, as a trained anthropologist with a white man's degree, I wrote it all off. Superstition. Jesus."

General Sutton said without hesitation, "Electric lights. A mineral survey team."

Wearily, Alf said, "Impossible. The reports go back too far. And I've spoken to a man who saw them, Phillip Waipuldanya. He was an ambulance attendant, a skilled mechanic. He's also a hunter, trained in the traditional techniques. You couldn't ask for a better observer. And it scared the shit out of him."

"Might have been worse." Looking intently into Alf's eyes, gripping his gaze, Lapp said, "It could have scared him out of his body."

Alf felt his heart cramp, falter for seconds, lurch again into action.

"What?" Fingernails drove into his palms. "What?"

The astronaut sat down on the bed's edge, touched his arm lightly. "I know," Lapp told him. "It happened to me, too."

Without any need to speak explicitly, they had bridged the gulf. It was untenable that Lapp might be lying, or intend some other meaning. Alf said, "You've been in there?"

"Not inside the Vault. Something similar, on a miniature scale. We have teams in Russia and the States working to duplicate the Vault's defensive fields. That's where I've been. I don't look forward to going back into it again."

"It didn't happen." Alf stared ferociously into the man's clear eyes. "Hallucination."

"It happened," Lapp told him. "Maybe it's hallucination. Harris Lowenthal insists that it is. He's our principal civilian psych consultant. I think I have news for him. It was real."

"We left our bodies."

"Sure felt like it."

"delFord," Alf said faintly.

"What?"

With animus, the anthropologist snarled, "Goddamn it, you heard me. We left our bodies. I don't believe it."

"Yes," Lapp said. "What did you say after that?"

Alf stared. "I didn't say anything."

"You said 'delFord.' William delFord? Do you mean you've already studied the OOBE literature? That's a rather strange coincidence."

"What the fuck are you talking about? I don't know any delFord. And what in hell is 'ooby'?"

From the corner of the room, General Sutton snapped, "Out-of-body-experience. O-O-B-E. Lunatic fringe. Occult pseudo-science. Captain Lapp, you're out of line. Dr. Lowenthal has accounted adequately for those hallucinations."

Lapp stood his ground. "He doesn't satisfy me, Joe. And I've been inside the gluon field. I know what it felt like. I believe Alf Dean's experience corroborates mine. And if delFord is still working on OOBE, we could usefully bring him in on this. Christ, yes, he's the perfect choice. I've read his Huxley reports. He's the only one in the OOBE regiment who's making any sense."

"Are you seriously recommending that we contact Bill delFord? Hugh, you shock me. The man's a . . . an anarchist!"

"Of whom do we speak?" asked Fedorenko.

"A West Coast nut who might have been a powerful research innovator," Sutton said, like a man personally affronted. "We worked together briefly. He's a transplanted Englishman, came over here—uh, to the States, I mean—in the early sixties. He did some very good psychophysical work in conjunction with specialists from the Department of Defense."

With a touch of mockery the Russian said, "Really? An anarchist?"

"That was later. The hippies got to him. Before that he'd married an American girl, got tenure at U.C.L.A.—and then walked away from it with his brain bent by psychedelic bullshit. He directs a place in California, Big Sur someplace, full of hairy freaks running away from the cruel, hard world. It sickens me to my belly."

In some puzzlement, Fedorenko asked Alf, "How do you know of this delFord?" Ponderously, he proposed: "The anthropology of 'hippies'?"

"Why is everyone asking *me?*" cried Alf in aggravation. "I've never heard of the bugger in my life!"

"But you mentioned his name."

"You're crazy. It *is* a lunatic asylum."

With abrupt decision, Hugh Lapp told Sutton, "I'm going to do just that, Joe. I think delFord could provide just the degree of off-center impetus this Project needs. A touch of English to keep the ball spinning." He uttered his own preemptive groan, but went on seriously: "Don't you find it significant that Dr. Dean raised delFord's name—and instantly blocked his short-term memory of doing it?"

"Not in the least. You mentioned hallucinations of leaving the physical body. Unconsciously, he then recalled the name of a self-styled 'authority' on the topic."

Alf objected strenuously. "But I've never read or heard of—"

"Right now, I believe we've taxed Dr. Dean sufficiently. In fact, I'm astonished that the medics haven't been in here yet to chase us out."

"It's your ferocious reputation, General. They're quaking in their boots."

"Me?" Sutton raised his eyebrows. "It's only psychic charlatans I eat before breakfast." He turned to Alf. "Accept my best wishes for your recovery, Dr. Dean. I'm returning to the States tonight, so I mightn't have a chance to see you again. No doubt, however, you'll continue to suffer the attentions of these two." He opened the door.

When they had all gone, Alf ground his large teeth together in furious bafflement. At least his headache had let up. He felt disabled, shockingly weak. The door opened again.

"Just one thing, Alf," Hugh Lapp's voice said apologetically. "I meant to mention it earlier. We're making arrangements for you to see Mouse later today."

"Thanks. I don't see why there's been any need for delay."

The captain stepped into his field of vision. "The boy has been behaving oddly. Nothing to worry about, though. He's a nice kid; I've been spending some time with him. Tragic."

"Yeah." With a deliberate show of insensitivity, Alf added, "Fortunately, he's tractable. I can take him with me on field trips without losing him. Until recently."

"Ease up on yourself, buddy. You could hardly be expected to take precautions against a teleportation system."

"I should never have left him alone." Alf caressed the

sweat on his face. After a silence, he said, "He's a good kid. We have him placed with a new stimulus enrichment program they're developing at Monash University, but they insist that it does him good to get out here occasionally with me."

"Lowenthal diagnosed Non-Specific Cerebral Dysfunction," Lapp said dryly.

"Dr. Fish used the same term. Wonderful, isn't it? Pinpoints Mouse's problem precisely." Alf exhaled. "His mother, Eleanor, was the last of the indigenous flower children. All incense and Indian dresses and mystical claptrap and whales and promiscuous communes. And LSD. She was knocking down a thousand micrograms a day when she got impregnated by some nameless hairy wonder. Of course, she considered the contraceptive pill unnatural, the stupid bitch. She kept dropping LSD doses of that magnitude during the five months it took her to realize she wasn't just getting back her puppy fat."

"Christ. Let's hear it for good ole Doc Leary."

"The acid got into Mouse through her bloodstream. He's been on a constant trip from the day he was born. Zonked, smashed, flying out of his mind—what there is of it. She thought he was going to be the new Messiah. My white sister."

The sheet had wrinkled and slipped from Alf's torso. The black man stared down at his own glistening chest. Incision welts made his flesh a barbaric shield.

They take the children and slit their bodies with rusty old razor blades, Alf thought distantly, alienated equally from the world of his genes and that of his adopted culture. Of course, no doubt razor blades are a technical advance over the ancient fire-hardened stick. Then they pack the open wound with dry soil and ashes, to contain infection and produce handsome, bubbling scarring. This is my people's notion of decoration, of manhood, he told himself.

He did not notice the astronaut leave, or hear the sick-bay door close quietly on his confusion and misery.

TWO:

THE BELLY OF THE WHALE

4. California

Down in the Pacific's flecked jaws, corroded by spume, a rusty automobile shell hung on the rocks, a gutted turtle. Bill delFord leaned out from the Institute's cantilevered deck, solid oregon against his bulging belly, and imagined he felt gusts of spray rising a third of a kilometer to blow in his face. Rain had desisted, but the dull, drenched ocean punished Big Sur under a winter sky.

I'm getting crotchety in my old age, delFord told himself. Like a talkback announcer's lagged tape, the reflection cycled in his brain. Its pseudo-objectivity shocked him, catching him unaware.

Jesus, I'm not that old, he thought. But it was thirty years since he'd teased the panties off his first girl in the back seat of a lumpy, borrowed Morris Oxford. He grinned at the memory. It had nearly shot his histology finals to rubble. What could compete with that moist, welcoming Brillo? Certainly not the nephritic truth that the parietal layer of Bowman's capsule, into which the glomerulus is invaginated, is continuous with the glomerular epithelium.

He stepped onto the shaggy lawn and bent vigorously back and forth, touching his sandaled toes, giving vent to hearty, full-bodied snorts. The brisk exercise cheered him immensely, as always. He almost found it in him to regard General Sutton's visitation with some avidity.

"Fuck the Pentagon," he muttered, with a ritual sign, "and all who sail in her."

From delFord's breast pocket his personal bleeper farted, juicy and antiphonal. He sniggered merrily, and started back through the damp grass to the large A-frame perched on the bluff. A sly gift from Benedict, his fifteen-year-old, the bleeper's slim case was an auditory jack-in-the-box, a maze of solid-state vulgarity and *joie de vivre* programmed to appall pompous dignitaries. It had exposed itself for the first time in the middle of an exquisite chamber recital in

Monterey; a D.A.R. dowager had bridled most satisfactorily at the brief squeal of a cow elephant in heat and drawn away aghast when Bill, stiffening in his seat, had collapsed again with coarse guffaws. He'd chided the impudent youth, of course, but kept and cherished the device.

The day brightened, and rays of splintered light gleamed beautifully from droplets trapped in a fern-spanning spider web. A large official automobile was parked in front of the glass-and-copper entrance, with a small official driver dozing peacefully behind the wheel. Bill delFord knew the species; the merest glimpse of military man would bring the driver's shoulders up, firm his features to instant alertness. How wonderful, thought Bill, to be so contained within the matrix of known and predictable necessities. How pitiful.

A spot of golden light caught his eye. Morning sun smeared the bronze plaque above the main doors. Commonplace after five years, the etched words failed to hold his attention; again, the chiding inward critic noted the dulling of his attention, its mere utilitarian focus. He stopped himself, took several paces backward, and looked up at the plaque. We're somnambulists, he thought.

The quotation was from Laura Archera Huxley, the visionary eclectic's widow: *It is easy for someone without scientific knowledge to accept an unorthodox approach. But for the people learned in any field it is very difficult to accept a conclusion totally different from that which they have formulated through years of work and study.*

Indeed. And thus had Aldous earned his peers' contempt, and the adulation of buffoons. And yet, delFord realized, he felt refreshed by the implied admonition. He wondered if General Sutton had paused here, minutes ago, to read the plaque, and imagined the slight tightening of nose and mouth. They need us, he thought, but they don't have to enjoy it.

Whistling, he stepped into the foyer. Erica indicated the reception annex with her chin, and grimaced. Bill grinned back without a word.

A pair of philosophical opposites framed the annex door. To the right hung his lovely Rothko, limpid and transparent, films of light blurred at their boundaries. Instinctively, the eye penetrated its planes to infinity, invited to a levitation of spirit. On the left was the more recent statement by Mark Boyle: planar, gritty, a surface of old pitted brickwork from the putrid Liverpool docks where he had spent his childhood. Anne's gift. The painting was in two planes simultaneously, the vertical wall of dark, purplish bricks, the horizontal of some pre-asphalt alleyway; in either orientation, a definitive, workaday squalor. The paintings, comparable in size, strained against each other, until the heart led the brain into their complementarity.

Janine met him with an earthenware mug of steaming dark-roast. It burned his fingers; he extended his right hand to the general. "Good morning, gentlemen. You're looking exceptionally fit, Joe. How's Barbara and the girls?"

"Fine, fine, Bill. Another grandson last month. And Selma?"

"Joe, you should give up all this military nonsense and get down here to the Coast. Selma's health has improved out of sight since we made the move." He sipped from his mug. "I gather you have some startling whizbang thingee you want us to road-test for you."

The general's eyes flickered to Janine. "Bill, I don't believe you've met these two fellows before." One was a dour, sandy-haired man in dark suit and tie. "Lennox Harrington, from Cal Tech. Lenny's been working long-distance with Cline and Rubbia on Weinberg's unification of the weak nuclear and the electromagnetic interactions." The other was young, an air force captain, a burly, eager type who surely possessed more brains than immediate impressions would credit. "Dr. delFord, Captain Hugh Lapp. Hugh has done astronaut training for the Shuttle program, and spent five months with Lilly's team studying cognitive distortion in the isolation tank."

DelFord ushered them to leather seats. "Of course," he said. "I recall your name on a couple of the final reports. You must be older than you look, Hugh. Maybe the military life does have some virtues, after all. And call me Bill; we work on a first-name basis here. Janine, nip out and make sure the kids are ready. Buzz me."

She departed, closing the door quietly behind her. Harrington visibly relaxed, though the muscles in his shoulders remained hunched and tight. What he needs to make him a human being, Bill thought, is about fifty hours of Rolfing. The implication was nervous-making. How could broken-gauge theory make a man so uptight? The man's muscular rigidity certainly had a more specific cause than general cerebrotonic blocking.

"As you've gathered," Sutton told him, "we have a direct interest in your work on out-of-body-experience. I'm afraid I can't give you all the background, but Lennox and a large number of colleagues have spent the last few months examining a curious effect with a bearing on your own experiments." He leaned forward and knotted his hands. "I'm having some equipment set up for you right now. Hugh will be seconded to your staff. Run this thing down for us, Bill. It is a matter of imperative national security."

DelFord regarded him with amusement. "I assume you're not out of your mind, Joe, but let me remind you of the security status of my merry little team. Alistair Jerison—"

"—is a member in good standing of the Trotskyite alliance Science for People's Liberation. Dr. Alice Langer is a spokeswoman for Sappho. And the rest of you are a bunch of left-liberal, freak-fringe intellectual bandits. I know." Sutton was angry, but contained the emotion well behind his bland sunlamped face; he *didn't* enjoy it. "Just take my word, Bill. The normal criteria have been waived. J. Edgar is reeling in his plutonium coffin."

"Shit," said delFord. "So they've finally found something bigger than the 'national interest.' I take it the Russians are involved?"

"What we're dealing with here," the physicist said, "makes the orbital docking exercise look like a picnic."

Briefly, Bill's stomach spasmed. You don't worry about OOBE's, he told himself, if the world's coming to an end. A muted buzzer sounded. DelFord stood up, and placed his empty mug neatly next to the bubbling percolator.

"Okay, guys," he told them. "Let's meet the gang. But let me caution you—your security reports might have us labeled as bandits, but you'd better *believe* it. We've devised our own methods, and they're not what you'll be accustomed to from the Pentagon." He held the door open as Harrington followed the general out. "Or the Cal Tech common room, either."

For a moment the astronaut trailed behind, studying a free-standing basalt, an Aztec rendering of Ehacatl, Quetzalcoatl under his guise as wind deity.

"You have a startling decor, Bill." He gestured at the muted mural of entwined Islamic geometric forms, the skinny bank of secretarial microprocessors, and the fleshy indoor plants.

"Yeah." Bill delFord walked beside Lapp as they went down the corridor to the Grope Pit. "The whole spread came to us by default, and we've tinkered with it. You can blame the OPEC upheaval. There was this sheikhling, Hosein el-Bagir Shah, who came to the States in the early sixties to learn the finer details of petroleum engineering, mixed with some advanced chicanery at the Harvard Business School. He was a devout Muslim and the hippie thing took his interest. I think his father had known Aldous back in the bad old days; anyway, the kid sank some spare millions in this setup, in memoriam, with some muddled notion of blending Sufism and high technology. Shortly after it was established, the price of oil skyrocketed and Hosein came to his senses. I hear he's doing very nicely."

"And you?"

"I was in the right place at the right time. He had it all locked in as a non-profit foundation, and there's still a trickle of money available to pay for upkeep and incidentals. Most of our funding—such as it is—comes from research contracts from NASA and several of the bigger foundations."

They stepped into a medium-sized room filled with sprawling bodies under lights with a warm golden tinge; heavy curtains covered one wall, blocking the natural illumination from the enormous sky. DelFord flopped on a large beanbag, waving his hands at the floor as the visitors stood perplexed. Sutton let himself down quickly, favoring the creases in his trousers. The other two, after some hesitation, sat on a single large fluffy mattress, Lapp with his broad back against the wall, the physicist hunched forward with his hairy shins exposed.

"Morning, folks. As you know, these gentlemen have expressed an interest in our work on ooby. I don't know any more about it than you, right now, but I'm certain we can depend on the general to have something piquant up his sleeve—like maybe a new device for detecting insipient Maoism by the radical absorption lines in the auric spectrum." A titter from one corner. Briskly, delFord introduced the visitors. "Obviously I needn't waste time returning the introductions; I'm sure our friends here have spent many happy minutes studying our files."

Tony Freestone shifted his great bulk, propping his elbows. "It's that big?"

"It is." Sutton refused to be nettled. "Ladies and gentlemen, let me say personally, and on behalf of my colleagues, that we're pleased to meet you. What Bill states so bluntly is true, but I hope you won't find anything unduly sinister in what is, after all, a routine pre-briefing procedure."

"Hell, no," said Alice Langer. "The price of liberty is eternal voyeurism."

Audibly, Lennox Harrington's knuckles cracked. He stared at Alice and said precisely, through tight lips, "At this moment a pair of army technicans is setting up a small piece of equipment in your main psychophysical laboratory. Outside, a truckload of soldiers is stationed with maser surveillance, two nausea-inducing subsonic generators, and a machinegun. The device the technicians are installing is capable of withstanding a ground-zero gigaton nuclear explosion. Perhaps this will enable you to grasp the need for caution."

In the ensuing silence, Bill delFord waited for Sutton to hit the roof. Instantly, he told himself: Don't be foolish. They've brought the thing here for us to study. Why should it matter who tells us about it? But he knew that Harrington's outburst had been a bad lapse. The strain, he thought, must have been immense. He let out his breath and realized he was trembling. The implications began to race in his mind.

Delwyn Schauble, the biofeedback specialist, began to giggle. "And you're telling *us?*" she asked with a squeak.

"We're not the first on the block," Bill said to her. "The Soviet Union has it, too."

The babble began; kids let loose in the playground.

"There goes deterrence."

"The N-country proliferation theorem—"

"Opportunities for reactor terrorism—"

"Poor old Teller, all those years—"

"And what the hell," broke through Alistair Jerison's booming voice, "does an anti-nuclear shield have to do with astral projection?"

"Let's have a little restraint in here," Sutton barked. He was met with unfriendly looks, but the room quieted. "The work your Institute has prosecuted on OOBE's may have a critical bearing on certain by-products of this process. Before we discuss the details, however, it's necessary for Dr. Harrington to give you an outline of how the field functions. Lennox?"

With distaste, the physicist stated, "I cannot pretend that this forum meets with my approval. There is no doubt in my mind that the so-called 'paranormal' phenomena with which you waste your time are a congeries of delusive—" He halted and licked his lips. "However, your work on sensory deprivation and overload may well contribute to a solution of our pressing difficulties. The device, as you have understood, is intended as a defense against nuclear attack. Do you have an overhead projector?" He was directed to the computer terminal and rapidly jotted down a series of equations with a light-pencil; they were displayed on a large wall screen. After thirty seconds of incomprehensible Hermitian scalar analysis, Bill interrupted him.

"Lennox, I'm sorry, but you've lost me. Could we have some approximation of the central data in clear? My math goes about as far as sophomore calculus, I'm afraid."

Lewis Carroll country, Bill thought. *He only does it to annoy, because he knows it teases.* But that was probably unfair. Lennox Harrington doubtless pitched his delivery more generously when giving advice to the ignoramuses of Military Intelligence, but the man was accustomed to the swift cut and thrust of his peers. Even this unruly shambles must project enough of the tone of an academic symposium to cue him in to high-powered exposition.

"I take it you are all familiar with the elements, at least, of quark confinement theory?" the physicist said impatiently. He pronounced it to rhyme with *cork* rather than *mark*. "Most subatomic particles are of the class known as hadrons. These, in turn, are composed of six kinds of quarks, paired into three generations, and distinguished by mass and other quantum values. Despite strenuous efforts, no one has been able to liberate the quark constituents from baryons and mesons, though they can readily be observed as point-sources inside protons, for example.

"Until recently there were several competing theories. Politzer and Bjorken attributed confinement to 'infrared slavery.' They held that the intrahadronic binding forces, which can be conceptualized as exchange particles called gluons, fail to obey the inverse square law. My own approach, using broken-gauge unification, saw hadrons as flux strings bearing the particle's momentum and energy, with quarks at the ends defining the additional properties."

"My God," Freestone said, "it's a Baggie!"

Annoyed, Harrington nodded sharply. "Kenneth Johnson at M.I.T. proposed that the quarks are literally held captive within gluon bags. Pouring in energy, the classic way to split particles into their components, merely expands the bag. The energy is translated into bag mass. Since then, Yoichiro Nambu has shown that strings are actually elongated gluon bags."

"You've built a bottomless bag," delFord said, tracing Freestone's intuition. "No matter how much radiant energy you pour in, it turns into a tougher fabric. What's the, uh, the elastic limit?"

"There is none." Harrington turned off the display and sat down gingerly. "You're only half-right. Quarks are generated, as well, and confined within hadron-sized bags. On the interface of the field, helium is created, which disperses as fast as it is formed. Under sustained nuclear or laser bombardment, of course, a fusion plasma envelope is produced, which decays when inputs are extinguished."

"Jesus Christ!" said Berys Marshall. Her gentle, grandmotherly face was pale. "You boys have been busy."

DelFord regarded the ceiling. His thoughts leaped like chains of sparks.

"Cities and agricultural belts get a perimeter of bag generators," he said. "The standard infrared detection satellites monitor a possible I.C.B.M. barrage launch. Up go the shields. If the intelligence was incorrect, no harm done . . . unless the bag field injures the people inside it. And it does, of course." He sat up and stared at Sutton. "Something happens to people under the gluon barrier, something intolerable. And you want us to find out what it is." He laughed incredulously. "An altered state of consciousness. Little wonder you came to us, Joe. We're expendable, and we're experts in deliberate derangement. A convenient combination."

"That's not true," the astronaut said sharply. "You're free to volunteer, as I did. The United States Government doesn't—"

"Oh, we'll volunteer, all right, Hugh," Delwyn Schauble told him softly. "They know we can't pass up a chance like this. Total exclusion of ambient electromagnetic noise. That's what it is, isn't it, Dr. Harrington?"

"Absolute interdiction," he said. "Nothing gets in; nothing gets out—including gravity waves."

"A space drive?"

"No." He drew back his lips unconsciously. "Einstein's Equivalence postulate has been disproved. Our protected cities won't be flying off into space; the inertial frame—"

"What does it do to people?" Bill asked the general. The room was utterly still.

"There is no observable effect whatsoever, detrimental or beneficial, upon animal test preparations," Sutton said. "Experiments with marine organisms like grunions, aquatic worms, and oysters, which respond to the lunar periodicity, show a temporary confusion of life cycle. Extensive reports will be made available to—"

"What does it do to people?" delFord asked again.

"Anxiety. Hysteria. Delusions of leaving their bodies. Mystical trance. In some cases," he said with retributive brutality, "it drives them insane."

"I see." Bill closed his eyes, bent his chin to his folded hands. "Out-of-body-experience."

"Yes." The general stood up, stretching his legs. "Think of yourselves as guinea pigs if it pleases you, if it caters to your damned paranoia, but the truth is that you crazy loonies come closer to being experts on this son-of-a-bitch than anyone else we've been able to locate who wasn't under lock and key. I read your last report, Bill, read it twice, carefully, and I tell you it distressed me. All of you people in this room—God Almighty, I know your track records. You could have been doing useful work, making significant contributions. Be that as it may. My superiors want you to take a shot at it. *Someone* has to make sense of it." He seemed genuinely in the grip of powerful, confused emotions.

"Sure, Joe," delFord said, aware of sudden compassion for the man. He sat up straighter and looked around the group. "Here's an idea I'd like to try out on you, gang. Romantic versus Classical science."

"Nice," Tony said at once.

Anne Hawthorne, their British psychologist, looked at Bill sharply. She rolled over, plucked her sari across brown knees. "I thought we'd got past binary, polar paradigms, Bill. Even Freud used a three-way system, and he had to keep replacing the parameters. And Lennox, here, wants six quarks for his *elements*."

Tony Freestone shook his great, jowled head. "The mind has an inescapable tendency to reduce to pairs.

Maybe it's the cerebral bilateral asymmetry. Pursue that—there's no reason why the dimensions need be seen as ends of a continuum; maybe they're orthogonal."

Crisply, Alice Langer stated, "For what it's worth, the distinction isn't new." Her knowledge was encyclopedic; she tended, as a result, to the pedantic, even in the Grope Pit. "There was a respected tradition of 'romantic' chemistry as late as the nineteenth century. Charles C. Gillespie discussed it in relation to the Jacobin—"

"It's a starter, Alice; I'm not looking for prizes for originality. Here's the sort of thing I had in mind. Classicism typically connotes a regime of well-ordered rules, unities, causality viewed as segmented chains, decorous generalities. While Romanticism, of course, is the affirmation—"

Sutton, staring around him with growing choler, snapped, "What the hell are you maniacs babbling about?" He looked at his watch. "The technicians will have the device set up by now. I suggest that we break up this merry antiquarian kaffeeklatsch and get to work."

For the first time, delFord felt truly angry at the man. "Joe, shut your mouth or get out. When you're in the Grope Pit and we're engaged in Heuristic Reciprocity, you contribute or you leave."

In honest bafflement, Sutton said, "We don't have *time* for philosophy."

"General, at Bethesda we used similar techniques," Lapp said. "Conceptual block-busting, lateral search—"

"Those methods are tactical," Anne told him. She eyed the astronaut with some interest. "Ours is strategic."

The tension and hostility in the Pit eased. As if there had been no interruption, Alistair Jerison said, "The Romantic/Classic dichotomy emerged in a specific dialectical context. Romanticism was a last-ditch attempt by a malcontent intellectual elite to regain the imagined freedoms of feudalism."

"Nonsense," the Cal Tech physicist said, to everyone's surprise. "If you take Thomas Kuhn's view, you might regard the normal conduct of scientific investigation as subject to the Classical constraints. Romanticism then emerges justifiably during the collapse of exhausted paradigms."

"Courtly love!" Anne cried. "The doomed, heroic quest for an object which by definition is out of reach. But isn't that the background to *all* science now, not just during paradigm upheavals?" She glanced around the group. "I mean, we don't just have experimental limitations anymore. There's quantal uncertainty, cybernetic random switching, Gödel's Proof. Our courtly quest is intrinsically unsatisfiable."

"Okay," Alistair admitted heavily. "But, in any case, ordered data only becomes knowledge, in the authentic sense, when it stands in meaningful relation to the active struggle for human liberation." Sutton groaned. "Romantic ideology imposed isolation on intellectuals. Classic culture was repressive, sure, but it remained social. The Romantic rebellion was decadent rather than liberatory precisely because it *rejected* the social context."

Bill delFord lifted his head. "Joe, were your experimental subjects put under the shield singly or in groups?"

The general blinked. "Why, each man went in alone, of course. It's standard procedure; it minimizes risks to personnel, reduces the variables under consideration—"

"I thought so. Good old positivist lab technique." Rising, Bill opened the soundproof door. "Okay, gang, that's it for the morning. Thanks for your help." The team stood up and straggled out. None of them continued the fierce debate. DelFord stopped Anne Hawthorne, holding her suntanned arm. "I'd like to try Hugh, you, and me under the field simultaneously. Are you game, Anne?"

"Fine." The woman looked slightly nervous, but she smiled as she glanced across at the waiting astronaut.

"I presume the dimensions of the field are adequate for three people," Bill said to Harrington.

"Certainly," the physicist said, taken aback by the abrupt change of pace. "It's an oblate spheroid four meters high, with the generator at one of the foci. We didn't intend the subject to be claustrophobic."

Testily, the general said, *"I'm* claustrophobic, goddamn it, and you're screwing the lid tighter every minute. Would it offend you too grossly if I ask for an explanation?"

"Three heads are better than one," delFord told him.

"Bill, that's not a working hypothesis; it's a blind shot in the dark. You don't lock three amnesiacs together to speed their recovery."

"How do you know?"

"I've seen men blundering around in battle shock."

"And do your psychiatrists treat them with solitary confinement?"

"Hmm. Yes, if they become violent—as they often do."

"That's not therapy; it's staff insurance. Nor do your reports list violence as a side-effect. My best guess right now is that Alistair hit the nail on the head. Your methods of investigation destroyed the social context your experimental subjects needed to sustain their sanity. The gluon field imposes a more savage quarantine on its victims than human beings have ever experienced. We're all linked together, Joe. Profoundly. Organically. The field severs that link, and your subjects bleed to death."

Sutton grunted in disgust. "Jung. Lilly. I've read my share, Bill, and there's not a single operational definition in the whole mystical box of tricks. Nothing testable, not one item you can put on a bench and measure."

"We'll provide your test, Joe. And if I'm wrong," he said with a grin which failed to convince any of them, "you can tie us up in satin ribbons and pack us off to the closest funny farm as a matched set."

On the way to the main entrance, delFord stuck his head around his office door and spoke briefly with Janine. Then they went out into the cooler midday air. Waves crashed behind them, at the foot of the vast bluff. They crossed the parking apron and left the paving, following a gentle grassy incline to the mandatory geodesic domes half-hidden in trees and shrubbery. A bird sang out; it, or its fellow, left a leafy branch and veered off into the gray sky. A large armored vehicle stood outside one of the black domes, ugly in outline against the somber solar-energy hexagons. On its roof, a maser mirror whirled. Sutton gestured to a patient, alert serviceman; they conferred in low tones. The general brusquely waved the others on to the entrance.

Against God's and Murphy's express ordinance, the army technicians had evidently experienced no difficulties in getting the device installed and phase-tested within the echoing barn. Among the litter of hastily cleared equipment, the gluon field was a prodigious bauble. Like a great curved mirror, an impossible egg of mercury, it rested without compressive distortion from gravity under the bolder arc of the Fuller dome. Bill gazed at it, dazzled, expecting it to roll from its unstable position and break into a myriad of smaller balls of spinning light.

Abruptly it was gone, replaced by a drab skeletal construction of bolted structural steel, an ovoid of wire mesh, a neat matt-finish box on a stanchion at one focus.

"It's activated and deactivated by a quartz crystal clock," Lennox Harrington told him. "Naturally, there's no way we can control it externally while the gluon field is energized. Our standard run is five minutes. You can alter that to suit yourselves—and override the programming from inside if the strain becomes intolerable."

Sutton was obliged to drag Bill away from the cage for the concentrated briefing session he'd prepared with Hugh Lapp and the physicist. The woman and the four men sat around a rickety table on stools, intently going over the documents and reports from previous experiments. Periodically, shadows shifted subtly as the mirror flashed into existence, hovered for five minutes, and extinguished itself.

After ninety minutes Anne leaned back from the table, stretched, and said, "I'm ravenous. I don't suppose we can have some sandwiches?"

"Not recommended," said Hugh.

"You're telling me." She pulled a face. "But that's the best we can do over here in greasy-hand territory."

"The only time I was in there, I threw up," the astronaut told her.

Anne nodded. "You must have the same catering service." Sighing, she asked delFord, "Enemas, too, I suppose?"

"I think so. And ten minutes of yoga before we pull the blanket over our heads." He glanced at the captain, and his mouth drew down ironically. "All our affective runs are done nude, Hugh. I hope you won't mind."

"I'll try to sustain my grief." His muscular shoulders moved. He gazed reflectively at Anne. She grinned back at him.

Minutes later, after she'd vanished into the bathroom with the enema bag, the men heard her vomiting in a businesslike fashion. Hugh halted at the door of the men's room and raised his eyebrows. "She's that nervous?"

"No. I'll be doing the same myself. It's a combination of common sense and Reichian relaxation therapy. Emptying the gut is a precaution suggested by your own experience. But I wouldn't recommend it unless you know how—it's a bit wearing."

DelFord came out naked, then kicked his sandals off at the edge of the cage. The technicians had positioned three aluminum-and-foam plastic harnesses during the briefing. Anne, eyes closed and breathing deeply, was already resting semi-supine in the central billet. Bill climbed up beside her and squeezed her hand. She really is a most attractive woman, he thought. How the hell does she keep that rich suntan? Her light brown hair, long and fine, was swept up carefully in a knot. He recalled the feel of that hair, and briefly the sadness came back to him. Their affair had been short and intense. Then he thought, with amusement: She's lusting after our honest captain today. The myth of astronauts. I wonder how long it'll take her to have him in bed. Not long, he decided. Hughie's no slouch, unless I miss my mark.

Lapp crossed the floor, stolid in his nudity. He held something metallic in his fist; after he had clambered up and slid into place, he leaned across Anne and handed it to delFord. "I took it out of your shirt pocket," he said. "It was barking at me. Like a Pekingese."

"Oh, shit, Janine must have a call for me. Joe!" he yelled. "Will you phone the main building and tell my secretary that we're in the middle of a run? If it's Selma, tell her I'm in bed with Bob and Carol." He placed the bleeper on the black box at his head and said, "Everyone ready?"

"Sure."

"Let's go," grunted the astronaut; he was pale, and his voice was tight.

"You heard what the man said," Bill told Harrington. He saw the physicist's fingers jab a sequence of buttons on the central generator, then close a clear cover across them.

"The field activates in twenty seconds. Don't hesitate to cut loose if the experience is unbearable."

Bill delFord ceased to exist.

The universe stopped at a concave sweep a couple of meters overhead. Flickeringly, the internal lights came on, dimly, with a faint buzzing. Vestibular canals signaled vertigo, free fall, acceleration. A sharp scent of sweat and urine moved in the air. Nobody home.

Abruptly, tinnily, a massed choir of male and female voices cried joyously: *Hallelujah! Hallelujah! Hal-le-ee-luu-uu-jah!*

An elephant trumpeted, and a bloodhound belled. There were the imperative hoot of a fire siren and a pompous British voice clearing its throat and saying, "Unaccustomed as I am to public speaking," the scrape of many chairs as a multitude made good its escape, a symphony of cash registers, a speeded-up male Japanese saying, "My feet are getting closer," a lavatory flushing, and a moist, protracted, lubricious fart.

In the incredulous silence, there was a strangled, hysterical gasp.

"Our Farter, Which art in Heaven—"

Peals of silly giggles.

"Fart for art's sake."

"Sewerealism?"

Booming guffaws, like drunken oafs.

"Don't talk such shit."

"You taking the piss out of me?"

"What a bummer! It's just pouring out."

Bill delFord did not exist, but some wiring diagram thought in desperation: This is no proper pastime for a philosopher. We need—

"—Sir Karl Pooper."

"The Open Society and Its Enemas?"

A shriek of drawn-out laughter. "No. That's Jean-Paul Farter." A pause. "The existenchilist."

"She was only a stable-hand but all the horse manure."

"What a handicrap."

"Golf? Not athletic enough. Prefer the shit-put."

"Never made the elimination finals."

"No. Team was pruned down."

Pain in the chest, in the diaphragm.

"Clear your head with Diarretics."

"Diuretics?"

"Shitology. Turdomancy. Movement of the future."

"A tissue of lies."

"Wipe the Opposition."

"Support the Turd World."

"Sounds like fecism."

"Troops in jake-boots? Flushing out the Privy Council? Establishing the Dung Dynasty? You're potty!"

The giggles came in convulsive, uncontrollable waves. Finally they ceased, and bodies rolled in their harnesses, hands knocking against sweat-slicked flesh and, finding it, touching, palping. Legs kicked and opened.

"Lapp me."

More silly giggles, in the swaying, terrible nowhere, and a shockingly blatant sound of slurping.

The universe returned, in a deluge to crack the head. Bill delFord screamed, piteously, and clamped palms over ears, elbows striking together. He was elevated; the light of souls beyond souls, crystalline glory, intolerable hubbub of infinite conversation; white radiance enclosed him, lifting him in a moment from his body, which hung below in the silvery bubble (but that had gone already?), showed him with his mouth slack and inane tears of mirth under his eyelids, his arms moving out to batter the woman beside him, who turned, her thighs spreading in invitation, and the other man shifting in weightlessness to bring down his head; all of this in an instant, imploding; and he fell back into his body, aghast, bereft, clinging to the spheres of endless light. . . .

The astronaut lifted his face in stupefaction and humiliation, banging his head against the wire frame. Anne moaned, and her face filled with a deeper flush. Groaning, Bill reached up and took the bleeper in his hand. He hurled it with great force across the floor of the dome. His stomach ached abominably.

"If you're still hungry," he said, "let's go eat lunch."

Lapp ignored the jibe. Glancing from the shattered bleeper to delFord and back to Anne, his face tightened with delayed understanding. "I'm sorry."

"Don't be silly," Anne told him. Lightly, with affection, she jabbed his arm, swinging down out of the cradle. "Par for the course. Here at Huxley, we're famous for letting it all hang out."

Obliquely, Bill said, "Ancient history."

"What he means is, we had a little fling and that was that. Nice while it lasted, though." She gave Bill a friendly hug. "Hugh, how did the subjective effects compare to your previous test?"

Instantly Lapp was all business. "The out-of-body phenomena, virtually identical. All that cretinous punning? Totally new. Frankly, I'm astonished. My jokes might be pretty bad, but kindergarten humor hasn't broken me up like that since I was four years old. What in hell happened?"

They paid no attention to Harrington, who hopped anxiously from foot to foot, trying without success to insert his suddenly irrelevant technical questions. General Sutton remained aloof on the far side of the test area, isolated by his manifest disapproval of the proceedings. Bill shivered, and slipped his feet into his battered Indian sandals. The dome was solar-warmed, but even in California the chill of winter leaked into a large enough convecting space. "Not kindergarten, Hugh," he said thoughtfully. "Small children don't know the names of too many philosophers of science. Good grief. Sir Karl Pooper, indeed!"

"I agree," Anne said. "That wasn't clinical regression. I think it was something more frightening than that—as though our brains were switched off. No, that's not right. As if conscious awareness was closed down. I felt as if my mind were functioning at the level of a . . . an indexing program. Pulling pieces of data out of memory and juxtaposing them on the instruction of some puerile sub-routine triggered by your goddamn crude farting bleeper."

"A computer terminal," Lapp mused. "Operating mechanically, without any true intelligence. Certainly without a trace of mature judgment." He scratched at his head, a curiously childlike gesture. "But why should external shielding screw up the brain's interior software . . . or hardware? Whichever."

"By golly, I think maybe my hunch was correct all along," Bill said with wonderment. "We've proved Carl Jung right. The gluon field literally cut us off from the collective unconscious. It left us isolated. Absolutely severed from the rest of humanity. Just the three of us to anchor one another, linked in a hermetically sealed bubble. . . ."

The technicians, he noticed, were jockeying for advantage, staring with blatant enthusiasm at Anne's naked body. He glanced down at his own uninspiring belly.

"I think we'd better get our pants on," he said in a low voice. "Joe would really be pissed if the vice squad put the arm on us at this point."

5. California

At three in the morning, the hour the beasts in tight leather boots prefer when they come to take you away, Bill delFord roused blurrily to the sharp knock on his door. Selma's regular breathing had not altered. He lay on his back, the formless dread of nightmare slowly ebbing. In dream, he reminded himself hazily, the voluntary muscles relax entirely. Occasionally the sense of paralysis leaks through, permeating dream with the terrors of captivity, threat, claustrophobia. Yet that inchoate sensation can also trigger tranquil illusions of levitation, he thought, of floating, of leaving the mundane body. . . . His heart jumped, hammering, as the brisk knocking was repeated.

Jesus! he thought. Selma stirred, grumbling, as he reached for the small digital clock beside the bed. Three-oh-seven. I'll kill the bastards, he thought in rage. His wife's bare leg was hot against his; the disparity in their nocturnal temperatures was a cause of wonder to him, and of annoyance when he awoke in the night—it made the reentry to sleep doubly difficult. He was half out of bed when the door opened quietly and his son Ben looked in.

"For you, Dad," the boy said laconically. "He insisted."

"Thanks, son," Bill muttered. He pulled his old threadbare Chinese gown around his shoulders and padded from the room, closing the door behind him. The boy stood uneasily in the hall. "Go back to bed, Ben. I'll tell you all about it in the morning."

The uniform was not one Bill recognized. He poked at the grit in the corners of his eyes and glared angrily. "Do you have any idea what hour—"

"My apologies, Dr. delFord," the man said in a low, clear voice. "General Sutton sends his compliments. Could you dress as quickly as possible? We have a chopper standing by in Monterey to take you to the air force base in San Jose, where you'll meet a U.N. courier jet."

DelFord's temper lost its last strand. "You can tell

Sutton to take a flying fuck at the—" A heavy boot blocked the closing door.

"I'm sorry, sir, but my instructions are clear. We don't have time for arguments."

There was a sound of footsteps and another figure came out of the darkness. "At ease, soldier. There's no need to harass the doctor." The man stepped into the dim illumination provided by the nightlight. Bill recognized him: Bryant Gellner, an ex-colleague from U.C.L.A. in the early seventies. He wore the dark suit and deft protocol of a U.N. diplomat. "I'm sorry to wake you, Bill." He extended his hand. "You're looking well for a man pulled out of bed at this godless hour. I was caught on the radiotelephone, or I'd have done the honors myself. Very well, driver, you can wait for us in the car. We shouldn't be long."

"Bryant, you presume on our acquaintanceship," Bill said without grace. "I'd gladly invite you in for a drink if the sun wasn't over the yardarm somewhere in the Indian Ocean. What the hell's Sutton playing at this time?"

"The general's in New York at this moment and he's not getting any sleep, either. In fact"—Gellner smiled—"I imagine you're four or five hours ahead of him in that respect. If we can bid the doorstep farewell, I'll explain everything in the comfort and privacy of your own home."

"Ah, shit." A distant shimmering danced at the limits of Bill's sensations, an invisible flickering, an inaudible buzz. It increased as he passed the silent telephone. In an illogical flash of insight, he conjectured that he was perceiving the sixty-cycle hum of the electrical devices and conduits in the house. Something had rasped his nervous system to an irritated, preternaturally acute sensitivity. That dream, he thought suddenly. It was the gluon field. The blank eternity of inhuman nothing, the explosion of light, the experience of floating out and away from my body. "Sit down," he told the diplomat, pulling out a kitchen chair. "I'll fix coffee."

"Thank you." Bryant Gellner was impatient, but he had clearly decided that compliance was the swiftest road to persuasion. "I trust we didn't wake your wife."

As he took milk from the refrigerator, Bill saw for an instant a fuzzy wash of violet light like ocean phosphorescence at its back. "She's literally slept through earthquakes," he said. "Why can't it wait?"

"I don't know," the U.N. man said frankly. "But whatever it is, I have a hunch there are lights going on all over the War Room Big Board."

The nuclear shield, Bill told himself. Pouring coffee, he was mildly surprised to find himself so calm. I've lived on the San Andreas fault for years at a time without breaking into a sweat. Maybe this is the same.

"A preemptive strike?"

"I don't *want* to know," Gellner said, his hungry eyes denying it. "There's a very curious U.N. flap on, very contained, very tight. None of the hoopla of a ritual scare. I doubt that it's the big one, but someone's remembered leaving the kerosene near the fire. That's a Mach 3 bird they have waiting for you at San Jose. I hope your circadian rhythms are in good shape."

DelFord stood up. "Do I need an overcoat?"

"A light suit would be fine." The diplomat smiled sweetly. "It's summer down there."

"Good Christ."

He awoke Selma as he was leaving. "Big silver bird kidnaps your Willy. I don't know how long I'll be gone. The mad bastards seem to think it's urgent, so I'll doubtless find myself perched on my ass in the middle of Chile twiddling my thumbs for a week. Then they'll decide they meant the other Bill delFord and pack me off home with a set of scenic views and no explanation. I'll call you soonest." He kissed her, tweaked her fleshy buttocks fondly as he leaned across to turn off the lamp, and departed regretfully. At Ben's door he paused for a moment, and was dumbfounded by the light snores he heard. Adolescents, he thought, shaking his head. Gellner had preceded him out of the house; Bill went into the chilly night air and found the gray limousine, all its lights out, parked several houses away.

The diplomat opened a back door for him. A glass partition sealed the passengers off from the driver, presumably a security device. As his hand touched the vehicle's frame, Bill sensed a mild, soapy texture against his fingers. He stepped back, rapped on the driver's window.

"You've got a short from the battery," he informed the soldier. "There's current leaking into the body work."

The driver looked at him steadily and said nothing. Shrugging, Bill climbed in next to Gellner.

"It's a complex heterodyning signal, sir," the soldier's

voice said from a grille in the partition. "Pink noise. It neutralizes bugs, and scrambles maser detection spy-beams bounced off the vehicle."

DelFord turned and stared at Gellner. "Golly," he said. "Isn't it exciting?"

The helicopter lift to the air force base did nothing to improve his mood. He hated the rowdy, clamoring things. After the effortless, nearly silent limousine, the chopper's vulgarity was an affront to the sleeping night. Falling toward earth, they slipped over rows of similar machines waiting neatly for the next convenient opportunity to spray human flesh with flaring petroleum jelly.

A stern, blue-garbed officer met them outside a gray concrete building. He wore a gun at his belt. Gellner tendered documents which were examined routinely. "Good morning, gentlemen. Mr. Gellner, you're requested to call New York. Just go right through."

They strode through a brightly lit green-gray corridor that managed to convey the dullness of blight. The place was first cousin to every military structure Bill had ever seen; it nauseated him. The diplomat made his call under an opaque plastic privacy hood. A wizened gnome, cap grimy and askew, told delFord that his courier was fueled and ready for takeoff. Gellner returned. "All clear. I'll see you off."

In a small bay at the back an electric runabout awaited them, post-box red. The gnome gestured them in. His collar appeared damp; it drooped. Somehow, in spite of the smooth, efficient motor, he managed to make the machine lurch. The five-hundred-meter ride to the jet's cruel wedge was no less eventful. Bill found himself grinning. Although they crossed perfectly flat tarmac, the little man was able to create the impression that they were galloping over rubble or worse.

They climbed out under a swept-back titanium wing and the red vehicle veered into reverse. The gnome sped off without a word, bucking as he went. There was just the merest hint, through the cold dark wind, of a derisive belch.

"Is he always like that?"

"So it's said." Gellner stood at the foot of the access steps, gazing after the little machine in admiration. "It's his way of deflating the pomposity of bureaucrats and the vanity of the nation's favorite sons. He's a dear old thing.

I believe he shot two saboteurs dead a few years back while they were trying to plant a bomb in *Air Force One*. Radical maintenance men, if you can credit such a thing." He gave delFord a bland glance and offered his firm handshake.

"I see." Bill grinned at him. "I'll try not to defect."

The polished fuselage was innocent of portholes. Inside, cunning ergonomics engineering had contrived a mahogany conference table flanked by soft-backed stools bolted to the deck. Aft, six comfortable lay-back chairs faced a series of television screens and a small computer terminal. No doubt there was a bar tucked away in there somewhere. Seated in one of the chairs, bleary-eyed and friendly, was the astronaut Hugh Lapp. His chin was penumbral. Bill checked his watch and nodded to himself with furtive pleasure. The stigmata was, indeed, very nearly five-o'clock shadow.

"Ah, the cunnilingual captain."

"Greetings, sage." The astronaut patted the padded chair next to him. "Strap in; we lift off in thirty seconds."

Bill glanced around, blinked as the hatch was closed and sealed from the outside. "Just us chickens?" He dropped heavily beside Lapp. A red warning light blinked above the bank of monitors. The roar of engines, which had been increasing since he'd entered the jet, reached a screaming crescendo. A sudden pressure on his torso thrust him back into his yielding seat. The tremor of vibration was gone, and the pressure increased.

"You might enjoy watching this," Lapp said belatedly, pushing a button. One of the screens brightened, revealing the geometry of runway lights falling away vertically at fantastic speed. Somehow the display seemed more real, in the ambience of this surrealistic exercise, than any direct view through the double-glazing of a porthole.

Maybe only what we take for granted seems real through a window, Bill mused. The extraordinary seems more natural when it comes to us via an instrument. Television tells us of war and catastrophe in exotic lands. It shows us men in clumsy suits kangarooing upon the moon. The only exciting things I've ever seen through a window, he thought, amused, were my big sister's big tits when I was twelve.

Curiously, Lapp chose that moment to say, "It's not the same, is it, Bill? We can up the magnification"—he twiddled a knob, and the distant lights slurred and expanded giddyingly—"or put it through an infrared transducer, with mini-computer enhancement"—and the image leaped into slightly discolored clarity, the suburbs knife-edged in their ranks—"but it's not the same as a raw eyeball. You get the feeling it's all being patched together in a studio."

Fortunately, Bill's neutral grunt was not taken as disagreement, or the younger man might have gone on to defend his opinion. As it was, Bill felt a brief sad sentiment of loss, as though in this gap between them the generational abyss had deepened. Ludicrously, it summoned an echo of that hateful, ineluctable failure of sympathy he detected in his relationship with Ben, the severing one by one of those precious links of deep fellow-feeling which had once existed between father and son. Others would grow to replace that earlier, simpler trust, he knew, but there was enough truth in Freud's shrewd conjectures to spoil forever the comradely myths of more archaic dynasties. For a moment the strands of his reverie wound together, in an almost hallucinatory visual memory of the astronaut's embarrassed face lifting from Anne's lewd embrace.

The jet leveled out at twenty thousand meters. This data was provided on a digital readout, which stated as well that their indicated air speed was twenty-nine hundred klicks, roughly Mach 3 at their altitude. Lapp unbuckled his seatbelt as a green light flashed. "We've got good weather all the way until we reach the turbulence at the Rock."

"You seem to know a hell of a lot more about it than I do," Bill said tiredly. The Rock of Gibraltar? The Albanians have seized it and towed it out to sea, threatening the traffic of Free World and Communist ports alike. The single weapon proof against the anti-nuclear screen. And they've done it with heinous Maoist astral thought projections. "Does your advance knowledge extend to the location of the drinkies? I could use a bourbon."

Lapp went forward, opened a panel beside the terminal, returned with Bill's bourbon and a sturdy measure of Southern Comfort for himself. "That was a freaky experience this morning. Yesterday morning."

The instant relaxation Bill felt was clearly a psychological effect, since the alcohol had not had time to diffuse through his bloodstream. "Hugh, I'd rather we talk about our destination."

"Sure. Let me tell you a story. What you're about to hear is known to less than a thousand people in the entire world. The decision authorizing this briefing has been ratified by the President of the United States and the Central Committee of the Communist Party of the Soviet Union." Lapp was, suddenly, no longer the boy spaceman; a note of command had entered his voice.

"I'm all ears."

"Way back when, the third lunar landing mission took off for the Fra Mauro uplands. *Apollo 13* was commandered by Jim Lovell, with Fred Haise as LEM pilot and John Swigert replacing Tom Mattingly, who was grounded with suspected German measles. Mattingly lost his chance at history, though he still doesn't know it. Do you recall the flight?"

"Not particularly. Space flight is a goddamn wasteful boondoggle, even if NASA does fund most of my fun." Bill watched the ground monitor; faintly, morning light was streaking the Earth. "No offense intended."

"I'm amazed, Bill," the astronaut said with some sharpness. "That's the sort of narrow, reflex response I've come to expect from cocktail party accountants and vitamin-deficient health-food fanatics. I think you'll change your opinion.

"On April 13, 1970, the Number Two liquid oxygen tank exploded in the service module. The landing mission had to be abandoned. They were not on a 'free return' trajectory, and they needed a major burn to avoid falling into solar orbit. M.I.T. computers ran out an optimum program, and Lovell altered the trajectory so the spacecraft would swing past the moon and switch them back to Earth. As they rounded the moon, out of radio contact with Mission Control, their instruments were thrown into a tizzy by signals from a crater on Farside."

DelFord felt his tongue cringe from the liquor. With wild surmise he said, "Intelligent signals?" Then his common sense returned. "A Russian base. But I thought their space technology—"

"No, Bill. The signals were overlaid on half their instrumentation tapes. As soon as the craft emerged from lunar shadow, Lovell employed a contingency security measure: he masered the unknown data to Mission Control through a comsat in synchronous orbit, which microwaved the signal down to the sixty-four-meter dish at Goldstone in California."

"You really *do* mean—"

"I do. Defense Department computers examined the lunar signals and concluded that beyond question they represented a non-human, extraterrestrial intelligence. The signal itself resisted translation and has done so during the intervening decades. The most favored current hypothesis is that it's so garbled with noise we'll never retrieve it."

"So we're not alone." His abrupt, soaring delight startled delFord. Inner space was his realm; he had never felt anything but contempt for those who sought comfort in celestial chariots. Yet this was intelligence, he told himself. Minds, capable and dextrous, other than human. Moved by passions as alien, perhaps, as those which Lilly had posited for dolphins. He snapped his head forward intently.

"You said that was back in 1970. What's happened since then? Contact?" Suddenly, the whole thing rang false. "There were other *Apollo* missions, *Skylab,* the *Viking* landings on Mars for the Bicentennial. . . . Oh. I dare say they couldn't cancel that last program."

Hugh nodded, teacher commending an apt pupil. "In fact, *Apollo* was run down faster than originally planned. But, of course, if there'd been any major inexplicable deviations from the announced itineraries, interested parties all over the world would have pricked up their ears at once. All launches are alarmingly public, to those with adequate equipment. Keeping the facts restricted has taken the most massive, thorough security operation of all time."

Bill helped himself to more liquor. "You mentioned the Soviet Union."

"It was inevitable. Both nations have so much hardware in lunar orbit now it'd be impossible for either to monopolize such a phenomenon for long. One of the Soviet's *Luna* series automatic probes picked up the signals some months later. It was diverted to a soft landing in the crater. That was the field they'd specialized in after they forewent manned landing missions. As it was, a top-ranking Russian selenologist managed to tip off his American counterpart at an international congress at Baku, Azerbaijan, in the U.S.S.R. Plans were already afoot for the *Apollo-Soyuz* docking, which helped ease tensions. There was no alternative but for both of us to pool our data and form a joint security screen."

"What happened to the Russian scientist?"

Hugh gave him a thin smile. "Poor old Anatoli Kubolayev came within a hair of the firing squad. In the event, though, it was a *fait accompli,* so the Central Committee gave him a severe reprimand, a medal, and put him in charge of the Soviet end of the project. In the meantime, a covert U.S. military launch put a modified *Viking* survey craft into the aliens' crater. Its findings complemented those of the less sophisticated but more mobile *Luna* probe. They were perched on the remains of a complex built somewhere on the order of twenty-five million years ago."

A deep, numinous chill worked through Bill's bones. His eyes drifted to the monitor showing the vast, snow-covered terrain, a sunlit relief map, they were crossing at such speed. We're heading for the Pole, he thought; following a Great Circle path. It would take them—where? Eastern segment of the U.S.S.R.? Japan, with some slight course changes? But he was wearing a summer suit. Australia, he told himself in astonishment. The enormous, empty island continent at the edge of the Pacific, a bleached, sunburned place, as he recalled, as far removed from this icy landscape as it was possible to conceive.

Yet he knew that his parameters were too narrow. The land below him and the land he was aimed at like an arrow were old—far older than twenty-five million years. The Oligocene, he thought. The Pyrénées and the Apennines had already been born, and the Alps of Europe were getting uplift surgery. To the far west, a land bridge had linked Alaska to Asia. Or was his geology out of date, retired by plate tectonics? He felt a terrible weariness. How little time there was to know everything, when everything changed so fast, so much. The land below him, and its mirror on the world's far side, was old—did it learn? Or did it merely suffer change? Harsh, inhospitable to man and beast, it was of the Earth; it knew the long cycles of climate, its rocks wore down under ice or sun to sand, and its sand turned when it was permitted to soil, and as the planet wheeled the soil received sun or water and brought forth flowers in profusion. No terrain on Earth was utterly barren of life; nowhere had the land suffered the frigid nights and the scorching days of the moon's marias and mountains. Life was possible, below, in the howling winter, at the world's extremities, even if it was not welcomed. But the alien complex had waited patiently through twenty-five million years of lunar desolation. . . .

The astronaut sat in decent silence while Bill regained himself. Deftly, then, he took a reel of magnetic tape from his jacket and wound it into the audiovisual control panel. "I have some videotapes of the alien installation. This has been edited down from a series of *Viking* and *Luna* probe transmissions. Considering that the data had to be transmitted from the surface of the moon through a relay satellite in lunar orbit and a second comsat to Earth, the quality is pretty good."

A NASA emblem briefly lit a second screen, followed by an identification tag. Then Bill was looking along a vast, black scarp, its upper edge brilliant as molten metal. He drew a deep, reflex breath, felt himself falling into the blackness, felt the enormous gulf of ebon sky above that sun-scarred cliff merge with the black of the inner crater wall to form an emptiness that seemed to suck at his soul. . . . The camera angle started to shift, panning across the crater; the moment of paralysis was broken.

Lapp registered his expression. "It's awesome enough; I think you'll grant me that. These shots are from the modified *Viking,* which landed just at the beginning of a dawn period. The camera is now tracking toward the source of the signals. You can't see anything much yet because the crater's far wall blocks the sun, so they've edited out . . . ah, there we are."

Bill's pulse jumped. The floor of the crater, far below, had sprung into visibility. Without atmosphere to scatter light, the image was preternaturally acute. For a moment, in the loss of its customary cues to depth, his eye was baffled. This segment of the moon was not the gray-tan-brown of all the lunar features he'd seen portrayed in the past. If a giant had taken a huge black glass ashtray, heated it until the glass was ready to flow, then flung a titanic cube of blue steel into it so that streaks and ribs and filaments of glass had exploded outward to cool and set in grotesque patterns, his work would have looked like this.

"My God, what happened to it? A spacecraft impact?" A forgotten image leaped to his mind: the catastrophic detonation over the Tungus *taiga* in June, 1908, the colossal cosmic fireball which a journalist named Baxter had claimed was a crashed interstellar craft. Brother to this ancient ruin?

"No. it was definitely a base of some kind. We've code-named it 'Selene Alpha,' though to date we've found no further traces of the aliens elsewhere on the moon. That mess, as far as we can tell, is the end result of a nuclear attack against Selene Alpha."

"Nuclear?" Finally the pieces fit together. He could have kicked himself. The vast metal cube, tilted and battered, had not been volatilized, though the crater in which it stood had been devastated by those stellar fires. "The gluon shield. It was protected. That's where you got it."

The astronaut leaned forward, pressed his hands together until the bones cracked. "We weren't ready to build the screen, Bill. Our theorcticians are still tearing at their hair. Selene Alpha was partially protected by a gluon shield system, but the weapons which attacked it were even more advanced. Most of the critical mechanisms overloaded, fused into slag. There was just enough for us to work from. Our experimental rigs are at the stage of Fermi's Chicago football stadium pile. But there's more to it than that."

The picture had shifted to the vantage of another robot probe, this one situated on the glassy crater floor. Sagging, one corner sunk in melted rock, Selene Alpha loomed into view. It was magnificent: a lonely, timeless, equivocal tribute to some ancient species who had conquered the stars before humanity's ancestors had left the African grasslands. And perhaps, Bill brooded, it was tombstone, as well, for many of that race must have perished in the nuclear blast. Or had they found their escape? Had the screen donc its job, as a fuse melts by design under power overload, even as its components flared to slag?

"If the Alpha complex is a ruin, what sent the signals the *Apollo 13* crew intercepted?"

"Alpha isn't entirely a ruin. All of its mechanisms were solid-state—no moving parts. Apparently, the few still in operating condition recognized the crew as living beings within orbital range and switched themselves on. We're assuming the signals constituted a part of the aliens' navigational network. Their technology was fantastic, Bill."

Indeed, he thought—considering that even some residue of the system works twenty-five million years after a nuclear bombardment. If it had all been abandoned in mint condition, he knew, such longevity would still have been all but inconceivable.

The picture had jumped again. Now the camera was crawling slowly around the Alpha base, jiggling up and down and in and out of focus as the clumsy servomechs tried to cope with the slippery glass surface.

"Hey!" Bill cried, and immediately felt foolish.

The Soviet machine moved stupidly on, past the great dark jagged rent. Then Earth ground controllers had responded, stopped it, turned it gingerly back. A searchlight sprang into life. The robot lumbered into the airless, lifeless, devastated structure.

Time ceased for delFord as he followed the slow, careful investigation of the crippled complex. He forgot he sat in a U.N. courier jet hurtling across the North Pole; he forgot how strange, indeed daunting, it was that he should be privileged to view this incredibly secret film. From time to time the astronaut beside him commented quietly on the picture, detailing various conjectures concerning this melted lump or that peculiar shape. Bill said nothing at all, lost in appalled wonder, until the searchlight caught the great, glimmering, cloudless map.

"The Earth. But the continents—"

"As it was during the late Palaeogene. As you can see, most of Europe is under water. The Low Countries, and Germany and Poland, are inundated. There's a seaway from France to Russia. The Americas still haven't joined, and much of their coastal regions are drowned. Australia's only slowly breaking away from Antarctica. The Himalayas are being built as India collides with Asia. It's a remarkable map; you can't tell at this distance, but it's holographic and can be magnified without loss of detail to the degree that single trees and animals can be identified. It's told us more about the pongid predecessors of Ramapithecus and other primitive hominids than all the fossil records of paleoarchaeology. But of course the most significant feature is—"

"—that violet flare of light in central Australia."

"Exactly. We infer that the site so designated was a base belonging either to the beings who constructed Selene Alpha, or to those who destroyed them."

Bill felt his pulse pounding wildly as the robot camera tracked more closely across the vast map to zoom in on the point of light. The nimbus glowed steadily around a huge pyramidal pile of eroded sandstone, a shaped mountain. "The Rock," he said.

"Ayers Rock," the astronaut told him. "It's a natural monolith in the middle of nowhere. The sand has cut it down a lot since then. The alien base itself is nearly three kilometers under Ayers Rock. It's protected by something that makes our gluon shield look like mosquito netting. We call it the Vault." Lapp looked down at his hands for a moment, spread his fingers wide, closed them convulsively into fists. "Bill, thirty-six men have died so far trying to get into the Vault. A couple of weeks ago, an adolescent autistic boy blithely walked out of the place—into our tunnel, three fucking klicks deep in the earth—and told us we were going about it all wrong. Well, not 'told,' exactly. He's barely capable of speech. But he's very hot with a pencil. If he was a member of the Spiritualists' Union, they'd call what he's doing automatic writing, and take up a collection.

"The only problem is, Doctor, we don't have the faintest idea what it is he's trying to convey."

THREE:

A CONCLAVE OF THE DEAD

6. Ayers Rock

Poor Selma, Bill delFord thought distinctly. Caught in that cold bath for days on end with her toe, swollen tremendously, jammed in the plug-hole. The courier's indirect lighting brightened as he lay blinking on his tilted couch. Reaching up, he brushed the small silver-chloride electrodes from his forehead and consulted his watch. God only knows what time it is at whatever longitude we're racing down, he thought. He hadn't corrected his timepiece. With the aid of the sleep-induction electrodes, he'd rested supremely well for a little over four hours. Despite the flat, conditioned air, with its taints of plastic and alloys, Bill felt the wholesome recovery rightfully due to nine hours in his own bed.

A rufous symphony in abstract expressionism was displayed on the ground monitor: red, mottled desert, long rounded shadows of summer daybreak. Bill was hungry. He lit a cigarette and went forward, searching for wrapped sandwiches in the discreet bar. To his delight, he found several cartons of milk, and a turkey on cracked wheat. The automatic timer had roused Hugh Lapp when he turned back with his breakfast.

"Plain milk or chocolate?"

The astronaut reached unerringly for the brown carton. "Where's the hot dog?"

"You're sick, Lapp, sick. Is this tomorrow or yesterday morning?"

"Beats me, Doctor. The Earth's flat. I *know*—I've seen it from the outside."

An amber light began flashing above the television screens. A crisp voice told them: "We're on the fringes of the heavy weather now, gentlemen. Better strap up and hold tight. It'll be a rough ride in."

"Thanks, Carl," Lapp said. "How long before we land?"

"Five, ten minutes, sir. There's a wild old storm blowing down there. They have so many cross-winds this morning we'll go the final thousand meters in Vertical Descent Attitude."

Already the hull was thrumming as the edges of the weather buffeted the jet. They lost altitude and speed. On the exterior screen the parched red Earth became obscured by vast cumulo-nimbus clouds.

"I thought this was a desert."

"The Vault," Lapp said. "It doesn't like being goosed. Fortunately, the E.M. field disruption doesn't extend this far up, or we'd be dead."

The engines bellowed as they dropped toward the thundercaps. Bill gulped his sandwich and grabbed the arms of his couch. They fell into blackness.

Had the jet possessed portholes, the morning sunlight would have been whipped away from them exactly as it had from the screen. It was necessary for Bill to remind himself of that fact, for the screen somehow had lost its power to convince. Its heavy gray might as well have indicated a malfunction in the circuitry. I don't *want* to believe it, he realized.

His stomach lurched, and his hands went into the air. It's trying to kill us, he thought irrationally. For seconds they dropped in the air pocket. Then they were flying normally again, battling against the purely natural force and power unleashed in every storm. He gave the astronaut an unconvincing grin.

"Sorry about this, Bill. Usually we come through the weather zone in heavy trucks, but my superiors thought no time should be lost getting you here. You can start worrying after we've landed."

Then they were through the cloud, and rain was streaking the camera lens. Thousands of meters below, the land was a dark sodden obscurity. Lights danced across the picture, were lost again. Had he seen, for an instant, a great black kite-shaped mound, distorted to a wedge, its edges eroded by an eternity of scouring sand?

"We're very close to the Rock facility now," the pilot told them. "I'm rotating the jets through ninety degrees for setdown, so don't be alarmed if we drop a little."

The engines faded to a whimper, letting the howl of the storm enter the layers of insulated hull. The drone became a growl, picked up power again, and the courier settled vertically into the nest of brilliant lights which had swung slowly into the screen. The sensation was little different from a fast descent in an elevator well. There was a slight jar and the engines screamed, then died.

"It's still pelting down, gentlemen," the faceless pilot told them. "I've ordered a plastic umbilicus. If you just stay seated for a moment, we'll make base without getting our tootsies damp."

"Fine, Carl," the astronaut said. "Thanks for the smooth ride."

The external viewer showed two drenched ground staff, water cascading from their yellow sou'westers and macs, guiding one end of a huge concertinaed plastic cylinder toward the jet. At its other end loomed a coppery geodesic dome the size of a football field.

"I'd have been just as happy with a pair of stout umbrellas," Bill grumbled.

"They fall into the way of treating people on these kinds of planes as celebrities."

Bill blew his nose. The sound of heavy rain persuaded him that nothing had changed with the translocation of hemispheres, that winter had skidded ahead of him with its gloomy burden of colds and drab skies. The door swung open. He followed the astronaut into the dead, smell-numbing grayness of the umbilical tube. At the far end, a pair of beefy military men was waiting for them.

"General Vladislav Logunovich Sevastyianov, Colonel Thomas Chandler, this is Dr. Bill delFord, our expert in weird shit."

Chandler grinned. He was a ruddy man, mesomorphic and sleepy-looking. "Your brief sojourn in California has corrupted you, Hugh. Welcome to the madhouse, Bill."

The Russian shook delFord's hand perfunctorily. "I am delighted to meet you, Doctor. Perhaps you would enjoy some breakfast?" He had a West Point accent, and Bill came close to laughing outright.

The dome was enormous. A wide access corridor circled the perimeter, branching off into specialized areas clearly designated by signs in Russian and English. Evidently, security distinctions prevailed even among the many men moving in U.N. uniforms about the corridor. Soldiers with open holsters stood at the entrance to certain passages, checking papers before permitting entry.

The Russian general, as far as Bill could make out, was in charge of surface operations. An American counterpart controlled all the on-the-spot investigations into the Vault, at the end of the prodigious tunnel that plunged back and forth more than two kilometers into the earth. Colonel Chandler headed the U.S. team on the surface, and doubtless the Soviets were equally represented below. Cold war protocol, Bill thought, in Dante's Inferno.

Nor could that be the whole story. Every three months or so, the entire bunch swapped roles, and there were frequent surface furloughs for the scientists and military working in the claustrophobic horrors of the deeps.

Bill found the whole place increasingly distasteful. He responded, inevitably, to the faint background zing of excitement, the authentic note of nervous delight in risk and the determinate response to risk which every barroom warrior tried to recapture from the single great episode of his drab life. But Bill had always hated regimentation, and the sight of this well-oiled military machine stifled him, transformed him into no more than an object of impersonal scrutiny. It was hard not to feel that if some functionary decided he constituted a threat to the place he might be wiped out of existence without the smallest trace of compunction. It was the opposite of Zen ego-lessness. It was a vile exercise of inordinate power to a machine's end. The fact that the Vault itself, relic of some unspeakably ancient paranoia, might effect the same unthinking extermination was not comparable. The Vault was precisely alien, without human intention. To find the same qualities in men always made his skin crawl.

They paused outside a door marked: DO NOT ENTER—AUTHORIZED PERSONNEL ONLY. A pair of recessed television cameras studied them from the corridor ceiling. The colonel stopped a passing private, turned to delFord.

"You must be uncomfortable after your trip. You can take a shower in your quarters, have a bite to eat, maybe catch up on your sleep."

Bill glanced at Lapp. "Well, I could use some coffee, but if you—"

"That's a good idea, Bill," the captain said briskly. "I'll be in conference for an hour or so, so make yourself at home. You'll have the room next to mine—I'll give you a yell when I'm through. Just one thing." He tapped delFord on the chest. "If you do have a shower, go easy on the water. We're in the middle of Australia's biggest desert."

When the private deposited Bill at his door, the man

hesitated and said, "Uh, sir, what the captain said about the showers—"

Bill smiled at the boy. He seemed hardly more than a year or two older than Ben. "That's all right, son, I know."

"The rain—"

"Really, I quite understand. My friend the captain has a distorted sense of humor."

The private smiled uncertainly.

To Bill's delight, he found a tray waiting for him when he emerged from the shower, replete with ham, flapjacks, maple syrup, a tall glass of orange juice, and a pot of coffee. A serviceman had bundled up his sweaty shirt and underclothes, and laid out fresh garments. The new shirt was white, and in the correct size. Someone had been doing some forward planning.

"Sir, the general conveys his compliments and would like you to make yourself familiar with this information before the conference begins." The soldier handed him a sealed package. "If you need anything at all, sir, there's a buzzer by the door."

"Fine." The moment the door was closed Bill threw the package on the bed and sat in front of his breakfast. He scoffed the orange juice (freshly squeezed!) and single-mindedly pushed food into his face. Belching, he got out of his towel and into his clothes, opened the seals, poured another cup of coffee, and sat back on the bed to read. His face still felt hot and tight, but the electrical flicker had gone.

The document had been printed on premier stock by a nimble word-processing machine, bound sturdily, and stamped SITUATION REPORT in gold. Much of it bristled with hideous equations. Bill stopped flicking the pages and started in at the beginning. He skimmed the historical résumé Hugh Lapp had covered, but forgot his coffee when he hit the details on Ayers Rock.

The events following the discovery and exploration of Selene Alpha moved straight into tragedy. A year earlier, and a little more than five kilometers from where he now sat, the search for the alien base on Earth triggered a totally unexpected disaster.

The map on the moon had shown that the aliens of Selene Alpha were deeply interested in Ayers Rock. Yet the Rock itself was nothing more than a monolith of hardened sandstone rising almost vertically three hundred forty-eight meters above a virtually barren desert plain that extended for more than one hundred fifty kilometers. It was little more than an enormous mound, but its size was startling: nearly nine kilometers around the perimeter.

The Oligocene hologram showed it as an eroded pyramid. Clearly, it had been there for scores of millions of years before Alpha was built on the moon.

Had it been carved into that shape? The conjecture seemed insane, but it led to testable hypotheses. Perhaps an alien base might exist inside the Rock, like the tombs of pharaohs found buried deep inside manmade pyramids. X rays were not powerful enough to penetrate such a massive outcrop. Instead, the team employed natural radiation: cosmic rays pouring down isotropically from space, solar neutrinos detectable in huge tanks of industrial tetrachloroethylene. Such techniques were fairly new and presented great practical difficulties, but eventually one essential fact was established: Ayers Rock was solid stone.

Yet the aliens had marked the place distinctively. Assuming a ground installation existed, it had to be *under* the Rock. The research crew began concentrated probing of the deep strata.

As the probes echoed back from twenty-five hundred meters, the twenty-one men at the instrumentation post died in a single explosion. Their equipment fused into melted desert sand.

The data they had been telemetering out, however, showed results at the moment of the explosion. There was a mass discontinuity at two-point-eight kilometers. The Vault.

Nor did tragedy end there. Cautiously, heavy machinery was brought in to begin drilling an access tunnel. Another ten men died, confirming that the Vault would not tolerate substantial electromagnetic activity in its immediate vicinity.

A raft of speculations had been advanced to account for that effect. Bill found most of it, as described in the Situation Report, utterly beyond his grasp. The best bet seemed to lie in Lennox Harrington's realm. Most phenomena in the universe, perhaps all, appeared to be generated by a limited number of underlying symmetrical interactions. But that symmetry was not visible; it was "broken spontaneously," and expressed itself in radically variant forms. The Vault suspended symmetry-breaking between two forces—

electromagnetism, and the weak nuclear force governing radioactivity.

"I can't stand it," Bill said aloud. He put down the report and went for a piss. For a moment he regarded the buzzer, and wondered if he could persuade someone to bring him a drink. It seemed unlikely. The coffee had gone tepid, but he refilled his cup, anyway. Groaning, he picked up the report.

By pretending the equations weren't there, he managed to make some sense out of it. The Vault unkinked kinks—but only in the presence of electromagnetic fields, charges in motion. The fields suffered a "gauge glitch." Maybe it's like a laser, he thought, and the power comes from the Vault. E.M. forces suddenly thought they were weak nuclear forces, and multiplied. Nuclear protons turned into neutrons, emitting positrons and neutrinos. Neutrons did the reverse. The beta-particles, plus and minus, got together fast and annihilated, turning into gamma showers of hard radiation. The neutrinos and anti-neutrinos ran off at the speed of light. In a brief, lurid flash, flesh and metal and glass and plastic convulsed in radioactive meltdown.

It was appalling. However it managed it, the Vault was a killer—but only if you offended it with electromagnetic fields, or by venturing into its proximate defense zone. That last, it seemed, was optional. The child and his uncle had come through unscathed. Others who'd breached the zone had left it babbling, and were now full of fluphenazine. Three had come out only mildly dazed; sent in again, they'd died instantly. It didn't make any sense, but it looked as if there were rules.

There was a knock at Bill's door. The astronaut came into the small room. He had a black, wiry man with him, apparently another civilian.

"Sorry for the delay." Hugh glanced at the remains on the tray. "Just as well you've already eaten; it could be a long session."

"When can I see the kid?"

"Later today, maybe. He's scribbling again. It's almost as though we wound him up. Or he heard the jet arriving. Bill. this is Alf Dean, the guy who teleported into the Vault."

"Hi." Bill regarded the Australian with interest. It had not occurred to him that Dean had joined the team. Given the man's grueling ordeal, he'd assumed he had been flown out for medical and psychiatric treatment. "Tell me, Alf, have you noticed any peculiar sensory effects since you were brought out of the Vault?"

"I spent several days hallucinating pretty wildly, if that's what you mean. They tell me I was rather sick." Slumped in the doorway, Alf Dean still looked ill.

"Sure. More specifically: When you were back on your feet, did you notice anything when you were in the vicinity of electrical equipment?"

The anthropologist considered him warily. "Yeah, for a while. Flickers of light, a sort of, uh, visual hum. I was worried about epilepsy for a few days. How did you know?"

"The same thing happened to me after I came out of the gluon field. Hugh?"

The astronaut shook his head. "Believe me, I would have hollered."

Bill tucked the Situation Report under his arm. "Let's not keep the general waiting, or they'll cancel our leave."

The conference room was long and dull, furnished in pale Scandinavian dreck. Half a dozen men lounged at a table bearing briefing folders, pads, felt-tipped pens, jugs of orange juice, and a couple of programmable Texas Instruments calculators. A computer terminal stood in one corner next to a shredder and a Xerox four-color copier.

Sevastyianov rose from a foam-and-blond-wood armchair as they entered. "Gentlemen, I would like you to welcome Dr. Bill delFord, whose field of competence is altered states of consciousness." A restrained mutter of welcome. The Russian gestured around the table as the three men found their places, naming names. A couple were recognizable; one was electrifying. A gray-bearded civilian studied the newcomers with focused, intent intelligence, pushing his glasses more firmly to the bridge of his nose. Victor Fedorenko, Bill thought, impressed. The man everyone was tipping for the Nobel in physics, following his astounding experimental success in proving the reality of tachyon radiation. Not to mention his much publicized criticism of racism in the Soviet Union. They must have needed him badly, Bill thought.

"Let us begin this morning's session with a review of the group trial under the gluon shield. Dr. delFord, you have the floor."

Bill stuck to the facts, and was brief. He remained unsure of the connection between the Vault enigma and the experience he'd shared with Anne and Hugh. Presumably the Cal Tech field was seen as a diminutive version of the Vault's primary defenses. His report evoked animation in the men before him.

"Sounds like the stuff we got from the guys who came out of the Vault with their wires crossed," said one of them. "Except that they stayed that way. Bill, you seem to be relating this to your previous research. Can you amplify that point?"

DelFord glanced at the general. "Is this the right moment to—"

"Go ahead, Doctor. Until Mr. Lapp suggested that your special expertise might be helpful, I do not believe that any of us had heard of out-of-body-experience. Personally, I must confess that I am still highly skeptical."

The astronaut winked at Bill. You bastard, delFord thought with some affection.

"Okay, I don't blame you. The study of OOBE's isn't new, but it's been dogged by crackpots. It got a boost in the right direction a few years back, when some of us were awarded the estate of a miner named James Kidd, who'd set up a bequest to investigate survival after death."

There was a snort from farther down the table.

"Don't blame me, brother; I'm an agnostic. The fact is, though, a hell of a lot of people have reported the experience of, well, physically leaving their bodies and trucking around the neighborhood with nothing on but their souls. Fallout from our tank experiments in sensory deprivation and overload led us to correlate the details. We found considerable consistency from astonishingly diverse sources."

"Sergeyev's bio-plasmic body hypothesis," said a heavily accented Russian voice. "The Kirlians proved that long ago."

"Wrong," said Bill. "Radiation field photography is completely irrelevant. The so-called 'aura' is the creation of fields applied externally, with a lot of volts."

"Corona discharge," said Lapp. "The air molecules are ionized, and get mixed up with organic crap and outgassing. I thought," he added with a satirical scowl, "you Commie atheists would have got on to that long ago."

Bill cut them both off before a dispute could get started. "Let's stick to OOBE's for the moment. My Institute has concluded provisionally that some cases of 'astral projection,' as it used to be called, are authentic. We've had people identify distant places in great detail while they experienced projection. And the vital signs agree. We get decrease in alpha rhythms, and a drop in electrical activity in the occipital or visual cortex. The greater decrease is in the right hemisphere, where most E.S.P. data seems to be handled."

"Damn, it does correlate. We found the same states from EEG printouts on the guys from the Vault."

Alf Dean said, "The same thing has happened with Mouse. They get a drastic reduction in his EEG when he's in trance state."

Bill sat back and poured himself an orange juice. Christ, I've got to get my hands on that kid, he told himself. An engineer began a droning report on the status of some new protective clothing his group was testing, aimed at the paramount task of getting a man into the Vault, and out again, without poaching his brains. His attention drifting, Bill became conscious of the white buzz, the flicker hazing the table. A recording system, he decided. The absence of a secretarial flunkey had surprised him, but of course these days the tapes went directly to secure word-processors. He gazed along the table. That sleek prick Lowenthal, the psychologist, looked away. The bastard thinks I'm a madman, Bill thought with a breath of anger. My God, the ancient Egyptians knew more about OOBE's than that Skinner rat freak. I wonder what the Aborigines thought about it. They were here long enough. "Shit," he said, lurching up in his seat.

Fedorenko had just begun to speak. The physicist stopped at once. "Yes, Dr. delFord?"

"I'm sorry, my mind was wandering." You're not in the Grope Pit now, fuckface. In this hard-line company, his question would seem merely ludicrous. They were not accustomed to the non-logical starters of Heuristic Reciprocity.

"Feel free to speak. We cannot afford to be governed by the rules of formal debate." Unlike the general's, Fedorenko's accent was a slightly thickened version of Oxford/Cambridge British. It reminded Bill of Anne's, rather than his own "red-brick" Liverpudlian. As a very young man, the Russian physicist had worked in England on radar systems, toward the close of the Second World War.

Sevastyianov was giving him the nod. What the hell. Bill

leaned forward toward Alf Dean. "Do the local Aboriginals have anything to say about the Rock?" It *was* ludicrous. Oligopithecus savagei might have been on the scene twenty-five megayears ago, but any word-of-mouth observations would have got a mite garbled in the interim.

Fedorenko apparently did not think so. Raising an eyebrow to Dean, he nodded in grave approval. The black, clearly far from recovered after his ordeal, seemed happy to allow Fedorenko to pick up the ball.

"A penetrating question, Doctor. We did not consider the possibility at the outset. The earliest date for man's arrival on this continent is roughly fifty thousand years ago. Selene Alpha was a radioactive ruin long before that. Until Dr. Dean's unorthodox appearance in the Vault chamber, we had not bothered to consult any anthropologist familiar with the local ethnographies. Of course, we had provisional analyses from exocultural specialists from our respective space programs."

Unconsciously, the physicist had picked up a calculator, and his fingers played at random over the keys. "Ayers Rock is the traditional domain of the Pitjandjara tribesmen. Fortunately, by the time we started our probes the team was authorized by the Australian Government to relocate the Aborigines outside the area—"

"Which wasn't easy," Chandler cut in. "The bleeding hearts started screaming 'concentration camp' when we shifted the blacks." The colonel stared blandly at Dean; clearly there had been words between them on the subject.

It was Fedorenko, though, who scowled angrily. "I used the word 'fortunate' only because the lesser evil forestalled a potentially greater one."

There was a shadow in the room. Bill found nothing of sympathy within him. No doubt some of the men here had colleagues among the dead, among the ruined bodies in the melted desert. Though the mourning was done, some dull ache remained at the uselessness of their deaths. Yet these men in their military uniforms, and the civilians who served them, had shared, perhaps, in the deaths of scores of thousands. With a surge of hard bitterness which surprised him, Bill thought: The gluon shield might be used by just such men to murder thousands of millions. This time men had perished searching for traces of creatures from the stars, surely an enterprise touched with nobility, but there was no simple, honest way to grieve their passing.

Chandler had thrust his chair back gratingly. "Yes, Dr. Fedorenko, those men are dead, and more might have been if we hadn't used our muscle. Hell, I watched my boys coming out of Danang with their bellies blown open, with their guts flopping out in the sun."

"Thank you, Colonel," the huge Russian general said dryly. "I do not believe there is any need to stand."

Chandler sat down. "With respect, sir, I have to stress that we're moving into unknown territory. The excavation accident didn't stop us from reaching the Vault chamber. We *must* get in there. The knowledge locked into that one facility will advance our technology a hundred years, maybe more."

The general raised his formidable hand. "I believe we all share a common motivation. Dr. delFord, your conjecture about Aboriginal legends was an inspired one. It also occurred to Dr. Dean."

The Australian straightened in his seat. "I'm no expert on the Pitjandjara tribe, but I've had all the journals flown in during the last couple of days and it fits. As Victor mentioned, they've been relocated for their own protection. That's a tragedy in its own right, since it's only in the last decade that they'd started coming back from the Missions. They have clan territories adjoining Ayers Rock, and I believe their sacred mythmakers had a lot to tell us about the Vault. Most myths are regional—one of theirs isn't, and it's found among tribes thousands of kilometers away, tribes that don't share the same language."

"The Rainbow Serpent," Bill said, nodding. "Hugh told me you were looking for bones when you found the Teleport Gate. But isn't the gate itself the source of the myth?"

"That was my first thought, but it doesn't go nearly far enough. Let me explain. Like most Australian Aborigines, the Pitjandjara believe that during the *tjukurapa* times—the world's creation—a number of cosmic entities performed various stupendous and valiant tasks which ultimately gave the universe its present shape and laws. When the Dreaming mysteriously ended, hills, watercourses, boulders, and so on appeared wherever these deeds had been done. Ayers Rock itself is a huge catalogue of these mythic beings and their deeds."

"You figure they were aliens?"

"Certainly not." The anthropologist looked offended. "In the main, this is standard cosmogonic material, an animist version of Plato's theory of Forms. The beings commemorated in myth are the great totems: the Lizard men Kanju and Linga, the Willy-Wagtail woman Tjinderi-tjinderiba, the Mala Hare-Wallabies, Kulpunya the Spirit Dingo. These all obviously derive their liturgical importance from the daily search for food, shelter, and safety. They're the stuff of legend in any equivalent pre-technological society. But there's one creature which is quite different from the other *tjukurapa* figures—the Rainbow Snake, known to the Pitjandjara as Wanambi."

"Jung would probably locate it in the collective unconscious," Bill said. "If I may say so, I'm irresistibly reminded of other phallic potency symbols—Quetzalcoatl, the Plumed Serpent on the pyramid temple at Teotihuacan, the Midgard Serpent, the Egyptian Buto, and the Great Serpent of the Hittites who fought the weather-god. It's certainly a common primary process image emerging in altered states of consciousness."

"You did not mention the most famous one," Victor Fedorenko said softly. "Satan—the Serpent who tempted us to our ruin with knowledge."

"Oh, fuck," Lowenthal said with disgust. "Why don't you come right out with it and tell us there are some things man was not meant to know?"

The Russian physicist smiled ruefully. "Harris, Pavlov would have loved you like a son. Did you know he used to fine his students every time one of them uttered a mentalistic word? Bill, Dr. Lowenthal is our chief psychologist. He holds a low opinion of our working hypothesis. If you would find it amusing to witness an excellent mind weaving Ptolemaic epicycles around a barren world view, ask Harris for his explanation of the automatic writings produced by young Mouse Dean."

"Gentlemen, gentlemen, I must insist on decorum," the general growled. "Such personal exchanges are unseemly."

"I don't maintain that the Serpent is an archetype or a Freudian symbol," Bill said quickly. "I'm merely stressing the great geographical and historical ubiquity of the image. Alf, are you attempting to relate the Wanambi to this more general datum, and also to the Vault itself? If so, I'm tempted to side with Harris."

"How else does it add up? Look, I'm a structural-functionalist. I once wrote a paper tearing the shit out of Castaneda, and I'd stick by it. I'm no fan of the occult."

There was something wrong with Dean's breathing, and he paused. His pupils seemed contracted. "Bill, I don't know how they did it, but I think the Pitjandjara sorcerers were tuned into something from down in the Vault. They couldn't understand it, so they expressed it in terms of their own hunting-gathering view of the world. It's built into their legends."

Pointedly, Lowenthal turned away from the discussion. Yeliseyev laughed with delight. He was the Soviet Army engineer who had headed the design team for the tunnel down to the Vault. "Despite our colleague's skepticism, I've heard stories from Science City in Novosibirsk that make me wonder. Perhaps I was too quick to accept the Kirlians' claims. But psychics have certainly achieved effects we engineers cannot match. So they offend us by calling themselves sorcerers? We must watch and learn. Sneering is no substitute for open-minded study."

"Two weeks ago," Alf Dean said, "I wouldn't even have considered such a possibility. Since then I've seen what this godawful place can squeeze out of a kid with massive cerebral damage."

"Jesus! The entire project is reverting to the Middle Ages." The psychologist swung around, nodded toward Bill without meeting his eyes. "Bringing in this mystic from the lunatic fringe went against my express recommend—"

The general's tone was ominous. "Dr. Lowenthal, you will observe the civilities."

"There's a radical distinction," the man said angrily, "between being open-minded and having a hole in the head. So, okay, little green men in flying saucers set up house on the moon twenty-five million years ago. We know that. Big deal. There's absolutely no warrant for jumping from that slender datum to the insane conclusion that they're alive and well and lurking under the Big Rock to gobble us up."

"No one—"

Bill said, blinking, "Gobble us up?" The room hummed with silence.

"Uh, the Wanambi isn't the most cordial beast in the world," Alf Dean admitted. "According to the Pitjandjara, the one under Ayers Rock is particularly bad news. It was said to live in a cavern beneath the Uluru waterhole, at the top of Tjukiki gorge. If anyone drank from the hole, or started a fire there, the Wanambi got a bit stroppy."

"The return of the repressed," Bill said feebly. The anthropologist took him seriously, and shook his head.

"Freud would find it rather tricky to account for the location of the Vault. It's almost directly under the Uluru waterhole . . . three kilometers straight down."

"If the tribal elders saw the weather outside right now," Lowenthal said scornfully, "they'd doubtless blame *that* on the Wanambi's foul temper."

Fedorenko pounced. "And in a sense they'd be correct. The meteorological disruption is due entirely to our interference with the Vault. But I imagine they'd be more discriminating than that. Bill, despite what you say about human auras, you might find one fact peculiarly suggestive. If the Wanambi is angered, it's said to appear as a rainbow before it kills the offender."

Incredulously, Bill said, "You think the Wanambi is an alien, still alive after all these millions of years? And the survey probes . . . woke it up?"

"Perhaps it has been awake all along."

"We can't take any chances," Chandler told him. "There are strong arguments indicating that the Wanambi is a representation of a living interstellar alien. If it is, we've aroused it. And it's not likely to be friendly."

"For Christ's sake!" Lowenthal said in fury. "Colonel, you've got Communists sleeping in the next room so now you need monsters under the bed." He splayed out fingers. "One: elements of Selene Alpha are still functioning after twenty-five million years on the moon. Two: the Vault has been totally sealed up for at least that long, in far better shape. Three: its activity to date bears all the hallmarks of automatic defensive equipment and nothing more. Four: the Teleport Gate is deadly, gives off pretty colors like a rainbow, and has Aboriginal KEEP OUT signs all over it. Five: the boy you're all pinning your absurd hypothesis on is clinically retarded, insane, and no doubt regurgitating chunks of information he's picked up over the years and recorded eidetically. Six: the answer's inside the fucking Vault, and if we get off our asses and develop a working shield to get us in there, we can flush out all this crap where it belongs."

Mildly, Bill said, "Why can't you go into the Vault? All I know so far is that it destroys electromagnetic fields. Surely the human E.M. output can't be powerful enough to trigger it off, or you'd never have gotten your tunnel dug."

"It's a bad place," Alf Dean said. His face was suddenly beaded with sweat. "If Mouse hadn't got me out, I'd be dead."

Fedorenko told him, "The Vault does . . . something . . . to men who go into it. It hurts their bodies and it wrecks their minds. Alf is the only one so far who has recovered after deep penetration of the Zone. At the fringes it's not impossible. Close to the Vault, it drives them irretrievably insane. They don't all die. There's not a mark on them." He struggled for further words, but failed to find them.

"The Wanambi zapped them?"

"Or maybe the laws of space and time are different inside that place. Perhaps they saw the *Ding an sich* unclad by the categories of perception we impose. Cameras don't work in there. The Vault does something to the chemistry of film emulsions."

Bill stared around the room, from man to man. They met his gaze in silence, faces cold and pale. Apprehension began to worm in his belly. He sought to deny it, reached numbly for objections.

"Harris is right. Nothing could live that long."

"Perhaps the Rainbow Serpent is an intelligent computer," Yeliseyev said quietly, "perfectly preserved until now by the Vault's force fields."

"We don't know for sure that they all died on Selene Alpha," the astronaut said. "They could have fled to the safety of suspended animation. NASA is working on it. We know they're from the stars—artificial hibernation is almost a prerequisite. Believe me, Bill, it's feasible that one or more of the aliens has returned to consciousness in the Vault, and is simply gathering strength and information before choosing to emerge."

Ironically, Bill asked, "To conquer the world?" But his mind presented the loathsome image of a giant snake coiled on a throne, an image from childhood, gorged on human meat, red eyes gleaming in the dark with dreadful intelligence.

"Or to set us free from ignorance and want," General Sevastyianov said ponderously. "Dialectically, as your horror story writers have never understood, it is certain that the more historically evolved a species and its material culture are, the more generous and humane its members will be. And one must expect star folk to be highly evolved."

"With nuclear weapons," Lowenthal muttered cynically, "and Gulag galaxies."

"Perhaps the aggressors have destroyed themselves in the interim."

A band seemed to be tightening around Bill's forehead, a white haze of gauze moving in slow waves over his visual field. They want me to go in there, he told himself. I won't do it. They must be insane. With as much false briskness as he could muster, he leaned on the table and said, "I take it the fourteen-year-old is the sole key you've found to date. Are there any testable indices which account for his immunity to the field?"

Major Northcote, the chief M.O., said, "There's nothing useful. The kid's been tested from hell to breakfast. He's a mess, but he was a mess before he went in. We have two facts. He was functionally almost totally aphasic. Now he babbles like a tape recorder let loose inside the Library of Congress. And his presence in the Zone somehow saved his uncle from permanent psychosis."

"Other than that," Hugh Lapp added, "semantic analysis of his verbal and written reports suggests that he has become a conduit from the hypothetical Vault intelligence to us."

"Sophomore sophistry," Lowenthal said. He opened the folder in front of him, flicked out several sheets of pale green paper. "If you wish to be edified by our spirit guide, delFord, I suggest you study these transcripts. Let's go back to the first interview with Northcote:

" 'However much technoenvironmental factors are determinants of behavior, the relationship between human beings, and their environment and technology, is mediated by their ideas and beliefs about themselves, their fellows, and, indeed, the universe itself. Myrna? Hello, is that— We seem to have a crossed— Appears to be little profit in it because the essential task of theory building here is not to codify abstract regularities— Why, this is hell, nor am I out of it . . . not to generalize across cases but to generalize within them.' "

Thunderstruck, Bill said, "And you don't find that significant, Harris? An aphasic fourteen-year-old—"

"Most of it," the psychologist stated dismissively, "is straight quotation from Clifford Geertz's *The Interpreta-*

tion of Cultures. The child's guardian, as you might have noticed, is an anthropologist. Let's go on:

" 'Viewing schizophrenia as a phenomenon of interaction within a given family makes the circumstances intelligible. Ill-advised attempts to transpose this emic apprehension into a systematic set of principles, as Laing himself has done more recently, results only in a parody of the etic approach he initially found inadequate.' We haven't been able to trace that, but it's almost certainly the residue of some overheard conversation. Does it sound to you like a communication from interstellar aliens, Dr. delFord?"

Bill had found his own copy of the green transcript, and his eyes sped down the neatly typed columns in pure astonishment. He put a cigarette in his mouth. "He's talking about empathy," he said distantly. "My God."

An italicized comment glossed: *The following two paragraphs are from Nigel Calder's* The Life Game, *1973, p. 130:*

> All too little is known, though, about why particular species or groups of species die out. New species may be in some respects "better" in the prevailing environment, but speculations about the genetic deterioration of the dying species turn out to be wide of the mark. For example, it was said that animals living a long time in a stable environment would narrow down the choice of alternative genes available in their populations, thus forfeiting all capacity for evolving once circumstances changed. This simply does not happen.
>
> Animals living on the ocean floor, at depths of more than one thousand meters, experience as constant an environment as any on Earth, yet they possess just as much genetic variability as species living in shallow water on land.

With high excitement, he took a thick pink bundle from the folder. This was headed: *Unedited copy of material written with great speed in pencil, Dec. 14:*

> Life of body social likened to life of social body as organism springeth from heredity and environment working jointly and separately thru mech of genetic determination and ecological adaptation so social group [two lines unintelligible] social noosphere like

unto genes specifying poss of individual within inhibitory selective influence of phys environ social innovation and choice akin to mutation and creative adaptation permitting breach of rules of universe of discourse bounded by prevailing order thus social phenotype mutable under influence of individual genotype and individ phenotype sculpted by changing social genotype while influence of mutation governed by control mech insects more phylogenetically stable than mammals cf societies capacity to permit polymorphic and polytypic variation itself element of social genotype in turn mutable in different degrees vector of prevailing level of immunity vigor of world three mutagenic agent metasocial environ in crisis culls ill-adapted social genotype in favor of low-level now viable line viability of mutagens and social immune rejection systems restraining them cf clonal inhibition of disease immunity secured by exposure of young to dead ideas.

Jesus, he thought. This is no *tour de force* of mnemonics. Fedorenko is right. The kid's a conduit, a leaking valve. From what? Not some alien presence in the Vault. The others, here, on the project? The collective unconscious? And the child is telling us something, something he knew with enormous certainty.

Out-of-body-experience, Bill thought. That soaring moment of cosmic awareness, the light, the terrible disjuncture from the body's limitations. Somehow the gluon shield triggered it. Somehow the Vault's defensive Zone works some still more radical breach. And drives men mad. Unless, he realized, the intruder is already mad. Without barriers, lacking ego boundaries. Fearfully, he thought: like the autistic boy, Hieronymus Dean.

Sevastyianov rapped on the table, bringing them to order. "Gentlemen, I think any remaining items on the agenda can wait until after luncheon. Thank you." He gestured to delFord. "I would like you to see the boy now, Doctor," he said in a tone which did not carry to the others straggling from the conference room. "I find your approach refreshing, delFord. To be candid, your colleague Dr. Lowenthal gives me a pain in the ass."

Bill laughed aloud. He knew it was true, but he hadn't expected to hear it. If he'd been wearing a uniform things might have been different. Or would they? Civilians were shit, weren't they?

"I appreciate it, General."

Hugh was waiting for him at the door. Somewhere in the dome, the weird kid was doing a Joseph Smith, translating the golden discs with the prism of his flawed mind. Bill delFord burned with eager happiness.

7. Ayers Rock

Although it was termed a dining room, the place was undeniably the officers' mess. Carpet softened the floor's concrete; grained timber paneling attempted to persuade the hungry that they were not under the arch of a prefabricated dome anchored in a waste of sand. Tables wore spotless linen; highlights gleamed from wineglasses. Bill sat down with Hugh and Alf, and their orders were taken by an unobstrusive fellow who clearly knew his stuff.

A palpable line segregated the Russians and Americans, except at one boisterous table where fists brandished calculators as often as booze. There was a boom of voices in dispute, friendly and passionately obscene, and a confusion of simultaneous translations.

"The engineers," Lapp explained. "A primitive species, bereft of the niceties of nationality." Pondering the menu, he nominated soup, schnitzel, and a complex sweet which involved a mango and an architecture of gooey flourishes. Alf Dean shuddered, and settled for chicken salad. Bill agreed with him. "Wine?"

"For lunch?" The Australian regarded him with horror. "We'll have Carlton Draught," he told the waiter with enormous conviction.

The beer's bitter chill harrowed Bill's root canals. Alf drained his own glass with a dextrous wrist, but stared gloomily at his salad. "This place has murdered my appetite. A couple of months ago I'd have eaten a brace of astronauts under the table."

"A girl I know did just that," Hugh said, pushing his soup bowl aside. "Right in the middle of the banquet she got down on her knees and—"

"You're an oral deviate, Lapp," Bill told him. "How in the name of all that's decent did you manage to raise a passing score on the psych profiles?"

"I may have gone down on that score," Hugh said instantly, "but I finally got my problem licked."

Bill found himself choking, and tried the beer again. "I've drunk worse," he decided. "What is it, kangaroo piss?"

"That was the original formula," Alf said, with a slow smile. "Unfortunately, a retired gentleman from Kentucky bought up the last of the animals for his burger chain."

"I always wondered why they called it fast food. Alf, I take it you're not on the best of terms with another colonel from the home of the brave."

"Chandler has an aversion to uppity colonials."

"The Ugly American? I'm sorry, Alf. 'There's one in every outfit.' "

"They've specialized in them here," Hugh said. "Wait till you meet Sawyer."

"The guy in charge downstairs?"

"Yeah. He's a Good Old Boy, with a bazooka and a Bible."

The salad dressing was superb, and the fowl virginal. Alf was still fooling at the edges of his. "I suppose you get used to being the policemen of the universe," Bill said. "And they'd hardly send any soft-liners to run a joint mission of this magnitude."

"I can appreciate the dynamics of it," Alf said, "but Chandler's attitude gives me the shits. Goddamn it! My people have been here since Chandler's ancestors were poaching from the Neanderthals. I don't recall any of us swearing an oath of allegiance to the Stars and the Stripes."

"They're always telling us Australia's a new country," Hugh said. "Me, I'm authentic first-generation American. If there hadn't been a brisk wind behind the boat, they'd have had to register me as an Atlantean." He gestured for his dessert.

It arrived snappily, and the astronaut monstered it while Bill forked up the last of his cucumber and yogurt. "Don't they have a weight limit for Shuttle crew?"

"Keep us on Tang for the final three weeks before lift-off."

"You remind me powerfully of my son, Lapp. He eats like a pig and has a smart mouth. Do you have any kids of your own, Alf?"

"No." From the second bottle he'd had uncapped at the table, Alf was pouring his third hefty beer, carefully monitoring the foamy head's dimensions and density.

"Married?"

"It broke up two years ago."

Bill waited. "Bad, huh?"

"I sent her packing. She had a big mouth." The anthropologist glanced grimly at Hugh, but the astronaut maintained a guileless expression. Rotten puns under control, Bill noted with approval. "Karen was always confronting people she hardly knew and asking for their life histories."

In a perfectly natural movement, Hugh Lapp was out of his seat and leaning relaxed on the table. "Got to run, gang. I'll check on Mouse and tell them to expect you shortly. No, no, finish the bottle. You won't get lost, Bill. Alf knows the way."

The engineers had departed, and a group of Russians were seating themselves, shouting for the menu. Not army men. It's a habit they contract, Bill remembered. If they don't bellow at home, it takes all day. "I'm not prying, Alf. Mouse is my primary concern. I need to know everything I can get about his background, and I gather his background is mostly you."

"Yeah." Dean brought one hand down over his face. "Sorry. Ask away. Medical stuff?"

"I can get that from the files. To be blunt, I'm wondering how a blond European adolescent has an Aboriginal uncle. Mouse is your sister's boy, right?"

"Eleanor is my step-sister. I was adopted by Iaian Dean several months after I was born."

"Ah. The genetics of it did seem rather improbable. Are such adoptions customary?"

"Far from it," Dean snarled. "The rule in this racist shitheap has been to segregate the tribal blacks from the part-Aboriginals wherever possible, and to keep both groups out of sight in case our repulsive presence frightens the women and children. Under the Act, blacks were detained by the authorities on reserves and compounds 'for their own good.' Vested interests, of course. We had no economic value, so they tried to exterminate us. There were no cotton plantations here, Doctor. At least the African slaves in America were housed and fed at a level comparable with other livestock. We weren't allowed to vote, of course, though they shoveled the gentle Jesus meek and mild crap down our throats. I was an adult before a referendum got us included in the national census."

The beer was abreacting Dean's hostility into loquaciousness. "Fully grown men and women were wards of the state. They needed permission to marry. I know this isn't answering your question, Bill, but it's the background. Half-castes—'yellow-fellers'—sometimes got raised in a white household, out of conscience or kindness. A lot of others were abducted from their mothers and sent south to orphanages, and sometimes whites adopted them. After all, they had halfway human genes. There was a trace of hope for them. But not for my kind."

Bill watched the dark face, its passion, its force. "You're a full-blood, I take it."

"Special case. Iaian Dean was a young army doctor with stars in his eyes. He was posted to Darwin during the war. His wife thought I was the cutest thing she'd ever seen. They'd had to cut me out of my mother's belly."

The double jump took Bill by surprise. Let the man tell it his own way, he decided.

After a lengthy pause, Alf Dean went on: "I went back later, you see. I wanted to know why my parents had given me away. They hadn't, the poor buggers. A Japanese bomb had blown my father to pieces and left my mother so revoltingly injured that she died three days later. A fucking Jap bomb, in someone else's war. They're all white to us, delFord. Puyungarla, his name was. Ngularrnga tribe. Most of them are gone now—just a few dirty old men and women hanging around the periphery of town eating scraps and drinking themselves blind." His voice faded. "Wanntukgara. She was beautiful. A beautiful black wife."

Dean's hand lost its loose grip on his beaded glass. The dishes had been taken from the table. Bill ordered coffee for them both.

"Do you regret your adoption?"

"Ungrateful, aren't I? Here I am, the best-educated boong in the whole country. The rest of them are lucky if they make it through high school. While whinging Alf

Dean teaches anthropology from the fine paper podium of a Ph.D."

Boong. A hideous word. Bill had heard it used several times since he'd arrived. A black human is not a human, but a boong. His heart went out to Dean. Compared with this man's horrific background, for all its superficial felicity and good fortune, his own battle up from the docks of Liverpool had been conducted by gentlemen's rules.

He prompted Alf. "The Deans had a child of their own sometime later?"

"Yeah. Resurgent fertility. Eleanor came late, change-of-life kid. And of course she resented me. Small-l liberal backlash. It was wonderfully baroque when she was little, having a black brother. By the time she was an adolescent, I was competition. She needed to go further out by her own efforts than I'd managed just by being born. So she hit the dope trail early and never came back. Mouse was an occupational hazard."

Mouse could wait. Bill diverted him back to his own history. "You went looking for your natural parents, and stayed to be initiated? I noticed the cicitrized marks on your chest."

"The Deans wouldn't tell me. But the Ngularrnga knew who I was. They told me what skin I belonged to, my totems, gave me a list of my potential brides. Pity about that; there were only two of them, both over forty. One had syphilis. I think they were relieved when I told them I was already married. But I stayed for six months. Ate dog food out of tins and drank Muscat out of plastic flagons. They put me through initiation. I'd been circumcised in the maternity hospital, so they covered me instead with these pretty decorations. You're looking at a Man of Silence, Bill. Alf Djanyagirnji. I can't hunt worth a damn, but I've danced the Lorrkun and Yabudurawa corroborees." He looked away. "They hate the dead, you know. Sing them off in the Lorrkun, beg them not to come back from 'Nother Place. *Cooma el ngruwar . . .*"

Carefully, Bill said, "But you didn't join them. A black American in your situation might have become, oh, a Panther spokesman, a civil rights leader—"

Alf acted as if he hadn't heard. "Christ, they brew a good pot of coffee here, I'll give them that. I can't hold my grog anymore. That fucking thing down there has knocked the shit out of my metabolism."

"Give me your wrist. Hmm, a bit sluggish. Your pupils are contracted rather more than they ought to be. I advise you to get some rest."

"Hang on. I'm all right. Anyway, I can't leave you to wander off through this place without a guide. It's a bloody maze."

His dereliction with Mouse? "Hugh'll roust me out. Come on, feller, I'll see you to your room."

"I haven't finished the Dean family saga. I'll spare you the heat-death of my marriage. Mostly, I was off in remote places doing field work, and my nice white wife, Karen, didn't want a baby. She considered absentee fatherhood an inappropriate way to raise a kid. We'd been married three years when my imbecile sister Ellie got herself pregnant and burned out the baby's brain with massive doses of acid. Since then, she's spent more time in the looney bin than out of it. My mother looked after Mouse for the first couple of years, but he got to be too much for her, and we started taking him at our place two or three days a week. When I got my lectureship I heard of a special program the Neuropsychiatric Department was starting for brain-damaged kids. We brought Mouse down to stay with us, and of course Karen copped most of the responsibility."

A tremor went through Alf's body. "I never understood how much she resented it. She certainly didn't take her anger out on the boy. Well, finally she shot through, and I got stuck with Mouse. Fuck." He jerked his eyes up and shook his head wildly. "That's not what I meant. I love that kid, I really do. And now he's stuck in a glass cage with wires in his head. Jesus."

"Right," Bill said briskly. "Point me toward your room. You need sleep more than I need information." Hoisting Alf to his feet, and waving away offers of help, he steered the ill man out under the struts of the main corridor which circled the dome's perimeter. "What's your room number?"

"North quadrant, forty-seven. I'm bunking with Mouse. Around to your right, there's a bilingual sign."

A crewcut P.F.C. paused, appraising them. Bill told him, "Private, get a medic to meet us in Dr. Dean's quarters. And if you can find him, I'd like Captain Lapp to join us there."

"Yes, sir. Do you need any help?"

"I can manage."

The side corridors were numbered with unusual rationality. Breathing hard, Bill opened the door marked N-47 and eased Alf onto the closest bed. A lieutenant with medic's flashes appeared almost immediately, with Hugh on his heels.

"Sorry, Bill, I should have alerted you. It clobbers him from time to time. I'm told there's no obvious organic cause for it. My hunch is he's in resonance with Mouse. Keep us informed, Lieutenant; we'll be at the Cage."

They walked quickly through the maze. Rain drummed dismally, gray noise from the high dome. In a low tone, over the clash of their boots on concrete, Hugh said, "The kid's scribbling like Dumas *père* on a writing jag. It'll knock you out." He fished in a breast pocket. "Better wear this or we'll hear every klaxon in the building." A large heat-sealed identity card bore Bill's photograph, thumbprints, and security rating. He pinned it on.

"We run Mouse in a shielded room," Hugh told him. "Don't ask me why; the physicists consider it a fail-safe precaution."

"Stuck in a glass cage with wires in his head," Bill quoted.

"Not exactly. It's a triple-walled Faraday Cage: copper interleaved with polystyrene acoustic foam, and NASA telemetry access. You get one hundred fifty decibels of attenuation on radio frequencies from fifteen thousand cycles up to about a billion. Magnetic fields are cut by about seventy decibels at fifteen kilohertz, though it drops off as you get down to sixty cycles. Hellishly expensive getting it here, and it doesn't faze the kid for a moment."

"Try a gluon field."

"Nah, too risky. He's an international resource."

An armed guard inspected Bill's credentials with more than passing interest, and did the same with Hugh's.

"Didn't you just come out of here?"

"S.O.P., Bill. That kid might turn out to be the super weapon of World War Three."

"Oh, for crying out loud."

They entered a dim room crammed with instruments, oscilloscopes gibbering blue and white pulses, little panel lamps flickering on and off like holiday ornaments. Two TV screens showed a teen-aged boy with a Medusa scalp of delicate wiring. His face could not be seen, but his posture was relaxed, almost torpid. The swift mechanical sweep of his right hand seemed something detached, tracking back and forth without cease across a flat, braced illuminated board. Beside him in a comfortable chair a bored attendant sat partially in view. A boom mike hung above Mouse's head; his regular breathing was just audible.

"There's no point going in; all the gripping stuff is piped through this room. The big computer's at the center of the dome under a mess of thermal insulation, but these word-processing peripherals are the major output systems. Copies of everything are slaved immediately to permanent file in the U.S. and Soviet sectors, but the snoops don't have any executive capability."

"I somehow imagined he used a blunt pencil."

"He did at first, before we got this little number installed. Mouse can't be persuaded to punch a keyboard, which is a drag, but I guess for a kid with half a brain he's not doing too badly."

A visual display unit in the observation room was showing a line-by-line update on the boy's scribbling, transposed on an adjacent screen into legible computer script. With a jolt, Bill saw that the characters were Cyrillic. A third V.D.U. came alive as he watched, presenting lines of English which rolled up and off the screen. An operator suddenly grunted.

"My God!" Bill said. "The child's a Slavophile. Has his political record been checked?"

"Three days ago he gave us a piece of poetry in Urdu. It threw the computer into some confusion. Didn't worry Lowenthal, though, the dumb prick. He still attributed it to a trick memory."

"The computer is doing the translation?"

"Right. See that board he's writing on? It's pressure-sensitive—digitalizes his efforts, and outputs a fair copy to the displays. Then the translating programs do their stuff, throwing preliminary English or Russian versions. If it's over their heads, they call for human intervention. Which happens surprisingly rarely—these programs are *good*. The Soviets cream their jeans every time they see our hardware, and weep at the software."

Bill had located the biomedical instrumentation, and was emitting little bleats of pleasure. A twelve-channel EEG fizzed in harmony with the electrical activity in Mouse's brain: right hemisphere pulses flat and fast, with no spindles; left hemisphere equally desynchronized and hardly more active. A Fourier wave analysis was displayed in a histogram below the individual channels, confirming an absence of OOBE alphoid waves. But the pseudo-beta pattern Bill recognized instantly from studies on the psychic Ingo Swann. Mouse *wasn't* awake, but he wasn't dreaming, either, and he had none of the slow, high-voltage theta or delta waves of coma or non-dreaming sleep.

"He's out of the body, I'd swear it," Bill said, grinning with satisfaction. All the vital signs from autonomic sensors seemed completely normal: pulse a steady seventy; basal skin resistance, from the thenar eminence of the left palm and the left forearm, at the expected level; respiration consistent with the modest effort involved in writing automatically; no G.S.R. anomalies. It certainly wasn't the profile of an autistic youth under stress.

"Captain," said one of the shadowed computer operators, "I think you'd better take a look at this." The other operator glanced up quickly. Bill peered at his insignia. A Russian. The man flicked a switch and began punching swiftly on his keyboard. Blue computer script continued to flow upward across the display screens.

"Shit. Give me a hard copy." Hugh Lapp leaned on the American soldier's shoulder, and took up the folded paper as it slithered from a Xerographic printer. A buzzer sounded.

"We have a hold on the translation," the American operator muttered. He ran a cursor across the screen. "Looks like idiomatic material."

"Here, let me in." The man rose and Lapp slid into his molded seat. He stared intently at the screen for a moment, keyed in an identifying header, and began hammering the input. The man at the adjacent terminal called a hard copy of his own and started to get out of his chair. Without looking up, the astronaut barked authoritatively in Russian. Undecided, the operator hesitated, nursing his sheaf of folded paper protectively. Again he stood up and began to push past Bill, who watched with a paralyzing sense of foreboding. Hugh came to his feet and blocked the door. He said something cold and definitive, keeping his hands at his sides. The operator shrugged and went back to his place. Hugh sat down and finished his task. The printer hushed, and gave him more paper.

"Judas priest."

On the television monitors, Bill saw the autistic boy lean back from his panel, right arm dropping by his side. The soldier in the Cage looked up and murmured something. All the V.D.U.'s had gone blank. End of transmission.

"What is it?"

"Crisis time."

A fierce red telltale lamp activated above the console, blinking twice a second. The astronaut took a slim plastic rectangle from his pocket, neater than a matchbook. It went into a slot beside the terminal keys. One of the V.D.U.'s scrambled, cleared. A tattoo of man-machine communication. Hugh lifted a phone from its recessed rack. "Lapp. Is the maser patched into High Roller? Mark." Four fingers came down together, and keys locked.

"You're C.I.A., you furtive son-of-a-bitch," Bill said.

Lapp's breath came straight from the back of his throat. "I'll never tell. Bill, you'd better clear out."

"No way. The kid's the reason I'm here. You can't clam up now."

"Sorry, buddy. Like your friend Lowenthal didn't say, there are some things man was not meant to know."

A high, sweet voice said, "Hubert Charles Lapp, Captain, U.S.A.F." It came from a speaker in one of the monitors from the shielded cage. "Operative Second Rank, active, National Security Agency, Fort Mead. Consider the document unclassified. Matthew, chapter eighteen, verse three: 'Except ye be converted, and become as little children, ye shall not enter into the kingdom of heaven.' It is advisable for Dr. Bill delFord to read the Kukushkin diary extract." Mouse turned, in the silence, and over his shoulder smiled with extraordinary innocence into the lens. "For your information, computer operator Dimitri Dimitrovich Joravsky represents the Glavnoe Razvedyvatel'noe Upravlenie."

Everyone remained stock-still. Almost simultaneously, three telephones buzzed, and a coded format started jumping across Lapp's screen. The astronaut's grim appalling expression galvanized abruptly into a spectacular grin. He dumped the printout into Bill's hands, and made a little bow in the direction of the Russian.

"What the fuck, Bill? Let's go with it. Read, read, enjoy. It's Doomsday evening and the kid wants you kept up to date. But don't try peddling it for mucho rubles to the

Military-Intelligence Directorate; I fear our friend Joravsky has an edge on the market."

Suddenly Bill delFord wanted no part of it. He looked down with uneasiness at the computer translation.

"You'll have to forgive my poor rendering toward the end," Hugh said. "The original hung the computer, but I think I've captured the gist of it." He showed his teeth to Joravsky, who sat motionless and tense. "Well, buster, we seem to have caught you cheating. How much 17-Tg-M have your boys ferreted away downstairs? Or is the point more subtle?"

In excellent English, the Russian told him, "Captain Lapp, I suggest we arrange a conference between our commanding officers."

Bill stopped listening. The first page was a copy of Mouse's handwritten Russian: hard, angular, adult. It was followed by the amended computer translation. His trepidation vanished. Hungrily, he devoured the communication from the Vault.

8. Ekratkoye Complex

NOVEMBER 12

Well, now that Nurse Kuenzli has at last brought me pen and paper, what am I to write?

It seems that my dogged habit of jotting down the day's doings in my journal has become something more than a simple compulsive ritual. (That it has indeed become compulsive is an astonishing discovery, considering how painfully I had to force myself, those ten years ago, to maintain regular diary entries. Discovering how peremptory the habit has become shocks me somewhat—as though in this respect, as well, I have become no more than an adjunct to one of my light-winking laboratory instruments.)

I am for the first time today mildly amused, if only at the minor paradox. What I began to write—nullified indeed by these words themselves, even if they are negated in turn by the circular triviality of my theme—was that the ritual of keeping current my pretentiously leather-bound journal has become so stereotyped I could not write without it.

These sheets of project-issue memo paper were fetched by Nurse Kuenzli when finally my monotonous complaints wore down her professional insistence that I should rest. The small success left me cheated and frustrated. I sat up in bed staring at the stack of virgin paper, irritably thumbing the retractable pen, and elaborated spurious conjectures.

Well. That exigency, at least, seems to have resolved itself. Perhaps (hallelujah!) I am, after all, more than a machine. To be candid, I suppose I first began my journal in the hope of allaying that bourgeois fear. After fourteen years in the neon halls of Novosibirsk, the human part of me was shriveling away, despite the fashionable banalities I could spout arguing the creative identity of science and art. I needed to speak human truth to myself, at least.

So much for the literary customs of the scientific animal. I am, frankly, indulging in the crassest diversionary tactics.

It is my belief that I am dying.

Why else would they have rushed me here? (I am unable even to give the place a name; Nurse Kuenzli adroitly skirts any direct answer to my question. "The doctors will be here shortly to examine you, Academician Kukushkin.") It's the damnedest hospital I've ever seen. A hospital with comfortable beds? Perhaps that is one of the side benefits of working in the most grandiloquent security operation since the *Sputnik* project.

(Perhaps I infringe security in writing these notes. Surely not: the medical staff must have clearance at least as exalted as anyone on the project. I was accompanied here by Aegis guards—I presume there's one or more on duty outside my room right now. Would they have allowed me pen and paper, for that matter, if they were concerned about security? No.)

My fears are doubtless without foundation. Apart from one extravagant vomiting episode shortly after today's anti-radiation shot, I have had no indication of illness.

My predominant sentiment is boredom.

That's my major complaint, and probably the explanation for my difficulty in starting today's notes. There's nothing to write about, except the unthinkable—and I shan't encourage morbidity by going on about that.

The whole cursed tasteful place, hopefully with the exception of Nurse Kuenzli, is, in short, intolerably tedious.

Writing about tedium is no less tedious. I shall lay down my pen and turn once more to the study of my navel.

LATER

I have been provided with a wristwatch. My own, together with all my clothes and personal effects, remains in custody. Presumably they will be destroyed to prevent further spread of the virus. The time is two-seventeen A.M. Try as I will, I cannot sleep.

The physicians have been to visit me.

Two of them. Lean, Gandhi-ascetic Zinoviev, who hurried me into the project infirmary after my nausea yesterday, and then called the ambulance which brought me here. I vaguely recall his somber manner from one or two bull sessions in the Rec Facility. The other man was a stranger, a short, hairy fellow of amiable mien.

"Good evening, Ilya Davidovich," he said, offering his hand. "I'm Sipyagin. I believe you know Dr. Zinoviev."

I nodded. "Would it be appropriate to ask why I've been brought here?"

Sipyagin laughed easily, stepped back as Iosif Zinoviev put his black case on the teak desk beside my bed and began laying out diagnostic impedimenta. "Of course," he said. "I daresay your removal here to Ekratkoye Complex was rather disconcerting."

"That's where I am, then," I said, none the wiser. Zinoviev gave me a sharp look, glanced at the shorter man, and started plying his stethoscope about my torso.

"A deep breath, please," he ordered. "I didn't know you were familiar with non-Aegis complexes."

"No," I said hastily between gasps. "I meant that I didn't know the designation of this hospital. Now I do." I was becoming quite rattled. "It's nice to know a place has a name, even if it's just a letter of the alphabet and doesn't convey anything to you."

Sipyagin came to my aid. "I know just how you feel." He hitched himself onto the edge of the bed and drew a folded sheet from his smock pocket. "Here, I brought you a map of the Complex. We expect you'll be staying with us for a few days. You have complete liberty, so long as you don't leave this building."

Zinoviev was peering at my facial acupuncture points with a tobiscope. He made another mark on the chart, took up a short syringe, and drew a small quantity of blood from my thumb. Sipyagin continued to regard me with benign interest from the end of the bed. My mental turmoil changed to exasperation.

"Well, look here," I said, "what on earth's all this about? I grant I was bilious this morning, but I feel perfectly well now. Why am I being treated as an invalid?"

"No, no!" exclaimed Sipyagin, waving his hands in the air. "You've received altogether the wrong impression. It's most unlikely that you're seriously ill, but"—with a sly grin and a gambit aimed perfectly at my self-esteem—"you *are* a very important member of the Aegis team, Academician Kukushkin, and we can't afford to take any chances."

I am ashamed to admit it, but his ploy was not without success. My face grew warm, a flush compounded in equal parts of pride and confused annoyance. "Well, yes, but—"

"We've reason to suspect," said Sipyagin, all briskness now, "that certain of the foodstuffs going into the Tse and Che kitchens this week contained impurities. A scandal. In short, Doctor, you're probably suffering from a minor case of food poisoning."

"Sabotage?" It seemed impossible. Besides, the imperialists were also working on the gluon shield. After all, their astronauts had made the original discovery of Selene Alpha.

Iosif Zinoviev gave a sour chuckle. He had packed away all his medical devices and stood at the door. "You have a suspicious mind, Academician. No, Aegis security remains unbreached. The impurities involve a fatigue-fault in one of the storage refrigerators. Unfortunate, but no machine is perfect. No more than any man."

"As to its seriousness," added Sipyagin, joining him at the door, "the facilities we have in this hospital are more than adequate. Set your mind at ease, Kukushkin. You might be in for a little discomfort, but we'll have you out of here in a couple of days." He nodded cheerily and strode out into the corridor. Zinoviev lingered for a moment, as though aware that I was far from satisfied. He had, however, little enough to add.

"There will be some pills brought in with your dinner.

Take them before you go to sleep. If there's anything you want, press the button by your bed." Dumbly I nodded, and watched his narrow back disappear into the corridor.

I was violently sick again after dinner. Oddly, I was afflicted by little of the enervation and wretchedness which usually attend nausea. About midnight, unable to sleep, I took advantage of my liberty and briefly explored the surroundings.

Despite my earlier presentiments, there was no guard at my door. The corridor was white and antiseptic, dully echoing. A different nurse nodded to me from her cubicle. I found a lounge complete with Max Ernst print and television, a pale-blue-tiled lavatory and bathroom. At the far end of the corridor, looking out on to a floodlit compound, was a heavily sealed entance, with three plateglass doors each separated by a space of three meters.

If my calligraphy is becoming shaky, it's as much due to anger as to belated exhaustion. Do they think me a complete fool? An ordinary hospital has no use for triple-doored Sterile Environment airlocks. Unquestionably, this Ekratkoye Complex is a center for bacteriological weapons research.

Food poisoning, my academic ass! Can there be any doubt that I have become the accidental victim of some experimental recombinant-DNA goddamn Doomsday virus?

NOVEMBER 13

I feel so strange this morning.

My sleep was broken and ruined by terrible dreams. I tossed and turned for perhaps five hours before Anna brought me a light breakfast. They were not nightmares, exactly, but torn and vivid pieces of my past—my frightened adolescence in the shadow of Stalin, my arid years at the university, my corrosive marriage. I had thought them forgotten, in every sense well buried, but back they came to haunt my night.

There's more to it than that—not pain; I'm no longer sick; my stomach is rested and hungry indeed. But a vague dis——.

I cannot find the word; a restlessness is what I meant, but I've gnawed my pen for five minutes in a sweat searching for the word, a dis—— . . . a dis—— . . . a *disquiet*—of course! Good God, the word just would not come until I dredged for it like some senile fool searching for his

Christos, what's wrong with me? The sweat is pouring off me, all for one cursed replaceable elusive word. Again! I had to stop and worry and hunt for that word *elusive*. Something is sick inside me; something hurts; I don't know what it is but dear Jesus

LATER

Anna, I am appalled to record, found me weeping. She was entirely sensible about it, gave me two large white pills, and left an eggnog beside the bed. I drank it a few minutes later and felt ten times better. When I rang she was good enough to fetch me another, which I sipped slowly while talking to her about herself.

I meant to note it earlier, before that lamentable frenzy burst over me. My little triumph! I have uncovered the charming lady's first name, and she now calls me Ilya Davidovich with hardly a trace of her previous professional distance. Sister Kuenzli no more; she is Anna, and I am her brilliant patient Ilya Kukushkin, and never mind the "Doctor," the "Academician." (I did Anna an injustice earlier, in demoting her to nurse. She is, of course, a graduate Sister with, it appears, qualifications in biochemistry and, of all things, psychiatry. My blushing tear-stained face!)

She is also beautiful, with plump rosy cheeks and a droll smile.

LATER

I've been trying to get into Stanislaw Lem's new novel, which Zinoviev fetched over for me from the Aegis Complex, along with a selection of my other books. I'm not enjoying it much, though. I've also tried to distract myself by going over the fifth equation of our unified-interaction model. There's something wrong there, I'm certain, but I'm having trouble concentrating on it.

The doctors came after lunch . . . well, during it, actually, but Sipyagin chatted away pleasantly while I finished my sweet. Hardly the meal one would have expected for a victim of food poisoning—slices of pork, an excellent salad, even a glass of tart white wine to refresh the palate.

My dark suspicions of last night seem absurd. Nevertheless, I remarked on the feast to Sipyagin.

"No reason to starve you, Kukushkin." He smiled. "Anyhow, the best way to cleanse your system is by offering it wholesome protein to work on."

I gave him a guarded glance. "You're sure of this poisoning, then? It couldn't be a bug of some kind?"

Zinoviev cleared his throat, an offensive sound. I am beginning to detest that man. "You can safely leave the diagnosis to us, Academician."

"Don't be too hard on the poor chap, Iosif," Sipyagin said. He adopted a speculative pose. "My theory has always been that intellectuals labor under the burden of what might be termed the Socratic phobia. Too well they remember the hemlock."

Zinoviev grunted, tugging out his instruments; I laughed aloud. It was a poor enough jest, but it soothed my anxieties. I thrust the last of the dessert into my mouth and submitted to their attentions.

Since they left, fears have crept back. It really does seem quite incredible that an ordinary base hospital, even one serving the most important military project of all time, should have a viral-contagion Isolation Environment as elaborate as this one. Perhaps the other beds are all full?

LATER

The time has dragged to five o'clock. I feel worse and worse, in some way which has little to do with my body's health. Whatever I mean by that. Well, I mean at least this: I have never *looked* better since my childhood. The tired old gentleman has been taking quite some notice of himself in the mirror today, trimming his raggedy beard, combing his hair. I even tried the nifty sunlamp I found in the bathroom, and my skin prickles with a slight burn. Does the crisp crinkle of Anna Kuenzli's smart uniform, the curve of her lips, the luminous blue of her eyes, explain all? No doubt, no doubt.

So. The fact is, Sister Anna visits me only too rarely. Certainly she has other duties, though she's taken time to tell me something of her pre-project life in a vast Life and Death factory in Leningrad. Like all of us, Anna must know tedium and loneliness here in our self-protective Security blockade, but her obvious love of life (the French phrase which better expresses that escapes me, damn it) seems to carry her through. She is not, it seems, married.

My real point is that I feel like hell. And I'm scared as hell. I took a further wander this afternoon, clad in pajamas of a wild and purple hue supplied by the base and smelling faintly of antiseptic, my feet in ludicrous fluffy slippers, and found beyond the angle of the corridor a single blank metal wall. I put my knuckles against it, a sharp rap or two, and had in return a flat metal clunk. It must be another door—there's no alternative way out—but it's thick as a vault.

I'm trapped, in short, in a luxurious prison designed to keep in not only viruses, but people, as well. What would happen if I smashed the first glass door in the airlock? Another metal wall smashing into place at the other end? I would not be surprised.

The map Sipyagin left me shows nothing of this; it is the barest outline of Ekratkoye Complex, labeled cryptically with numbers. These are useless without the key, which the doctor carefully tore away, although the L-shaped section I inhabit is hand-annotated. The map's sole function so far has been to guide me to an artfully concealed liquor cabinet in the lounge. I've brought the vodka back to my bedroom, but self-restraint prevents me from getting thoroughly sloshed. This is the *weirdest* hospital.

It is thirteen minutes after nine in the night.

My head is funny. Anna bent over me and her tits were pushing out behind her white dress and I wanted to give them a grab and a squeeze, but I didn't dare. She's real sexy. I groaned a bit so I could move and look up her dress but I didn't see much she was too quick. Get up now Ilya Davidovich she said and lifted me into bed.

I wonder if she saw my hard-on. Lets face it why should she get a charge out of me showing how randy I am God please believe me I'm truly sorry. It just stuck out and I didn't really mean it to and I got down quick as I could and hid but anyway why SHOULD she care when she can screw all them big tough Komitet Gosudarstvennoi Bezopasnosti cops and generals and little smiling bastards like Dr. Sipyagin for that matter. Let's face it.

O my god I feel reel strange why am I WRITING all this stuff anyway, I must be crazy, someone will see it and then I'll be in the shit up to my ears man oh man. Well I gotta coz Ive always written it down every night for ten goddamn years theres a funny ringing buzz in my ears I can see words jumping up and down in front of me leaking real fast out of the pen scrawly over the page, skid the page across the desk, what the hell, grab another one, its liking raping the page the virgin white page my god how corny Sister Kuenzli's no virgin for sure with tits like that rape rape sez the pen jesus jesus forgive me oh jesus its like all my brains were flaking off away out of my head an pouring down my ears like dandruff

NOVEMBER 14

I don't know what to do.

I really don't.

Habit, let habit show the way.

All right. Eight o'clock, maybe half a minute past. Ante meridian, morning of the day, an hour after breakfast and the doctors' silent visit, mutter mutter, or is my hearing impaired? I don't think they said much to me.

Go on, then, Professor Kukushkin, put it on the paper:

I no longer think that I am dying.

I think I am going out of my mind.

"Tush, Ilya," says beautiful, crisp Sister Kuenzli when I weep and clutch her arm most sexlessly and tell my fear, sob it at her, rant and hurl the plates sloshing messy on the carpet. "It's just a fever, Ilya Davidovich," says Sister Anna, crouching carefully and efficiently and cleaning up the mess, showing disapproval by turning her face away, showing fear (Or is that a delusion of my madness? And if so, she has every reason to fear me.) in the tightness of her muscles as she sponges up the milk. "The doctors will look after you, Ilya," she explains, voice stern but matter-of-fact. "It's just a touch of that poison still in your tummy."

Well, why no stomach pump? Why this fantastic setup in the first place? I might not be the most popular of men, but old Georgii Piatnitsky sits with me over chess, and Lev Kamenev enjoys a bout or two at quark theory. Why haven't they arranged clearance and come to console the sick? Too many questions which can't be answered, not consistently—oh, there're glib retorts to every one; I can think of plenty myself; but put them together and what picture fits the total bill?

There is, if I'm to be rigorous—what an agony it was

to find that word—that simple bloody word—the thought I had before: I've got some revolting disease mutated into existence by the foul-minded military geniuses I had hoped we were putting out of business, some viral filth which squats in my brain. How, how? Is it possible for a thing like that to escape their gentle care, flutter on the cold wind of the Steppes from Ekratkoye to Tse Complex, crawl on my skin, suck at my cortex? Christos, it's the conceit of a madman! What are Isolation Environments for, if not to prevent every chance of such a disaster? And why am I the only victim? The other rooms here are empty, four beds unmade, their ticking bare, one freshly sheeted.

Those terrifying words.

They bring it back, the howling numbness in my mind, my raped soul, my very intelligence seeping away like blood drained into sand. And still it's there, the humming roar in my head, the fingers tugging at my memories, cutting me to shreds, I can feel it chewing and gnawing, O Christ bring it to a stop if You exist, stop this dreadful suction in my head.

I must concentrate on *facts*. I'm losing the words, losing *myself*. I pick up books from the elegant desk and flick pages back and forth—the words are meaningless. I look at numbers and symbols, equations jotted in my own hand in the flyleaves, and *I don't know what they mean!*

Facts: my name is Ilya Davidovich Kukushkin, D.Sc., Ph.D.

I am one of the international team which jointly developed the theory of sub-quark parastatics.

With my colleagues and assistants, I have puzzled over ancient debris from the moon and constructed from it an anti-nuclear shield.

The shield is an oblate spherical parastatic gluon bag. With this screen, the two great industrial nations of the world will be absolutely safe from atomic attack. We have neutralized one another. This fact does not entirely dismay me.

How far my illness has progressed! The attack last night was no fleeting aberration. All the details, all the equations and engineering data concerning the shield are gone beyond recall, wiped away as if by a wet sponge. My whole grasp of physics and math, and yes, those delightful subtleties in which I rejoice, the musical structure and form of Webern and Schönberg, all gone, dear Jesus. I look at Lem and the words are not even words any longer—have I forgotten how to read Polish? Yes. And French is fading in my mind, German, English—like a smear of ice across a windscreen, my mind is blurring over and hardening into darkness.

Phooey on those silly old books. [Here Hugh had noted: *The following elisions and solecisms reflect the fragmentation of the Russian text.*]

I was reel bored waiting for lunch, and Sister said Try the TV. Well I did an guess what there was lots of bottles of cordial in the cubord. Sister K. give me some buns too but there wasnt much on TV except school stuff

Proly its all rite to rite on this cos i did before only i kant understan any of them big werds

Well I don't know but i feel pritty sad and glum which is thc werd my frend Ana sed.

Reel sad and glum cos it wood be nise to rite how i usetoo. Most times i jest sit hear and cry becoz there is a big pain in my hed wich is like a hole.

My hans are very big and klumzee and their are blak hares on them wich i kant rember it is very skary i think sister Ana is reely my muther but wen I tolled her she just went away very qick an i think she was sad or sumthin.

Well that is all i kan rite for now.

Ilya Davidovich. Ilya Davidovich. I. D. Kukushkin.

Thatz how i rite my name.

Horrses and kows an berds an fethers an hats an heds an fasez an nozes an muths an lips an eers an loleez

ilya davidovich

NOVEMBER 16

They gave me the antigen this morning.

The bastards the bastards the filthy depraved bastards.

NOVEMBER 19

Boris Sipyagin allowed me an hour in the sun today. Not, needless to say, in the compound—I still bear a potential pandemic in my tissues. Even so, a meditative hour beneath the glass roof of the Isolation sunroom was a relief.

My compulsion to keep the journal current has vanished these last several days. Understandably, perhaps; the sight of those tormented pages extruded while the 17-Tg-M Strain wrought havoc with my faculties is enough to destroy forever the urge to remember.

There remains, however, a grim and bloody necessity which transcends my reluctance. I must not falter. I must set down this abomination.

Three days ago, drooling and sucking my thumb, I lay curled on the floor as Zinoviev withdrew his needle from my arm. Sipyagin crouched watchfully at my shoulder, murmuring in a singsong, offering a rainbow-spiraled confection. "It doesn't hurt a bit now, does it, Ilya Davidovich? Good boy, good little fellow. Hush now, don't cry and we've got a lovely lolly for you, Ilya. Shush now, there, there."

That is the vile inhumanity of it: the vividness, those monstrous memories. Try as I might, as for hours I did try, I cannot blot it out. My degradation is scorched into my soul. But I no longer wish to forget. The obscenity they did to me must be recorded while the scar is livid.

I remember the gurgles dribbling from my lips. My hand clutched greedily for the sweet, pushed it into my mouth. Zinoviev motioned to the two hefty orderlies and stood back as they hoisted me into the big cot. Do you understand? It was as though I had withdrawn from my body, hung away from it, shackled in all the clarity of my most lucent perceptions to the shame of my humiliation. I could not cry out in rage. I tossed my limbs about in mindless contentment, sucking, sucking. Vaguely, my body heard muffled sounds. Clearly, in my awful detachment, I knew the sounds were Sipyagin clearing away the large polyethylene alphabet blocks he'd brought in the day before.

After they had left, I crawled around the cot, uttering an infantile babble, and only began to cry when I wet myself again.

Recovery was hours later. By six in the evening I was in full possession of every faculty but my self-respect. I doubt whether that will ever, *can* ever, be returned to me.

The two experimenters returned with the orderlies shortly after six and helped me to the bathroom. When I had cleaned myself and donned a fresh pair of pajamas, they dismissed the nurses and offered their rueful version.

"You cannot know how sorry we are about this, Dr. Kukushkin," said Sipyagin, features carefully grave. I said nothing, my face turned, like stone, to the wall.

Iosif Zinoviev grunted. "It is only fair we give you an honest account. You must understand, however, that everything you are about to hear is under the highest security classification."

"I'm sure the Academician understands," Sipyagin said gently. Gently. "You see, old fellow, you're the victim of a rather appalling accident. Ekratkoye Complex has been doing some rather advanced tricks with reverse transcriptase. Dr. Piatnitsky was involved at one point, and somehow you managed to pick up one of the bugs from him. Very nasty, indeed, and we'll all be cashiered if anyone hears about it."

I turned and looked at him with loathing, thinking of the troops massed along the Amur and the Ussuri. "You're all set now, aren't you? You and the imperialists. Once the Aegis screens are mounted, you can plaster the People's Republic of China with I.C.B.M.'s full of virus and slowly drive your divisions through the country cutting everyone's throats while they gurgle at you like happy imbeciles."

Sipyagin was sanctimoniously hurt. "You've been under great stress, old fellow, but what you're saying comes rather close to slander against the Motherland. It's very nasty stuff, this 17-Tg-M Strain, and it's a damned shame you caught it. But you must understand that we have to keep abreast of what our enemies are doing, in case the worst comes to the worst."

They were carrying on a rapid dialogue with their eyes. Sipyagin rose and patted me on the arm. Anna fetched me a meal after they'd left. I couldn't touch it.

Accident be buggered. These ghouls don't make that kind of error. I was injected with it during our monthly anti-radiation shots. They knew what they were doing, all right, the motherfuckers.

They *have* to use it. It's the way their paranoid minds work. Now they're potentially proof against nuclear retaliation, they are obliged to get in first. I wonder if they intend to take out the Americans at the same time. I don't doubt the stupid bastards really expect to walk in, take the key positions, vector the antigen, and congratulate themselves on a bloodless victory. A handful of the fanatics might lust after total obliteration of the Enemy, but I suppose the bulk of them view 17-Tg-M as the ultimate glorious evolution of humanitarian class struggle.

The fools. I know beyond question the inevitable reaction of their victims.

They will have to slaughter every single one of their conquered enemy. They will be forced into the genocide of half the human race.

How can they fail to sense the ferocious hate, the murderous, vengeful loathing I feel for them? The self-disgust, the degradation of everything which makes a man human. Do they know what it feels like to have all the dignity and self-respect crushed inexorably out of you, until you squirm like an imbecile in your own stinking shit? What would you do to those who had done such a thing to you?

And yet surely I am not the first of their guinea pigs. They must already have tried 17-Tg-M on criminals, on soldiers, on technicians and bureaucrats and housewives. They would leave the geniuses until last. Is it conceivable they'll realize the consequences of this filthy thing, before their own imperatives—and the shield, the screen I helped build, God pity me—force them to use it in earnest?

No. They will not be balked. The vision of consequences did not hold Stalin's hand from the Kulaks, or Hitler's from the Jews, or Truman's and Attlee's from Hiroshima. It will not stop them now.

I hear approaching footsteps. I am a dead man but first I will kill

9. Ayers Rock

On the tail end of his dream of death, Alf Dean heard the rap at his door and knew he was asleep. Life, said the dragon named Kukushkin, would be much easier if your brain was a telephone. The reptile wrung its double-thumbed hands in aggravation. You won't remember any of this, damn it. With dread, Alf told the dead dragon: I will. How could I forget? He rolled in his bunk. His brain waves speeded up and diminished in voltage. At the repeated rap he awoke, pajamas pressing his skin like an ill-fitted wetsuit.

"Sir, the general wishes you to join him in the conference room."

"Yeah. Okay." It was late afternoon, according to his clock. Mouse's bed was empty, of course. The stink of his terror filled the room; he must have been dreaming again. Nothing remained of the nightmare. "I'll have a shower and be right there."

"As soon as you can, sir."

Alf stripped off his sodden pajama top. "I don't think the general would appreciate it if I turned up in this state."

"I'll tell him you're on your way."

Beyond the hiss from the shower head he could hear the relentless drumming of impossible rain, the Vault's deluge on the Rock. Where did all the goddamn water *come* from? Fedorenko thought that a teleportation system was involved, more diffuse and less exacting than the grid designed to transfer complex organic structures of the order of living human beings. Or living dragons. Shit, where had that come from? He quailed under the hot water. The rain was pure distilled water, so it wasn't coming straight from the sea or from a buried water table. A lot of it seemed to vanish after it soaked into the desert. But it wasn't an endless loop—if it had been that simple, gravitational acceleration would have turned each droplet into a lead brick moving near the speed of light.

Another echo of his repressed nightmare came back to him in the corridor. Soldiers on guard stood braced and alert; each pair or group contained equal numbers of Soviets and Americans, and they seemed to be warily sensitive of their differences.

A guard inspected his identity card at the door and finally allowed him in. Sevastyianov gestured him to the remaining unfilled seat. There were at least twenty men in the room. Alf sought Bill delFord's eye; the man was tense, his compact body hunched forward across the conference table. Alf's apprehension found a focus. "My God, has something happened to Mouse?"

"The boy is well," Sevastyianov said curtly. "Please be seated, Dr. Dean."

Before each place at the table lay a single sealed folder, blazoned with security injunctions. None had yet been opened.

Sevastyianov studied each of the group carefully, his gaze tracking with an impassivity at odds with the stress Alf detected. Chandler sat at the general's right hand, face hard, in his element.

"Gentlemen," the Russian said finally, "I have to inform you that certain events this afternoon came close to precipitating nuclear war between the Soviet Union and the United States. Thankfully, that danger has now been resolved."

In a non-military gathering of this size, the announcement would have produced pandemonium. Here not a word was spoken. Alf felt his nightmare move on him, a crack of memory opening.

"The precipitating agent," he heard the general's deep voice saying, "was a communication from the Vault. There can be no longer any doubt that it is under intelligent control. And it has made what can only be construed as its first overtly hostile move."

The Russian paused, like an actor, giving them time. "You will notice that I discount the deaths and injuries we have suffered to date. These were passive responses, equivalent to trip wires triggering traps previously set. This afternoon, however, through the agency of the boy, the Vault attempted to provoke major conflict between our two nations."

The room had receded. Alf clutched at the table's edge, and the sealed folder slid under his fingers, tumbled into his lap. "The dragon," he heard himself blurt. "The dragon Kukushkin."

Bill delFord's face, a flushed moon, hung over him. "Jesus, it's patching through *him,* now. General, could we delay the briefing for a—"

"I see the implications. Go ahead, Doctor."

DelFord was steadying him, filling a glass from a jug on the table. Alf gulped down the orange juice, feeling like a fool. "I'm sorry. This damned thing—"

"That's okay, sport. Do you feel up to talking?"

"I'm okay." It was incredible. They'd just missed a nuclear war, and he was falling down because of a bad dream.

"Alf, you just mentioned a name. Where did you get it from?"

The anthropologist blinked. "Kukushkin? I don't know. Look, this is absurd."

"He was a colleague of Dr. Fedorenko. Has Victor mentioned his name to you?"

"I don't think so. Goddamn it, if you must know, I was having a nightmare just before the general sent for me. Do you really want to hear this garbage?"

"You bet. What do you think Mouse is doing all day long in the Cage? He's dreaming nightmares from the Vault, baby."

"Oh. Well, most of it is gone now. I think I've been having the same nightmare ever since I—ever since the Vault." He felt himself convulse. "All I remember is a dragon called Kukushkin. I suppose it should have been a bear."

From the other end of the table Lowenthal broke in. "General, is this penny-ante psychoanalysis necessary? I'd—"

DelFord said, "Shut up." To Alf, he said, "Nothing else? Was the dragon trying to tell you something? Maybe some message about Mouse, or something for the rest of us?"

Alf put the folder back on the table. It was damp with palmprints. Every face in the room was directed at him, several with deeply puzzled frowns. "That was what it complained about—the fact that we forget." He felt his scalp crawl. "One other thing. I'll leave you to work out the symbolism. The dragon was dead."

Bill clapped him on the shoulder. "Well, General, I'd say that puts the cap on it. It's trying to communicate."

"Thank you, gentlemen." The Russian waited for the room to quiet. "We shall defer discussion of Dr. Dean's remarkable experience. I ask you now to unseal your folders."

Alf gazed dully at his folder. The room rustled. He tore it open. It contained a single computer-written document headed: NOTES MADE BEFORE HIS DEATH BY ILYA DAVIDOVICH KUKUSHKIN, NOVEMBER 19. The Russian name pierced him like a thorn. He uttered an inarticulate cry.

"Indeed, Dr. Dean," Sevastyianov said. "This material was written by your nephew three hours ago, at the instigation of the Vault intelligence. I ask those of you who have not yet read the extract to do so now."

Confused and distraught, Alf forced himself to read the damning, terrifying words. Behind Kukushkin's stuffy diction he saw the mocking clever face of his nightmare's dragon. The Rainbow Serpent, he told himself. He shook his head, turning pages and absorbing the dead man's words at some distant automatic level of consciousness. Dinosaurs and dreams. Viruses. Doomsday in a laboratory vial. The voice of the dragon was heard in the land. With a colossal effort he restrained the silly laughter inside his head.

Sevastyianov waited stoically until the last man had closed his folder. He laid his hands on the table. "The material you have just read is absolutely restricted, as is everything you learn here pertaining to defense matters. All parties to this discussion, civilians as well as military personnel, are subject to battle discipline. Any breach of security, now or in the future, will attract summary execution without trial."

Again he allowed that to sink in. His eyes rested on Bill delFord, then moved to Alf. "This station remains under Yellow Alert War Orders. Tactical nuclear ordnance rings the Ayers Rock region, supported by massive program-targeted strategic firepower from Indian Ocean submarine weapons platforms. Within the station, customary need-to-know restrictions on command information have been partially relaxed, to provide the operational staff with the broadest access to multi-disciplinary evaluation in the shortest time."

While he was speaking, the general's aide had entered. Now he passed him a note. Sevastyianov scanned it, muttered briefly. The aide departed. There was an indefinable change in the room. Alf concentrated, sought to bring some resolution to his senses. Something— An absence. "Gentlemen," the Russian said, "it is a day for surprises. The rain has stopped."

This time there was no composed hush. Engineers and physicists broke into a frenzy of debate, the unmelodic song of scientists handed one crucial datum more than their hypotheses can hold. Finally, Sevastyianov rapped loudly.

"Another significant coincidence, no doubt," he said. "Let us restrict ourselves, for the moment, to the Kukushkin diary. I am authorized by the highest executives to tell you that the extract itself is genuine. It was retrieved after Professor Kukushkin's untimely death." He ignored the quite audible hissing curse from Victor Fedorenko. "The Academician's hysterical meditation on policy, however, is categorically repudiated. The *E. coli* strain coded 17-Tg-M, produced by recombinant DNA engineering, is *not* part of the arsenal of the Soviet Union, nor was it so intended. As Colonel Sipyagin made clear to Kukushkin, it was developed for experimental study only."

The Russian glanced at Hugh Lapp. "Due to satellite transmission of the document to the intelligence communities of both our nations by covert agents at this station, a rapid escalation to High Readiness was set in train." His voice deepened. "Although these illicit transmissions constitute a gross affront to the joint commanders of this station, I am under instruction to exact no retribution. The principals concerned may count themselves exceedingly fortunate." The astronaut, Alf noted, listened alertly without emotion. Was he one of the "covert agents" Sevastyianov was speaking about? If so, he showed truly remarkable self-possession.

"I repeat, the immediate threat of war has been averted. Since the primary source of the leak was the Vault itself, we may conclude that its intention was to provoke global preemptive holocaust."

"General," Bill said fiercely, "I must protest. That is certainly one possible estimate of the crisis, but hardly—"

The Russian scowled. "Dr. delFord, I had not finished speaking. I have made more than enough allowance for your status as a civilian. Please do not interrupt me again."

DelFord hesitated. "My apologies." His face was flushed with anger.

"Very well. The predominant military estimate holds the Vault responsible for this afternoon's general nuclear alert. However, those behavioral specialists who have already examined the Kukushkin document regard it instead as a potential key to the Vault. These interpretations could not be more polarized. Personally, in view of the most recent phenomena, I incline to the latter position. I direct your attention to the scriptural quotation which the boy delivered, presumably as a verbal coda. Major Northcote."

The medic rose. "I have been in comsat consultation this afternoon with Doctors Zinoviev and Sipyagin. It is their considered judgment that the effects of the 17-Tg-M strain approximate, on a temporary basis, the cortical disruption which afflicts Hieronymus Dean. Hence the panic. *Escherichia coli* is a bacterium we all carry in our intestinal tracts. A tailored variety, bearing a puerilizing plasmid gene in its cytoplasm, would multiply on release like a chain reaction. I stress, therefore, that the Soviet biochemists insist that 17-Tg-M is a disabled strain. It is viable only in the laboratory. Even if it escaped by accident, it would perish.

"For our purposes, though, the interesting feature of 17-Tg-M is its ability to generate a small endorphin peptide, arg-enkephalin. Endorphins are morphine-like substances, produced naturally by the human body. This one is not yet known in nature, though the probability is high that it plays a role in some forms of gross mental retardation and behavior defects. Apparently it binds so tightly to cortical neuron receptors that their function is massively reduced."

Northcote consulted his notes. "I won't weary you with the biochemical architecture. Fortunately, the Soviets have already isolated out the plasmid puffs from 17-Tg-M as independent preparations. These have very little effect on the pituitary until stimulated by further enzymes, at which times arg-enkephalin production is enormously accelerated. Stocks of the analogue are being flown here at this moment." Abruptly he sat down.

"You have a question, Dr. Fedorenko?"

"Yes. Was the major saying that you intend to use this substance on men going into the Vault?"

"It is a possibility we must explore."

"The idea is outrageous. Has the degradation of my colleague Kukushkin served no purpose at all?"

Komarov, the electronics expert, said, "Before we get sucked into the mire of Victor's ethics, let me report the progress of my own team. The null-suit is ready. I am confident that it will permit us to obtain entry to the Vault without relying on the peculiar oracular powers of our young Australian friend."

"Thank Christ for the voice of sanity," said Lowenthal.

Controversy began. Sevastyianov gave them their heads. This, after all, was the reason they had been gathered together and made privy to the world's dark secrets. Alf stared at his hands, listening to the absence of rain. In the conference room its drumming had been close to inaudible; now its truancy deafened him with intimations of significance. Skin, the tan already fading. Hairs like any animal's. The dragon had been covered in a fine down of feathers. Fingernails. He'd been chewing at them again. Beneath the skin, threads of blood vessels. On the tides of the blood, hormones: protein messengers, driven by the nucleotide messengers of his DNA. Tide and time. The bones beneath the veins, the sacred bones. Bill was arguing with Victor Fedorenko, insisting that the Vault meant them to use the drug from their mutant bacterium. How could one lift out and away from this web of flesh when that was all there was? The American had promised to show Alf the data from his OOBE studies as soon as the books were flown in from the States. As the arg-enkephalin was being flown from some bastard's laboratory in saltiest Siberia. A consensus seemed to be emerging in the discussion: they wouldn't use the null-suit until the drug was on hand. Both eggs in one basket. Only way to make an omelette. Did dragons go broody, hatching their eggs?

Bill touched his shoulder. "Let's go, sport."

10. Ayers Rock

Under the limpid, prodigious sky, the Rock Uluru was an orange-red Leviathan stranded by immense catastrophe in some limitless swamp, flanks scarred, tormented by stinging flies. It took an effort of will for Alf to translate the image to reality: flocks of finches soaring against the morning's katabatic winds, the purely natural downdrafts provoked by the massive stone anomaly. He tousled Mouse's hair, dropped his arm with sudden protective urgency around the boy's shoulders. The Vault's oracle took us to the edge of disaster, he thought, and then it guided us back with a single symbolic intervention.

The Beast, with Captain Hugh Lapp at the wheel, rocked through the red mud and lush grass of the new marsh. Alf had never been carsick in his life; he hardly recognized the faint nausea for what it was. It's damaged me, he told himself. Something has gone awry permanently in my hindbrain. I'm giddy most of the day, and when I lie down to sleep I wake up with nightmares of falling into infinity.

It was difficult not to respond to the Vault as to a force implacably malign. Yet it had hung out its rainbow in the sky, turned off its outer defenses at the very moment they were reading Kukushkin's explosive diary, dispersed the storm clouds which had brooded over the Rock for the best part of a year. At least the farmers in the eastern states will be grateful, Alf thought. They'll be praising God for the end of the drought. Perhaps they should be directing their thanks to the devil.

"It's big," Lapp said.

"It's stupendous," said Bill delFord, sitting on the other side of Mouse in the back of the Land Rover. "That goddamn hunk of rock is nearly as tall as the Empire State Building, and taller than the Chrysler Building. You could bury a city of skyscrapers inside it."

The fatuous comparison irked Alf. How much finer, he thought, were the metaphors of the black men who came to Uluru's caverns for worship. From this angle, from the north, most of the great scallops and buttresses were hidden, but even from here one could see the last camp of Linga, the Lizard-man, the boulders which were the food piles of the Mala women. On the south face, undercut deep into the stone, the pools which had persisted even through the millennia when the rainfall had been little more than a hundred millimeters a year were not merely a source of physical sustenance; they were Muitjilda Water, the blood of dying Kunia, and the waterstains in the ancient flaking stone were the bloodstains, petrified at Dreaming's end, of dying Liru. Lichen had once been the smoke rising terribly from the burning camp of the Sleepy Lizard. Gutters gouged into the furrowed dome of Uluru were the tracks of escaping Malas. Nothing here was merely mundane; each stone and cranny had been transvalued by the deepest emotions of men and women.

Alf recognized that his peevishness stemmed as much from a sense of dread, of contingency, as from any abstract legitimate grievance. He took his arm away from Mouse and opened the journal on his knee. For all his love of myth, out-of-body-experience was a postulate he still regarded with profound suspicion. Yet what alternative concept came halfway close to accounting for the appalling dislocation of reality he'd known as the Gate had hurled him on the trajectory of some incomprehensible equation into the halls of hell? He had spent the sleepless night reading an absurd concoction by a man named Robert A. Monroe; it startled him, as he read delFord's article now, to find the Englishman agreeing with his own incredulous scorn.

The vehicle's jouncing made his head swim. Alf sighed and put the journal aside again. All around, the sky's glorious cloudless blue was reflected back from the layers of water gleaming between clumps of glossy desert succulents, grasses, the gnarled roots of mulga scrub. The wheels spun and skidded, fighting for traction in the preternatural mud, but Alf knew that the endless mirror would be gone in weeks, perhaps in days, sucked inexorably into the thirsty soil. Then the true spectacle would blossom. Desert would be transvalued not in the austere imaginations of animistic nomads, but in the explosive biochemistry of a dormant ecology.

Already, despite the ferocious beating of the rains, the

air was stunning with the fragrance of golden cassias. Emu bushes, lewdly swollen, opened their languorous blooms like flame and embers; cinnabar, crimson, heliotrope—all the pink vaginal shades of promised fertility. The morning light slanted in through the tufts of spinifex, circled the needles of desert oaks in light. All the trees were bent: hard, angular plants, the bonsai of extremity. And presiding over all the living creatures, the silver-gray acacias, the white-cypress pines, the sudden fluid bounding of a distant mob of graceful red kangaroos, rose the awful measure of their transience: Uluru, red as granite, glowing sunlit like a brick just taken from a kiln.

Victor Fedorenko, seated on the left in the front seat, shook his head slowly. "It is magnificent. I have climbed in the Himalayas, where the snows block out the skies and one fears the earth is tilting, but this is—incomparable." The massive dip of the bedding, thrusting from the Earth at eighty degrees, caught the sun. "And this is just the residue of a pyramid more than a kilometer high."

Dreamily, Mouse said, "Great seal."

Alf laughed. "I thought it looked like a whale."

"Very like a whale," Bill agreed. Then he said, in a shocked voice, "My God. The Great Seal." He dug out his billfold, extracted a dollar note. Shakily, he said, "Maybe the Vault is an Illuminati plot."

Mouse greeted the banknote with enthusiasm. He seized it, brought it close to his right eye, rubbed it against his forehead. *"Annuit Coeptis,"* he said clearly. *"Novus Ordo Seculorum."*

Fedorenko leaned over the back of his seat and stared speculatively at the boy. " 'He favors our undertaking,' " he translated. " 'A new order of the ages.' It is an invitation from the Vault intelligence."

"By God, it's more than that," Bill said. He retrieved the note. "After all the mystical claptrap that's been babbled about the Great Seal, we finally know what the original was."

Lapp eased The Beast up onto the glistening tarmac of the abandoned tourist airstrip. His new course took them parallel to the north face of the great tor, the morning sun behind them. Thirty kilometers distant, vivid through the purified air, the tumbled monoliths of Mount Olga came into view past the northwestern edge of the Rock.

"This is the reverse of the Great Seal of the United

States," Bill explained to Alf, showing him the truncated pyramid at the left of the note, topped by its floating, radiant triangle and the unblinking left eye within it. "The design is two hundred years old, attributed to Franklin, Adams, and particularly Thomas Jefferson. I'd never noticed it before, but the damned thing's *not* a pyramid—it's a narrow wedge. It's a slice *through* a pyramid. And look at the angle of incline: it must be sixty-five, seventy degrees. But the usual slope of Egyptian pyramids was fifty-two degrees." He pointed at the striations furrowing the Rock. "That's closer to the line of Jefferson's design."

"You're crazy," Alf said weakly. "Gosse, the first white man here, didn't reach the Rock until 1872. Do you think Jefferson was given to astral traveling in his sleep?"

"Don't blame me," Bill said with some asperity. "It was the kid's idea."

Even at this distance, they could hear the moaning of the winds moving over the deep, eroded caves. The vehicle bumped off the end of the runway, heading for the road which looped Uluru. Good old Beast, Alf thought fondly. He had been heartily relieved when a group of project experts airlifted her in after her lonely vigil near the Tanami cave. Light danced from the red Rock; cascades of water were spilling in filigrees from the fresh pools on Uluru's lofty dome.

Ahead, casting black shadow across the delicate hues of the desert wildlife, a stupendous slab of stone leaned toward the Rock. A ribbon of pale sky shown between them. The slab was seventy meters tall, one-tenth as thick.

"The Rock's shedding its skin," the astronaut commented.

"That is exactly what it is doing," Fedorenko said. "The whole tor is composed of arkose grit, with several bands of conglomerate bonded by siliceous cement. For millions of years the surface has been flexing under a diurnal temperature range of twenty-five degrees Celsius or more, so that thin flakes constantly break off and degrade under the windblown sand. Exfoliation has been most marked in the west and the southeast; this slab is all that remains of a shell which once covered the entire tor. Since the Rock is so homogeneous, so solid, such weathering is wearing it down in a fairly even fashion."

Lapp found the tourist road and picked up speed. "I'd like to climb that mother," he said, and affected not to hear delFord's snigger of amusement from the back seat. "Unfortunately, the general has put it out of bounds. Maybe he figures the Wanambi is still ticklish." Nevertheless, he stopped the Land Rover at the western buttress where a curving handrail of chains rose in catenary curves up a natural ramp a kilometer long. Against the bright line of sky at the top, several "dead finish" acacias lifted gnarled, imploring limbs from the meager soil of narrow clefts. Alf found himself shivering, despite the heat which brought waves of mist from the drying earth. He opened delFord's article again, while its author climbed from the vehicle and urinated noisily into a muddy puddle.

A door slammed. Hugh and the Russian made their way carefully through the red-splashed spinifex toward the thirty-degree slope. Alf asked the boy, "Do you want to go with them, have a look at the Rock?"

Mouse rolled up his eyes until only the whites were visible and stayed where he was. Bill got back in, grabbed an oily rag, and wiped mud from his fashionable riding boots. "Feeling any better, Alf?"

"I'm okay. Do you publish much in the *Journal of Biblical Accountancy?*"

"Ah, the Monroe debate." Bill laughed gleefully. "Are you familiar with *The Worm Runners' Digest?*"

"I've heard of it. Scientific spoofs, that sort of thing."

"And serious articles, often a bit too novel or eccentric for the straight press. My friend Bjorn Bangsund decided the study of altered states of awareness was getting too stuffy, too eager to emulate the tired old shibboleths which had hamstrung academic psychology. So he launched the campus of Ard-Knox in Oslo, an imaginary university with faculties in disciplines such as Theological Engineering. I'm an honorary member of the Board of Deputies, with an advanced degree in Biblical Accountancy. Professor Bangsund delivers the annual keynote address. As I recall, his inaugural statement was a closely reasoned fiscal analysis of how much it profiteth a man to gain the whole world and lose his own soul."

Alf smiled, with a hunch that his leg was being pulled. The other two men had turned back, deterred by the slush. "Bill, why do you bother with this bullshit?"

"Astral projection? Because it's a hypothesis which helps organize the weird data we keep getting from our affect experiments."

"But Monroe—"

Bill passed the wet rag to the swearing astronaut. "What he says sounds nuts—but it's awfully close to the reports I've been reading on the ravings of your unlucky predecessors into the Vault. Tart took him seriously. So did Lilly."

"Yes," said Alf in exasperation, "but I thought this paper of yours was meant to discredit their gullibility."

"What do we discuss?" Fedorenko asked.

Bill gave him a brisk rundown on the author of *Journeys Out of the Body*. The book had appeared in 1972; its author was a middle-aged businessman who had been studied by Professor Charles Tart on and off between September 1965 and August 1966. He was president of two corporations active in media and electronics, and had opened a "Mind Research Institute" in Virginia in 1971. Monroe claimed to have discovered the existence of a transparent "Second Body" in 1958. According to his book, a ray had struck him from the northern sky as he lay snoozing on a couch. It shook him savagely, making his whole body vibrate. Months later, during a recurrent session with the vibrations, he unintentionally moved his "astral" arm out of his flesh. Medical and psychiatric examinations gave him a clean bill of health. With due caution, he learned to induce the vibrational state, control it, and leave his body completely.

"John Lilly has endorsed Monroe's findings in print. Tart has stated that—"

Mouse sat forward and said in his high voice, " 'It will be very tempting to dismiss Robert Monroe as a madman. I suggest that you not do that. Neither would I suggest you take everything he says as absolute truth. He is a good reporter, a man I have immense respect for, but he is one man, brought up in a particular culture at a particular time.' " The boy beamed at them.

"Christ," Bill said, "I wish he wouldn't do that. He'll get himself carted off on a diabolic possession rap."

"What were Monroe's claims?" Fedorenko asked. "I have heard of such cases in the Soviet Union."

"Oh, standard occult recipes," Bill said. "Relax with your body oriented north–south. Only he tried to put it on a statistical basis. That shot down a lot of trad ideas, if you take him seriously. It didn't depend on physical debility. There was no discernible relationship between OOBE's and lunar or planetary configurations. But he found that the auric body is subject to E.M. interference. In 1960, he zipped out while lying in a Faraday Cage carrying fifty kilovolts. He seemed to get tangled up in a flexible bag, and couldn't get through it. Another time, he was stopped by power primaries in a street."

"It sounds exactly like what happened under the gluon screen," Hugh said.

"That was just the start," Bill cautioned. "Most of Monroe's jaunts have taken him to a cosmos he terms 'Locale Two.' Heaven and hell, you'll be interested to hear, are just suburbs. It's the embodiment of primary process. The region of Locale Two closest to our world is populated by three nasty groups—the astrally projecting insane; those emotionally retarded dead who can't bear to tear themselves away; and a host of mean sprites indigenous to the realm. Bad trips for the novice." He seized the journal, found a paragraph.

"You'll love this. He saw God once. There's a blast of heraldic trumpets, and everyone—including transients like Monroe—respond with an instant reflex. 'Every living thing lies down—my impression is on their backs, bodies arched to expose the abdomen [not the genitals], with head turned to one side so that one does not see Him as He passes by. The purpose seems to be to form a living road over which He can travel. . . . As He passes, there is a roaring musical sound and a feeling of radiant, irresistible living force of ultimate power that peaks overhead and fades in the distance.' "

This time, Mouse had remained silent, but the astronaut had not. With a wheezing gasp, he bottled his mirth until Bill stopped reading, uttering small choking sounds that exploded into a roar of laughter. "Not the genitals," he said finally. "Not the genitals."

"Not everything in Locale Two is so transcendent, by any means," Bill said loftily. "For Lapp's benefit, I must point out that sex of a sort is practiced there widely, rather as we shake hands, or, if we are astronauts, as we practice sex widely." Hugh made another convulsive inhalation, and Alf was undone as Mouse began applauding enthusiastically, bringing his hands together like pistol shots. "It involves a total interpenetration," Bill added heroically, "of the astral bodies. This produces a tingly delight far surpassing mere genital play, you primitive swine."

"Of course," Lapp hooted. "God forbid the genitals."

"Thrilling as these disclosures are," Bill said, "they didn't exhaust Monroe's findings. At the end of 1958, he discovered a hole into a parallel physical universe, 'Locale Three.' The residents of this world are human, but they have a different history and culture from ours. They have eschewed electromagnetic technology, internal combustion, and the use of oil, making do with steam power and possibly nuclear energy."

"The Doppelgänger world," Fedorenko said seriously. He had not entirely approved of their unrestrained mirth.

"You bet," said delFord. "To Monroe's agreeable surprise, he found that he can take over his double's personality simply by entering the unhappy fellow's body. Over the years, he's kept tags on the double's rather gloomy life, including a marriage to a divorcée named Lea with two children, and their subsequent breakup."

The astronaut grinned. "What the hell is a NASA-funded research program like yours doing studying this kind of demented garbage?"

"Ah, you are too quick to reject," Fedorenko said sternly. "Must we not inquire of its source? You say this man has been tested in the laboratory?"

"Right. Tart asked him to identify some distant random numbers. Other OOBE's had succeeded with this task, but Monroe bombed. He explains that the rapid-transit system is liable to grievous misrouting, since the slightest distraction can divert the astral traveler to the wrong address."

"But you know the whole thing's crap," Alf said testily. "Half your paper here deals with cogent details Monroe left out of his book."

"Indeed," Bill said with satisfaction. He sat back with his knees up and his hands linked over his belly. "By a stroke of luck, we can compare this wholesome, apple-pie account with another version by Andrija Puharich, published ten years earlier in *Beyond Telepathy*. The good doctor cites the diary notes of one 'Bob Rame,' a successful New York media business—"

"Is this the Puharich who studied Uri Geller, the metal-bender?" Fedorenko asked with suspicion.

"That's him. A nice guy, Andrija, but gullible. Well, here's 'Rame's' story." He consulted his article. " 'In a desk cubbyhole, a piece of plywood had to be glued into place with cement. As I brushed on the cement, I noticed a feeling of lightheadedness and for a period I remembered nothing.' It was a pleasant sensation," Bill commented, looking up, "and one to which, when the occasion arose, 'Rame' had recourse repeatedly."

"An intoxicant?" Fedorenko asked, shocked. He had been ready to believe, Alf realized with aversion.

"You bet your ass. Right: 'One night, unable to sleep, at around two in the morning I went into the room where I had been working, obtained a can, and went downstairs and sat, occasionally taking a casual smell. . . . Then quite suddenly, as I looked at the can, I felt as if a ray or some kind of energy had come down from a low angle and bathed the upper half of my body. . . .' "

Lapp turned the ignition key. "In ethyl ether veritas," he said.

"None of this was in Monroe's book?" asked the Russian.

"Not a word," Alf said. "I would have supposed it to be of more than passing interest in such a case."

"And this subsequent inhalation was sufficient to trigger the OOBE's?"

"By no means," Bill said. The vehicle drifted past the southwest curve of the Rock. In the shade of several great flying buttresses, luxuriant growth glowed from protected pools. " 'Rame' began tuning in on various radio stations of the mind—"

" 'People were talking,' " Mouse quoted, just such a radio station, his unbroken voice carrying clearly over the growl of the engine, " 'mostly along the lines of jazz, foreign languages, odd music, and fast chatter.' "'

"*Shit!* That's unnerving," Hugh said, looking over his shoulder. "Is he picking it up from us by telepathy, or has he memorized the article?"

"I don't know," delFord said frankly. "I think it's coming from the Vault, but don't ask me to justify that." The boy was gazing raptly at a peregrine soaring on the boisterous drafts. "Anyway, after further nocturnal communion with the cement can, 'Rame' found himself floating four feet above the bed. As you can imagine, I was rather cross with Tart for letting Monroe get away with deleting the sniff-tripping from his book, and I whipped off the article to Bangsund—keeping it in the family, as it were. Then Lilly got into the act, defending Monroe's experiences by references to his own independent 'simulations of God,' and it was generally concluded that since Monroe's book was for general public consumption, his entrée to OOBE via the cement can was best kept as restricted information."

Angrily, Alf said, "Bill, you're avoiding the issue. Do you normally pin your research on the hallucinations of a cement sniffer?"

"You miss the point," delFord told him calmly. "Victor was right—you are too quick to judge. The cement fumes were a gateway, that's all, as acid and yoga and biofeedback and meditation are all potential paths of access to authentic OOBE. My complaint was that the details had been edited. But Monroe and others like him also cite case after case of veridical information gained paranormally while in the astral state. I think his fantasies are symbolism, as your dragon dream was symbolism, and we need to unlock their meaning. Now that I know about the Vault, I suspect that they are something more critical than that, something whose implications are apocalyptic."

Without prompting or preamble, Mouse said, "'I received the firm impression that I was inextricably bound by loyalty to this intelligent force, always had been, and that I had a job to perform here on Earth. The job was not necessarily to my liking, but I was assigned to it. The impression was that I was manning a "pumping station," that it was a dirty, ordinary job, but it was mine and I was stuck with it.'"

The astronaut put his foot on the brake so hard The Beast slewed around, pawing the road. He turned off the motor and stared at the boy. "What the fuck's it trying to tell us?" he said, a touch of hysteria in his voice. For the first time Alf saw how deep the man's tensions were, how considerable were his fears. They're going to send him into the Vault, he told himself. With the insight, his skin oozed sweat. He felt himself losing consciousness. Yet he heard Bill delFord saying in a placatory tone, "Just another quote from Monroe, Hugh. Maybe it's a random process, like flicking through a book and poking your finger at a paragraph."

"It doesn't sound like that to me." Abruptly, beyond the voices, Alf saw a tunnel of honeycomb tiles, brilliantly lighted. At an immense distance, he heard Bill saying, "The pipes were rusty and overgrown, designed to transport some energy supply to an extraterrestrial civilization. It's symbolism that crops up in Hubbard's Scientology and Lilly's simulations, though Lilly prefers soulless computers." A man in a white glistening suit was walking down the tunnel to a large opening. "According to Monroe, more than one consortium has been plundering this valuable material from the Earth for eons, with much competitive tussling between them." Other men stood behind him, tending instruments. The suited man swung around heavily at the edge of the opening, lowered one leg carefully over the side, and began his descent. They promised us there'd be a moratorium, Alf cried in fear. Just because the outer defenses are down doesn't mean— Someone was saying, "Hubbard's mystical idea of the thetan. Following physical death, they are obliged to go to 'implant stations,' where goals and trauma are imposed on them with crippling electric shocks." The man was walking tentatively on the lower level, toward something huge which Alf refused to look at. No, no, no! he cried without sound. His body was slumping into the seat. Mouse was a vortex of energy, prismatic, through which he plunged. There was a cynical laugh. "It would not surprise me in the least to learn that some luckless thetans are press-ganged into pumping stations by nefarious implanters." The man staggered, beating his gloved fists against his head. "He's asleep, let him rest. God, those colors are beautiful." The Rock's striations, coral and orange, folded like waterfalls of stone into the earth. "The other tors are stratified nearly horizontally. Ayers Rock is directly between Mount Olga and Mount Connor, certainly part of the same formation, yet something has taken the crust and slammed it up at right angles. Could the Vault engineers have—" Tottering forward, the man wrenched at his protective garments. He hurled them in every direction. His hair was on fire. Alf was paralyzed. The man must have been screaming, as the skin bubbled and charred on his face and hands, crisping like baked pork. Alf's stomach voided itself horribly, explosively drenching the seat, running across Mouse's leg. The boy touched his hair tenderly, keening. The man fell, twitching, his long underwear igniting at last from the heat of his burning body. "Jesus, get the poor bastard out of the car." Thick oily smoke billowed up and failed to hide the blackened, disintegrating corpse, for the draft from the Vault caught it up in eddies and streamers and carried it away as the body fell into glowing ash.

Alf's scream went on and on, high and shrill and driven.

Vacantly, he heard the crackle of the CB radio, saw Hugh Lapp put the microphone back and move into the shadow of The Beast, squatting beside him with a shocked, furious expression. "The stupid fucking sons-of-bitches," he was saying. "They couldn't wait for the drug. They sent another man in."

"He burned up," Alf said, crying. "He's all burned up."

FOUR:

BEFORE EDEN

11. Deep Time

From the jeweled, prismatic cavern of encroaching crystals, her plumage in dulled tatters, Riona rhal Nesh came screaming like some poor mad creature. Perimeter alarms activated, shrilling, as she broke the boundary in her wild charge to protected territory. Pongid sentries added grunts and terrified curses to the uproar before they recognized her as a person. Belatedly, one of them slapped the panic button OFF.

In the sudden silence, appallingly, she was still shrieking.

Abruptly, Riona seemed to realize she was safe. Her headlong dash faltered; she stumbled. Her screaming ebbed to wrenching sobs. Torn by crystals, she hunched on the deck and wept.

Anokersh huj Lers shot out of the Control-to-Perimeter express tube, darted a glance at the now immobile sentries, hurried to where the female lay. His talons rang against the metal of the deck, the ragged rhythm of his slamming heart.

Riona had been gone five "days." Anokersh could still scarcely grasp that she was safe. It was the first time any of them had returned from the tumorous Ancillary Core, ever, ever, ever.

A young medic was already bent over her, smearing the lacerated flesh beneath her feathers with an enzyme salve. Behind him, a slavey nervously attended the diagnostic float. He stood up shakily.

"Well?"

Muscles stretched taut across the bones of his muzzle. "Sir, just shock, I think."

Sedation baffled the female's fright. Her sobbing caught and choked. Anokersh lifted her in his own arms and carried her to the sentry bubble.

Stiffly formal, mastering his own shock with evident difficulty, the officer of the watch preceded them into the bubble. He helped the medic fold out a foam stretcher float and lowered Riona on to it. Gently, he removed the hands that clutched his upper arms. And with abrupt distress, and aversion, he saw the mutilation which had been done to her: the finger of her right hand was absent, surgically excised. The thumbs remained, pressed together over the stump with bloodless, unconscious intensity.

"Status?" Anokersh demanded without turning his head.

"We have this quarter of the Perimeter fully covered, sir," stated the officer. "I've ordered up reinforcements from Gamma and Delta. Nothing can get through now." His thin, dark lips drew back over incisors in a snarl.

"Any signs of pursuit, Sentry?"

"None, sir. The board's clear."

The medic reached across with another ampule of sedative. As the fine jet hissed against the pulsing artery at Riona's neck, her breathing slowed, relaxed. Lifting the exhausted female, the Director let her lean against his chest.

"It's all right, technician," he murmured. "You're fine now, it's all over." The sentry's shadow put bruises about her dark eyes. "That's all for the moment, officer," Anokersh told him. "Send in T'kosh huj Nesh as soon as he arrives. Oh—and allow Diitchar rhal Lers through if she comes up." The guard gestured his understanding and stepped out into the tense, arc-bright crystal coruscations of the Perimeter.

"Kersh?" The thin, injured face looked up at him. "Am I really home, Anokersh?"

He ruffled the soft, tawny down at her neck. "You're home," he said. "I'll be surprised if the whole mission doesn't know it, the racket you raised getting here."

"Tech temperament." Her wan smile was ghastly. He felt his abdomen tighten again. Despite every precaution, the Core and the ferals it harbored were slowly squeezing the life out of them all.

Distantly, the express capsule sighed, and a voice demanded peremptorily: "Where is she?" A slavey muttered. T'kosh came into the sentry bubble, the plumage at his limbs and torso quivering erect. His pupils were dilated. "My love!" He went down on his knees beside the float and took Riona to him, ignoring the Director.

Anokersh moved aside, conscious of the revived rage within himself. He left the couple to themselves, sealing the bubble behind him. Etched rainbows of light splintered from the crystal mass.

The sentry officer interrupted his brooding with a curt status report. Glare splashed the deck. With some hesitation the youthful medic joined them. "Director, it would be best if the female were taken immediately to sickbay."

"All right," Anokersh agreed. They went back to the bubble. T'kosh sat on the rocking stretcher beside his spouse, arm tight around her. His atavistic aggression display had subsided somewhat, but his plumage continued to ripple in barely controlled spasms.

"Kersh," he said at once, "we have to act. We've been too patient." The sharp-boned planes of the artist's face were rigid. "We must go into the Core in force."

As always, nausea burned Anokersh's throat. Riona gave a sharp little cry, and her lips twisted with the same reflex.

"Brother," Anokersh said, "you know that's not feasible."

T'kosh rose. "We must make it possible."

"Hush, my love," whispered Riona faintly, through the blurring clouds of her medication. "The Director is doing all he can to contain the crystal mass. You can't expect—"

"Expect? I *demand!*" The medic glanced sideways at T'kosh, aghast. "The situation is intolerable. I demand safety, for the mission, for the children in the still-cells, for the females." His eyes bored into Anokersh, pale fire.

And the cool voice at the entrance: "Ah, Riona, dear."

The exhausted female smiled from her float. Fury left T'kosh's blood-filled face for a moment. The Director turned, took his spouse's hand.

In the doorway, against the stark glare of the Perimeter arcs, Mistress Diitchar rhal Lers was sublime. Her eyes were shadow-masked in her perfect face; flame lit them. And though she had missed the outburst from T'kosh, her thumbs closed on Anokersh in that same struggle to express the unthinkable.

Like a huntress, like a mother, she went to the injured female. When she stood back, trembling, the golden feathers of her spine stood out; her tail whipped back and forth. "What have they done to you?" she keened, holding the maimed hand. The violence of her tone dizzied Anokersh.

He gestured the medic forward. "We'll talk with Riona later. For the present she must rest, recover her strength. We must learn what she can tell us of the feral pongids. And then," he growled, holding to that resolve which buckled and slid aside even as he spoke, "we shall look to action."

A piercing howl was exclamation mark. It rang in the bones above his auditory openings where the communication circuits were printed. The sound galvanized him.

"Break-In, Break-In!" cried a voice. The carrier whine vanished, replaced by the anxious tones of Control-Watch. "Director, return immediately to Control. There is a feral within the Civilized area of the craft!"

Anokersh huj Lers was already sprinting across the metal deck.

He hit the inter-deck express tube, slid into the cushioned capsule, activated the field. From the corner of one eye, he saw his spouse following. The capsule kicked, draining blood from his face. Almost instantly it belled and sprang open. He hurled himself across the Control Room, heard the bell of Diitchar's tube arriving, took in the patterned information of the computer displays.

"It's on the third deck," Diitchar decoded. She stood beside him, snapping the visual display screens from one loc to another.

"Third-deck study sector," confirmed the voice in their ears. On every side, officers sped through an all-systems check. The intruder would most probably aim to sabotage as much vital equipment in the people's redoubt of the craft as it could manage. Fortunately, it seemed to have no grasp of where those vital services were located.

Even so, the Director told himself, the feral can do a boning lot of damage if it isn't stopped immediately.

The screens before Diitchar flickered and hissed.

"It's using some kind of electronics-jamming mech," explained the voice. "That's why we didn't pick it up the moment it broke in. No doubt jerryrigged—it's failing already."

"No mechanism," dissented another voice. "Chances are this feral's employing some neural form of radiation control. What we're getting now isn't component degradation; the creature's under stress, and it's losing fine focus."

"Still on Level Three. Everything else sealed off now, sir."

"Good." Anokersh spun to face the tall, golden female at his side. "So that's why they let Riona go. She was a blind, a cover to get this one in."

Diitchar nodded. "They must think this feral is pretty important."

"He's important where he is now. It's the first wild simian to break through since the Core brought us out of our still-cells." He unclipped his formal cloak. Diitchar ran at his heels. With faint incredulity he found himself standing before the Always-Locked weapons room. It opened to his priority command. He grabbed up a power-gun, thrust in the charge cell, checked it.

"Kersh, what are you *doing?*"

"We're not going to . . . hurt it, sweetness. I'm going to drag it back here before it retreats to the crystal mass." He headed for the tube to Level Three.

People shouted as he ran; he shouted louder. Even on a mission craft, you don't contradict the Director under conditions of emergency.

Capsule field detonating. The tube kicked him out on Deck Three. A rough-and-ready militia, people backed by simian slavies, crouched at all points behind anesthetic synaptic distorters, covering corners, guarding critical installations. A bell chimed and Mistress Diitchar was beside him again, a power-gun in her hand. Anokersh grinned at her with a sudden savage glee. They prowled, looking for their impudent feral.

Information streamed into their printed command transceivers. It told them nothing. The simian had vanished again off the screens.

Then: "Power drain, Children's Orientation Center." They started running. A corner came up; two corpses huddled in the corridor, feathers charred and rank. Together, they hit the deck and skidded.

Fiery whiteness blossomed. The air was scorched. Cascades of golden sparks opened like murderous flowers.

"Communications," Anokersh murmured, flat against the deck. "Give me a private channel to Diitchar rhal Lers." She lay beside him, breathing deeply without a sound. He could have whispered directly to her now, but he needed to keep in touch when they split up.

"Control, cut the ventilation fans in this section and break all magnetic locks on service inlets." It was an expedient of desperation, but fortunately, he told himself, far from obvious to the wild pongid. For hundreds of millennia its kind had been forbidden any access to the electronically operated inlets. Other than that they had contrived for themselves, of course. . . .

"Fans and locks off, sir."

"Dii, edge back and go through the shaft," Anokersh murmured, not looking at her, intently watching the white-hot fountain erupting from the classroom.

"Yes." It was eerie, hearing her at his shoulder, as well as on the closed band. A slither, and she was away. Up ahead, metal from the ancient corridor wall glowed red, runneled sluggishly into a pool of molten slag. Once, when it was new and bright, that metal would have withstood the assault of a terawatt laser. But millennia of slow, inexorable quantal changes had weakened its formidable metallic glass molecular structure. Abruptly, the defensive wall of hot sparks died.

"Power source traced and cut, sir," said the Control monitor. Good, Anokersh thought, easing to his feet. That'll throw the pongid back onto its own resources. Carefully, he made for the corner, grimaced as the heat of barely cooling metal singed his plumage.

"I'm at the ventilator inlet over the classroom, Kersh." Diitchar's voice held a note of horror. "He—it's searching for another power cable."

"Drop through," Anokersh said, peering into the darkness for the entrance. He hadn't been up here for years. Light had gone when Control cut out the main regional power supply. "Distract it; I'm nearly there."

There was a thud, ahead and to his right. He saw the frame of a door, hurled himself through with the power-gun dialed to quarter-strength. There's no question, he told his clamoring inhibitions, of killing the feral.

Glo-strips marking the light switches gave the vaguest possible general light. Anokersh heard a cry, strained his eyes to peer into the gloom. Diitchar's power-gun blazed at the far end of the room. The dim-red energy beam snaked raggedly across the ceiling, went out again. In that brief moment his adjusting pupils caught his spouse struggling with a dark shape.

The Director raised his own weapon, fired over their heads. The red glow burned an image into his retinas, a momentary picture of Diitchar toppling across a Teaching Machine as the pongid struck her with a huge, five-fingered fist. There was a crash as she fell, and then silence.

Anokersh used the distraction, for all that his heart

faltered in anguished rage. He slid in away from the door, hunched himself against a wall. There was no telling how sensitive the feral's vision was, and he had no wish to be silhouetted against the dull illumination of the molten wall outside. He ran his tongue over the roof of his mouth, found the switch for his printed transceiver, and pressed it off. There was no telling how sensitive its radiation perception was, either.

Across the room, in the murky blackness, flesh scraped metal. It's found Diitchar's weapon, Anokersh surmised. He circled silently toward the sound's source, avoiding the glo-panels, wondering frantically if he could dial to full power. Cool and heavy in his hand, the gun's upper stud pressed his central finger. The thought of death was unutterably repugnant. He left the setting at quarter—paralysis strength.

"TODAY, CHILDREN," a hearty voice boomed, "LET'S TALK ABOUT THE CRAFT WE LIVE IN!" The Director's heart contracted, and his feathers stiffened in reflex dread. Then he placed the recorded voice, and his pulse thudded back to stability. In groping for Diitchar's gun, the pongid had accidentally activated one of the Teaching Machines. Evidently the Machines were serviced by an alternate power circuit.

Useful, Anokersh decided, eyes aching with the futile effort of trying to pierce the darkness. The noise will mask my movements, he told himself. I can move faster with less worry. The same held for the feral, but the creature was not, he assumed, familiar with this area of *The Soul.* Anokersh huj Lers had at least been brought up in it.

"WE LIVE," roared the recorded voice, "IN A LARGE METAL EGG MADE BY GROWN-UPS MANY, MANY YEARS AGO. IT ISN'T A REAL EGG, OF COURSE, BUT IT'S SHAPED LIKE ONE. AND IN SOME WAYS OUR HOME *IS* LIKE A REAL EGG. IT PROTECTS US FROM TIME, JUST AS A REPTILE'S EGG PROTECTS THE TINY CHICK INSIDE IT."

The room stank with a curious unpleasant odor, the stench of a foreign biochemistry. It was an appalling reminder of how far these ferals had deviated from the slavey simian stock. Half a million years, at least, Anokersh thought. The figure was beyond intuitive appreciation; it meant nothing and everything. I wonder if my sweat smells as bad, he thought, to the feral.

"THE EGG IS CALLED *THE SOUL,*" the Teacher informed him at the top of its voice. "CAN ANYONE TELL ME WHY?"

There was a moment of silence, while the idiot circuits listened for a response in the vocal frequency range appropriate to its usual charges. Anokersh listened, as well, nerves trembling, for some clue to the pongid's position.

"NOBODY KNOWS?" the robot tutor chided buoyantly. Another terror had placed clammy hands on the Director. If the feral took time to draw off power from the Machine's source, he'd be faced by a more terrible weapon than his gun. On the evidence, the wild pongid itself constituted an irrevocably lethal arms system. "WELL, CHILDREN, OUR GREAT CRAFT IS CALLED *THE SOUL* TO REMIND US OF OUR SACRED MISSION. FOR WE ARE ALL ON A TREMENDOUS JOURNEY, LITTLE ONES, A MOST HOLY VOYAGE TO CARRY THE LIGHT AND JOY OF KNOWLEDGE TO OUR REVERED ANCESTORS. ONE DAY YOU WILL UNDERSTAND MORE FULLY—"

Anokersh hardly heard the old familiar words, strained against them, through them, for sounds of the feral. He moved cautiously across the large room, made for Diitchar's unconscious body. She, at least, would not be hurt further if he could help it.

Reaching out, his hand encountered something soft. He jabbed the snout of the power-gun into it. No movement. He realized that he'd found his spouse, and sagged.

Faded-ember lightning split the darkness. It missed them, burned a scar across the console of the Teaching Machine. Parents of all, Anokersh screamed within his skull. It's found the burn-setting on her gun!

". . . SEVERAL DISCRETE GENERATIONS OF PEOPLE." The programmed voice jumped crazily. Anokersh was cold, cold. He could not bring himself to alter the setting on his own gun.

"SPACETIME IS AWASH IN TERRIBLE ENERGIES," the tutor was roaring. Its tone had changed; now it was more measured, academic, directing its deafening banalities at an imaginary audience of adolescents. "THE GENETIC HELIX CANNOT WITHSTAND THE TUMULTUOUS SIDEREAL BOMBARDMENT TO WHICH WE ARE SUBJECTED, ON OUR ACCELERATING PARAREAL-TO-REAL TEMPORAL RATIO, WITH-

OUT THE MOST STRINGENT PROTECTION OF PHASED UNIFIED FIELDS. THIS IS WHY YOU, AND YOUR TRAINED PONGID ASSISTANTS, HAVE BEEN QUICKENED FROM EMBRYOS STORED IN STILL-CELLS. DUE TO THE DELETERIOUS EFECTS OF SUCH FIELDS ON FULLY DIFFERENTIATED ORGANISMS, SUCH PROTECTION CANNOT BE AFFORDED TO THE ENTIRE CRAFT. I REFER YOU TO THE M.H.D. TAPES IN—"

The voice bawled on, its dry detachment mocked and made absurd by its epic aural impact. How did the hideous creature hear me, Anokersh thought, through all that? His hand moved across Diitchar's muzzle, felt breath against his skin. He exhaled in relief. Gently, gently.

Then he turned, moved away from her, and waited for another bolt of fantastic heat. He sensed that the feral was tearing at the side panels of another Teaching Machine, desperately seeking external power.

At that moment, sound stopped. His ears roared in the silence. Someone in Control had remembered the alternate cable to the tutors. Anokersh thumbed the power-gun to its widest possible beam and pointed it in the air. A broad red shaft swathed the roof.

Shadows danced. One of them was the feral. A sizzling bolt snapped in his direction, over his head, as he dropped. He had its location. Throwing himself forward, he triggered the weapon to paralysis intensity and blasted at the hulking figure.

Incredibly, his aim was precisely accurate. The pongid loomed toward him, beam still blazing, and crashed onto the deck in catatonic seizure. He leaped to it, snatched Diitchar's stolen gun, and cut the beam.

Shuddering with reaction, he crouched on his haunches and tripped the circuit in his palate. Behind him, Diitchar moaned and he heard her struggle awake. "Okay, Control," he said, "I have it. Put the lights back on."

The pongid was hairy, flat-faced, stupefied from shock. At every synapse of its central nervous system, neurotransmitter vesicles had been numbed into inaction. A pair of slavies put their heads cautiously around the cooling, jagged edge of the entrance to the passageway. The Director recognized them: Lazy-Legs, an elderly gray-haired male, and Apple, a bright female who helped Stezna do Nen in the medical bay. He ushered them in, and they lugged the unconscious creature onto a float. The young medic who'd treated Riona—was his name Jik huj Lod? Anokersh wondered confusedly—went straight to Diitchar and gave her an analgesic shot. She disdained a helping hand. Anokersh regarded the scarred corridor. Damage to the craft appeared moderately serious, but not critical. Together, they followed the slavies to the utility tube leading to medical bay.

"Do you think there's any chance we'll be able to communicate with it, Kersh?"

He looked with disquiet at the dormant form on the bobbing float. Heavy tufts of bristle, a brown deeper than bronze, sprouted from its leathery hide. The relaxed, open palms were naked; like the slavies, the creature possessed five manual digits, only one of them opposable. Its visage, in narcotized repose, was horrifyingly akin to its tame cousins, but the skull bulged threateningly above beetling brows, and the wide nostrils twitched above a slack mouth crammed with spittle-shiny grinders. Anokersh shuddered slightly. The feral's cranial capacity might well be greater than his own—but did it, too, resonate to some element of the damaged Ancillary Core? His mind veered from the blasphemous possibility. The thing was an isolate, like all its family. And it had not been trained by scrupulous schedules of reinforcers, as the slavies had been, from birth.

"Communicate, Diitchar?" They stepped aside as Apple and Lazy-Legs eased the float into a surgery module. Within the confines of the med bay, the creature's musky stink was more a throat-choking affront than before. "I can't believe that it's more than an animal, Mistress. It's governed by instinctual reflex nets." The slavies were strapping it down securely; Anokersh glanced up and nodded as the medical chief came in, extending his depilated arms. "Well, Stezna, it seems all the hullabaloo was worth it. I know you've always been anxious to get a close look at one of these fellows."

"Director, Mistress." Bowing in perfunctory deference, Stezna do Nen looked worried. "Permit me to congratulate you both. But I trust you appreciate," he said acutely, "the difficulties this raises. In a sense, this is a moment we've all been avoiding and delaying as long as we could." His eyes flickered over the metabolic outputs, and his bare arms shuttled automatically over the hardware, preparing a suitable pharmaceutical cocktail.

Anokersh said nothing. Stezna shrugged, laid the jet-injector against the creature's short, thick neck, and unsnarled its synapses.

Its eyes snapped open, startlingly blue, and flicked around the module.

For an instant it caught Anokersh's gaze and bored into him with raging intelligence. It can't be, the Director thought, quailing. It *must* not be. Then with a dreadful scream the feral surged against its bonds.

Fantastically, one of the foam-covered steel bands appeared to give slightly, creaking. The pongid swelled its powerful chest again and tensed for another assault. With mild reproof, unperturbed, the chief medic sequenced an anesthesia field on his panel. The pongid slumped again, filleted, and its eyes dulled. The great mouth parted.

"You fools," the feral said, with a barbaric accent, "don't you understand yet that you are doomed?"

Anokersh stood utterly frozen, and watched the creature sink once more into unconsciousness.

12. Deep Time

Amid the woe of the Going-Hence, the genuine grief of the dead ones' clan-kin and the conventional wails of the rest, Anokersh huj Lers stood somehow apart from his central role, deeply troubled by images of the unconscious feral. In the purple gloom of the Great Concourse of the Dead, his eyes moved automatically from the keening mourners to the huge slabs of pack ice adrift in the cold black waters beyond the weather shield, the vast furled streamers of pastel aurora painted on the darkness by Winter's hidden sun. Illusion, he thought, all of it. But it was a kind deceit, even a necessary one. To know entirely, in this moment of Translation, that the infinite sky was an arch of ancient metal, that the slapping frozen sea was a metal deck, would be a recognition close to insupportable.

Yet it was not the holographic illusion which disturbed the Director, but some deep stirring of anguish he could not name. The pent feral was its occasion; that much he knew. Beyond that, he was aware only of the general terror which the cancerous crystal mass provoked in him, the Ancillary Core which now stood, for all the people, as much a symbol of dread as of peace and hope. Anokersh shivered, and drew his priestly robes about him in the season's dusk.

A new note entered the lamentation. The floating catafalque appeared, solemn and splendid, flanked by four clan-kindred males. Under the illusory purple sky, the dead males were hardly distinguishable from the living, except for their awful stillness. The bier came forward, through the sobbing crowd, and settled in the apparent ice at Anokersh's feet. Diitchar, silent at his side, touched his arm; he turned and took from her the long ceremonial knife. Light stropped its grooved, chased blade.

Again, some undefinable premonition of the feral stole over Anokersh. He hefted the knife angrily, lifted it in the sight of the gathering. I am Sacerdote before Director, he told himself. Or was that a meaningless distinction? As commander of *The Soul,* were not his sacred and his mundane roles conjoined? He could not dismiss the feral's mad, impossible words: *Fools, you are doomed.*

"People," he said aloud, and was surprised at the ringing steadiness of his voice, "we are come to the Place of Birth and Re-Birth."

"We are gathered," the many voices chanted, though some continued their sobbing, "to rejoice in the Translation of our comrades."

"The Nesting Place and the Resting Place are One."

"Where the children are made," the people murmured, calming now under the ritual, "the discorporate congregate in their wisdom."

"Where the semen and ova of Consciousness are joined, the Flesh is brought forth. Where the Flesh passes away, the Consciousness of the Dead is born into Eternal Life."

"The Flesh returns to the Flesh," the people said, in the twilight of the night season, "and the Spirit goes on in the Spirit."

"Our sorrow is right and proper," Anokersh told them, "for our comrades have gone away from us. Yet they go only to await us. Their Spirit has not perished, even as their Flesh shall not perish. Let us find joy in our grief, for as we revere the bones of their death they shall comfort and guide the blood of our life."

Lesser Sacerdotes took up the antiphony as Anokersh stepped forward. Diitchar carried the golden bowl, placing it carefully as the dead ones' kin lifted the bodies, their poor singed feathers flaking away in the dim air, and carried them in turn, reverently, before the knife and the vessel. The blade slashed, opening the necks. Blood, ruby-red, held from clotting by the medic's post-mortem injection of heparin, gushed into the deep bowl, misting in the chilly air. Anokersh felt his own pulse quicken as he gazed at the splashing libation. His mouth filled with a spasm of saliva, and his belly quailed, as always, in a contraction of incipient nausea. With abrupt insight he recognized the emotion as an analogue of the dizzy faintness which took him, took them all, when any attempt was made to grapple with the problem of the feral pongids. A spearing migraine burst above his eyes. The insight was lost on cross-currents, swirling eddies that evaporated—

He forced his attention back to the corpses before him. Drained of blood, they lay once more on the stainless steel of the catafalques. Plaintive, the ancient chants closed their dying fall. How inappropriate it is, he thought, so far from the true Place of Birth and Re-birth. A pitiful sham. He felt, in that moment, abandoned, forsaken. We are the instruments of a great purpose, he rebuked himself. We have no rights of complaint.

Soon the dead would speak, resolve his doubts. He momentarily caught the clouded eye of the Intercessor, swaying in her filmy cloak, half-deranged already by the sacred drugs. Swiftly he moved forward into the crowd pressing to the biers. It was shameful, an abrogation of tradition, that all the craft's crew were not here, yet the exigencies of their plight precluded it. At the Perimeters, watch officers must stand at their posts, governing the slow pongid sentries. Others still must remain on duty in Control, lest the ferals somehow seize this opportunity to redouble their mischief.

"People of the Mission," he said, "we come to do homage to our brothers, who passed from our midst defending the integrity of *The Soul*. For Ghine do Lod and Thali huj Salder, death has been more than Translation; it has been their glory. Now we do them the final honor, recalling as we eat and drink in their memory those last moments when they faced without fear a foe more terrible than the mute forces of nature—" He choked, and in silence took from Stezna do Nen the heavy surgical lancet. It buzzed against his thumbs as he activated the rapidly vibrating blade.

Standing by the body of Ghine do Lod, he had a sudden image of Riona's brutalized hands, the excised fingers. Was it a parody of this sacred rite? Trembling, he thrust the image aside and addressed the corpse. His first incision slit the downy skin of the belly from groin to neck. Stezna, and Jik huj Lod—the dead male's clan-kin, Anokersh noted distantly—stood to either side of the catafalque in ceremonial robes; they reached forward and peeled the opened skin from the body, exposing the layer of subcutaneous fat, which gleamed dull yellow under the auroral sky.

Two clean strokes continued the incision from neck, across the deep rib cage, to lay back the skin of each arm along the scaly ventral undersurface. Two more extended from the groin to the taloned feet. As his acolytes eased back the burned skin, shriveled and hard in patches where the feral's energy blast had seared it, Anokersh deftly took the surgical knife through tendons and gristle, severing the muscles to the powerful slashing weapons of the feet. He placed the dismembered feet in a silver vessel brought to him by his spouse, and moments later added the relaxed, bloodless hands.

In the cold breeze, plasma oozed from the raw flesh, sticky under his fastidious touch. Jik and Stezna, familiar with surgery, swiftly rolled the skin to the corpse's muzzle. At Stezna's muttered reminder, Anokersh incised the scalp; freed, the pelt came away and was folded gently over the jointed extremities.

The chief medic passed a power-saw to Anokersh. A diapason of grief rose from the gathering as the Director trepanned the skull. A stench of burning bone moved on the air. Anokersh slid his thumbs into the cranial cavity, and drew forth the small double-lobed brain; it came out with a moist, sucking sound and slipped into a waiting vessel.

The sheet of banded muscle tugged at the vibrating lancet as he bent back down over the belly, slicing into the abdominal wall. Stripping back the muscle, he removed one by one the internal organs: the massive, looping intestine, the kidneys, liver, heart, the pink sponge of the lungs. He took particular care with the gallbladder, lest he rupture it, loosing its bitter green fluids.

Eviscerated, the corpse was almost unrecognizable. Litanies soared and fell, ambiguous voices. Anokersh completed the paunching, taking the bright specialized instruments from Stezna and laying them aside, slick with dark juices. He butchered the carcass, then, jointing the limbs, carved the flesh delicately away from the bones in long strips and slices. The final disposition of the spinal cord, the ribs, the pelvic girdle he left to experts; the bones must, where possible, remain inviolate.

At last he rose. The mortal remains of Ghine do Lod lay all about him, piled raw in the sacramental vessels. An acolyte fetched him scented water; he washed his hands, shaking slightly from the tension, and turned to the corpse of Thali huj Salder.

The quivering pitch of the wake tightened even further when finally he put aside the hot knife and once more dipped his aching hands. In the consummation to come, the dismantled dead would speak, make utterance from that pinnacle of illumination which the quick might never attain unaided. The sighing, half-exhalation of exhausted pain, half-exaltation of expectant mystery, broke again and again against that tension like the indigo waves of the numinous, icy holorama. Anokersh lifted his arms and sang:

"In this Place of love and terror let us lose
ourselves.
"As each of us speaks in the common tongue,
"Each is a syllable of the Great Utterance.
"We commend to the Parents the lives of these
newly dead,
"Ushering them into the Womb of eternal delight."

In the swift blurring of his perceptions, the echoing multiple overlays, Anokersh heard the massed voices join his in the invocation; one voice, not his, not Diitchar's, not maimed Riona's, not any of the several voices of those strong figures bent toward him in the dusk:

"We ask as a People, each clinging no longer to the isolation of the finite ego-self, for the blessing and wisdom of that multitude-made-One gone before us to beatitude."

And a single voice once more, his, yet in the streaming

lambency a voice speaking from no fixed place, no single throat, as he bowed to the golden bowls, the silver vessels, and distributed the raw gobbets of flesh, the succulent meat of their brothers: "Let us eat and drink of our comrades, Ghine and Thali, that as their cells mingle with ours the ancient covenant of Peace shall be affirmed, to take life neither in hot anger nor cold calculation, and the wisdom of the discorporate Spirit announce itself in our midst."

Hungrily, in an elevation above greed or revulsion, Anokersh tore at the strips of tepid meat with his carnivore's rending teeth, gulped at the sweet feast, sent his snout again and again to the salty liquid. With enormous tact, then, he drifted back from the banquet, his tongue seeking the last of the blood adhering at his mouth, and awaited the benediction from the Intercessor's lips.

When she spoke, it was in a high strange quaver, drug-slurred, an utterance to the One People from the pseudo-soul mapped in the Ancillary Core.

"Life returns on its way into a mist, its speed into its quietness again: existence of this world of things and men renews ultimately their never needing to exist."

She choked, spittle at her lips. "Again knowledge will study others, wisdom is self-known, and muscle masters brothers; self-mastery is bone; content may never need to borrow, ambition will wander blind, and as vitality cleaves to the marrow leaving death behind. The universe is deathless, because having no infinite self, it stays infinite. Clarity has been manifest in heaven and purity in the spirit. Consciousness has no death to die." The Intercessor sagged; her feathers drooped, her tail jerked spastically. Strong hands, her clan-kin, took her at the armpits and held her erect.

The Director looked into her foggy eyes and asked gently, through her, "Do we speak with Thali huj Salder, with Ghine do Lod? Tell us, comrades, was your Going-Hence a good voyaging? Are you sojourners in bliss?"

Her eyes reeled. Syllables stammered. Anokersh felt cold, colder than the chilly, contrived breeze. The dead took up his physical dread and spoke it aloud from the Intercessor's clattering jaw:

"A a a cold a k k k cold coming we had of of of it. Just the worst ti time of the year for a j j journey."

Thali's widow screamed. This was not the way of it. All

the dead were at rest, among beatitude, dandled in the temporary peace of the Ancillary Core, awaiting their reconciliation with the Race when the Mission's voyage was done, when at last in the completion of that million-year epic the protective gluon shield might be let down, opening once more the Soul Core to the delirious flux of universal consciousness. Yet the Ancillary Core was diseased, Anokersh knew with horror, as he had always known and denied; their temporary haven, their greater extension, their life was run amok. He laid his hands on the fragility of the Intercessor and shook her. "Tell us of beatitude," he demanded desperately. "Speak to us of your Passing-Over."

She threw back her head and howled like a mindless pongid slavey.

"We are running to the Children's Orientation Center," she cried shrilly. "Yes, we hear it ahead of us. It looms. O Parents of All, it burns with a fiery nimbus. A power cable, torn from the wall, is in its hand. Sparks fly in a scorched cascade. Heat blooms from its touch. We are on fire, we burn, we burn. It turns away. The hull is melting. We are dead. Oh, Thali, I can't move. There is no pain, Ghine. Can we be Translated? I didn't know it'd be so cold. What's the humming? I can't hear you, Thali. Everything is so dark and cold. That terrible buzzing, that screaming saw. Are they eating us already? But I'm not dead. *I'm not dead!*"

Anokersh stood aghast. The dead were lost, trapped in their terminal agonies. Never before had he witnessed a post-mortem communication from anyone who had died brutally, in pain, without the comfort and the songs of their companions. Those who had vanished into the cancerous Core zone and had not returned had been beyond reach of the Intercessor; he had assumed that they were not yet Gone-Hence. Now he saw another, more appalling possibility. Had they perished in this agony, caught in a loop of meaningless loathing? But the Old Ones, the Parents of All, were sketched in the Ancillary Core. Surely they would reach out, guide and comfort the dying—

Silence fell. Stezna do Nen glanced up from the diagnostic float which monitored the Intercessor. He scowled at the Director, but said nothing. When the female spoke again, all the harsh shrillness was gone. Her voice came with a tranquility near to woodenness.

"We move in the Birth Canal. The light is deepest red. We float. There is small resistance to our contractions. Ah! The bodies lie below us, ahead of us. Alas, the plumage is in sorry array. Communications, give me a private channel to Diitchar rhal Lers. How strange, it's leaking. Dii, edge back and go through the shaft. We leave the shaft. Here the light is golden. Ah! Ah! Are you the Parents? How sweet, how warm. Such light! It flows, it gusts, it is a wind, there is a fine taste of blood. We have come home."

The terror slowly ebbed from Anokersh. Head lolling, body rocking slightly, the drugged female hung in the arms of her clan-kin. Aurora shook the sky. Diitchar took his hand and squeezed it tightly. Abruptly, the somnolent female jerked up her head and stared directly into his eyes.

"Confusion is here. We must not rest. Anokersh huj Lers, there is peril to the Mission. Other voices jabber. Do you see? Attention must be paid! Knowledge will study others. At the interface. Corrosion is here. Our tongues are bound. One has said to you, you are doomed. The jabber must be stilled. See to it." Then the blinding potency was gone from her gaze; she slumped utterly, and Stezna was at her side with an injection jet.

There was little enough remaining of joy, of harmony, of reassurance in the ceremony. With a stubborn loftiness, Anokersh saw it through to the end—the farewells to the departed, in formulae ill-wrought to suit those restless, minatory beings, the reminders to the living-in-flesh of their Mission and the gift they bore, a benefice locked away from their collective reach, the final sacramental partaking of the last shreds from Ghine's and Thali's bones, and the consignment of those dull, pale remnants to the cryogenic mausoleum—but panic gnawed at him, reduced him untimely to the isolation of his ego-self, stole the charity from his words.

"Mistress," he said urgently to Diitchar as the gathering dispersed uneasily, "we must go down at once to the feral."

"I know it."

At last he dared admit the truth to himself. "The wild simians have found more than sanctuary in the crystal mass. They have broached the resonance. The computers have been in error." His words stumbled at the blasphemy:

"The souls of another species have intruded within the Ancillary Core."

His spouse turned her golden head. "I have known this since the creature first spoke. They possess intelligence. They have evolved."

"First we must hear what Riona can tell us."

The artist T'kosh huj Nesh had taken his spouse back at once to the Recuperation bay at the ceremony's end. Initial exhaustion and the stress of the Going-Hence had brought her near to incoherence. She rested on a null sleeper under the soothing solar panels. Questioned, she could recall little. She trembled at the gateway to hysterical fugue. Only fragments of her ordeal remained, and those she resisted: blurred endless periods of vague horror; stark images of crooked, humped, bloated monsters whose ancestors had once been pongid slavies—images which hinted more at nightmare than truth, for the selection pressures shaping the pongid they had seen must have been ferocious; running, tripping, torn by the blade edges of the shimmering crystal Core. And among the nettles of that awful time were other people, others who had been stolen into the prismatic jungle. Sane or insane? Riona could not remember. For her, the boundary was too imminent. . . .

Stezna do Nen woke up the creature for them. Anokersh leaned close to its flat face as the induction currents brought its cerebral rhythms accelerating up from the nadir of coma to the rapid flutter of alert awareness. For a second time he felt shock as the blue eyes opened to pierce his soul with their intelligence. The pongid turned its head aside with distaste.

"Take your rancid breath away. I smell the blood of your kin, and it sickens me."

Anokersh brought up his arm deliberately and slapped the creature with tremendous anger. The sound of the blow was unbearably loud, and pain closed his thumbs across his palm; the Director came close to cringing from his action. Blood gushed from the creature's nostrils, brighter in this light than the blood he had drained from the corpses of his brothers.

"You shall speak only to answer us, animal." His fury returned, and a gross, unfamiliar lust worked from his belly to his groin in a wave of heat.

The beast snarled. Its teeth were square and flat. Along

its scalp, bristles rose. It said nothing. Foam-padded steel left it barely space to breathe.

Diitchar, with cold sardonic contempt, said, "Animal, do you have a name?"

"If I were an animal," the creature told her with equal scorn, "I would have a name like Frizzle, or Rutter, or Muncher. Do you take me for one of your mute, pathetic monkeys? My name is my own, and of no importance to you. I do not think you will mistake me for a snake."

For all the barbarous slurring of his speech, the beast's diction was comprehensible. Anokersh was filled with an incredulous loathing, tinged with curiosity.

"Let us be magnanimous," he said. "We shall give you a name commensurate with your status. Prisoner"—his tone hardened—"why have you come here?"

The nasal bleeding had ceased; congealed clots clung obscenely at the Prisoner's whiskers, along its broad upper lip. "I am only the first," it said thickly. "Soon the tribes shall be ready to follow. We shall crush the snakes beneath our heels. We shall drive you interlopers whence you came, to the dark places beyond the world's circle."

Cant, Anokersh thought. The rhythms of ritual, of rage clarified to banality but retaining still some link to the dynamo of emotion. He was thunderstruck, as much by the implications, the near-comical misapprehensions embedded in the pongid's outburst as by the continuing absurdity that an autonomous sentient could utter any intelligible words at all.

Sharing his astonishment, Diitchar rhal Lers forgot her hauteur. "We, interlopers? Is your ignorance so entire? There is no world beyond the fields and metals of the hull. This craft, this island, is the construct of our Ancestors, of the Living People—yes, even the crystal mass which you bumptious vermin infest." Her anger returned. "We have been generous too long. Anokersh, the stench of the creature offends me."

"Go, then," he said shortly. A vortex had hurled itself at his head; he felt the blinding migraine return. With betrayed surprise, his spouse stared at him for a moment. Her tail snapped twice against her legs; she turned and stalked from the room.

The Director scarcely noticed. Curtly, he told Stezna, "Put it to sleep, and leave us."

"Without an orderly?"

His head shot up. "Can it harm me under anesthesia? Do as you're told."

"You fear the truth," the Prisoner began. It went into coma in mid-word, and Anokersh brooded over its inert bronze form, alone, with pain.

Half a million years *The Soul* had plunged untended in the terrible dark, he knew. In all that remorseless time the quantal flicker of the electronic computers had governed her course, under the command of the patient dreaming dead mapped in the Ancillary Core. In cycles of placid generations it had hatched out the slavey embryos, fed and trained the creatures, used their marginal motility and skills in maintaining the deserted craft. And all the while *The Soul* accelerated, hurled by the energies of sundered quarks, plunging like a meteor into the appalling vectors of para-reality.

—And the supernova had flared in the cruel crucifixion of an instant, only tens of light-years distant, all the raging fire of a galaxy ignited, its fifty-five-day half-life compressed by the craft's monstrously elided ratio into a savage shrieking pulse of piercing radiation. . . .

External gluon shields faltered. The Ancillary Core was sleeted with a sidereal howl of hardest radiation. Had any crew walked the decks of *The Soul,* they would have perished in the instant of auric overload. Had they, impossibly, survived, had their groins—against the Mission's plan—retained fertility, they would have brought forth nothing viable. But the seed of the people was safe, locked under that central and most precious seal which guarded as well the Soul Core itself. It was the slavey stock that suffered mutation, that groaned for a hundred generations in cancer and deformity, retreating from the damaged computer's scrutiny and the mindless zeal of the unscarred lines of newly quickened pongid servants; retreating, yes, into the dreadful heart of the injured crystal mass.

And there they had evolved. Anokersh whimpered. The beast on the float before him, leashed and passive, was the child of ten thousand generations of an imploded, unspeakable ecology. It bore the desolating heritage of an intelligence—an intelligence!—shaped in total confinement.

He stood over it, his nostrils shrinking from its musk, the tender flesh of his palms pressed against its brutal, rhythmic rib cage. Its pelt was warm. Even in coma, the pulsations within that bulging cranium, the chemical messages below dream on their voyage from synapse to nerve, were charting their echo in the Resting Place of the People. Anokersh was cold; he shuddered; he brought the talons of his thumbs gouging down the animal's breast. He knew at last, without reprieve, what must be done.

13. Deep Time

Into the effulgence of the arc-lit crystal mass, his plumage imperial, Anokersh huj Lers stepped like a prince. He bore no energy weapon; the people dared not risk such potency falling into the hands of the ferals. The guns he and Diitchar had used to subdue the intruder had been returned to the locked weapons room. In one hand, tightly, the Director held a powered knife, a modified butcher's implement from the protein abattoirs. Behind him, their talons clashing on bare metal, a dozen strong males passed the Perimeter line. All the shades of light flickered for an instant to shadow, and then brightened once more; the alarms had been reset. They went forward into feral territory.

T'kosh huj Nesh came up beside him, warily, the knife an extension of his artist's hand. "Kersh, how did the computers let it get this far out of control? We should have been quickened thousands of years ago."

They moved swiftly into the tunnel. The metal walls were an intellectual abstraction behind the sharp-edged mounds, the stalagmites, the frost spurs, the glancing violet stars and corona of the glacial Ancillary Core. They stepped carefully, keeping clear of the murderous crystal spines. The lancing icicles grew denser as they penetrated to the Core, a spectrum of jewels that hurled the eye into infinities of confusion. A male stumbled, his foot pierced; as he fell, blood matted his feathers from a hundred small wounds. His companion caught him as he cried out, held him tottering on one foot. Jik huj Lod bent, smeared the torn limb, squirted a covering. The male limped ahead, his knife thrust forward against a malignity for which none of them had truly been prepared.

Why? Anokersh thought. Because the computers had been damaged, because the vast array of pre-planned scenarios had failed to include the possibility of biological subversion among the slavies? Because the reliquary of the Ancillary Core, the accumulated wisdom of three million years, had collapsed crucially from homeostasis to random growth? Because, quickened at last, brought to adulthood by the crippled programs half a million years too late, this generation of the crew had been smug, comfortable behind the Perimeters, betrayed by their confidence in the science of their species and their secondhand sense of mission? But these were hardly answers to T'kosh's question, Anokersh knew. His crawling skin told him that the ferals were watching, awaiting their advantage. His mind swam. We are no suitable heirs to the Old Ones, to the Parents of All, he told himself bitterly. We are as defective as the wild ferals.

He stopped short. Light split and danced at the intersection of what had once been a bay of the Core. The male behind stumbled against his heel, cursed. Anokersh spun about, his thoughts febrile and agitated. He lifted his knife.

"Listen," he said urgently, "what are we doing here? We have some blurred notion of reprisal. It's not enough."

T'kosh said angrily, "We can bring out the poor bastards they have imprisoned here."

"The Ancillary Core must be repaired," said one of the males from the Engineering Clan. "These animals have to be stopped before they—"

"We have only two options!" Anokersh cried harshly. "Don't you understand? We have to come to terms with the ferals, accept them completely—or kill every last one of them."

Blood rushed, clashed with the frenzied babble.

The Director seized T'kosh huj Nesh by the shoulders, yelled into his face. "You know that we can't allow them to remain in the Core!"

A primal fear brought the artist's lips back to the sharp

bones of his muzzle. "Kersh, these are the sacred places of our—"

"Can we exterminate the ferals?" he screamed remorselessly, shaken with nausea.

"How can you speak of killing?" T'kosh asked in loathing, pulling back from the Director's grasp. "Have you become a wild beast, Anokersh? Have you abandoned all decent—"

Lurching under the cataract of light, brain afire, the Director caught the chains of logic and instinct and brought them clashing together. "Brothers, the ferals have entered the collective soul of our people. They sit camped at the perimeters of our consciousness, of our being, of our ancestral heritage. It is no more possible to plan the deliberate death of a feral pongid than to consider the slaughter of one of our own brothers or sisters." Distantly, he saw one of the males bent over double, heard the retching. His own body cramped into agony. He said the appalling thing that had to be said. "Brothers, we *must* destroy the ferals."

"Anokersh," T'kosh said with terrible intensity, "be silent." The artist turned to the others. "He was right. Reprisal is madness. We must turn back."

The ferals leaped at them, then, howling in a travesty of speech. "Do you see?" the Director cried, his powered knife useless in his hand. "They have nothing to restrain them." He saw the crude metal club coming at his head, a curve inexorable as gravity. The blow caught him at the back of the head.

When he tried to reach his bruised, abominably throbbing head, tight bonds held his arms.

In the dim light, he saw that most of the crystal mass had been hacked away from the hull. The pain was overwhelming. He opened his eyes again. Most of the power had long since been cut from this sector, but the autonomics had been obliged to leave some cables alive—those adjacent to the hull, and to the Ancillary Core maintenance systems. Even so, he observed at once, there was clearly little enough electricity for the ferals to waste any on illumination and warmth. Unbelievably, their deranged ancestors had somehow contrived a jumbled, makeshift closed ecology.

Rude, open tanks extended on every side, dull with ultraviolet lamps, atrickle with hosed chemicals. Vegetation straggled from the simple hydroponics vats, heavy with seeds. The blunt, herbivore's teeth of the invading feral flashed in his mind. No, he thought with sudden understanding, they have no restraints. Sixty million years of carnivore inhibitions stood behind the People. But these creatures, he thought, might not hesitate to kill their own kind. There would be no genetic prohibition against the slaying of intelligence.

"To your feet," a voice slurred. A wave of feral musk and sour sweat assailed his nostrils. He struggled up, looked into the blotched face. The pongid cuffed him; pain cracked through his head. Groggy, Anokersh stumbled across dry vines, unruly runners from the crude food vats, urged on by ungentle shoves. They have been isolated for ten thousand generations, he thought. Yet they speak our tongue. Are they so deeply in resonance with the Core? Or have they adopted the speech of their captives?

They came into a better-lit clearing. Perhaps the outer shields inhibited the growth of the crystal mass here, for the impervious metal of the hull was visible under a thin skin of the memory lattices. The Director faced a scene beyond nightmare.

They have bred for intelligence, he thought, recoiling, but their flesh is ruined.

Grotesque shapes moved in the twilight. Near his feet, a hairless pup spat at him. Another cowered, scratching at the scabbed white scales that covered its body. Malnutrition, he realized. Carcinomas in their food supply. Our presence on *The Soul* has driven them to desperation. Until the machines quickened this second generation of the people, he thought, the ferals must have made forays into the stores. Now, with the slavey guards under living command, the ferals are penned utterly into their redoubt. It is no wonder, he told himself, that they hate us.

An ancient creature jabbed at him with a strip of metal. Its teeth were rotted. Anokersh turned his head away, his gorge rising. With sudden clarity he knew what was required. He triggered the printed transceiver, sub-vocalized direct contact with the control computer. His feral guard looked at him suspiciously and failed to determine what was amiss; it shoved him into the center of the clearing.

He gave the machine the Priority override code. Step by

step, in precise mathematical language, he instructed it and put its systems on hold. He switched to his spouse.

"Diitchar, they're detaining us in the vicinity of Hull-Sector Seventy-one. Can you trace us?"

"Praise be to the Parents!" her voice cried. Then she said, "Kersh, the sensors have come up on the Board from Seventy-one." They had been quiescent since the computers sealed off the damaged pongids thousands of years before.

Several of the reprisal party were shoved into the clearing beside the Director. T'kosh lurched against him; hobbled as he was, Anokersh nearly fell. Praise the Ancestors, he thought, that I refused to allow Diitchar to come with us.

Her voice told him that she'd traced a service route to the clearing and entered it as an available sub-routine. Muttering, he ordered the program to spring the magnetic locks on access inlets sealed since the isolation of the defectives.

The beasts formed them into a straggling crescent, separating them, pushing them to their knees on the matted deck. There were groans, sounds of rustling; extraordinarily, nobody spoke. Some paralysis of the will held each of them. T'kosh huj Nesh bared his fangs. Blood welled from his mouth. Since Riona had disappeared and returned, hatred had gnawed at him like acid. Muscles contracted under his plumage. His bonds held, cut deeper into his flesh.

"Don't, brother," Anokersh told him. The artist's eyes, half-crazy, stared in contempt. "T'kosh, we'll . . . wait for their move."

A dark icon, his face was ugly with fury. "You have forfeited command," he said. Several ferals moved toward them, fists bunching. "You would not turn back. Now you demand—"

"Hold your tongue!"

T'kosh brought his teeth clashing together. And his eyes widened.

A jabber went up from the spectral, brooding gathering of deformed ferals. Anokersh twisted about. A pongid female stood at the edge of the clearing, an aureole of crystal light spearing from her dark, gravid body. At her shoulder, denuded of plumage, leaned the first person they had seen since their entry into the feral sanctuary. Anokersh heard the name wrenched from his heart:

"Chalzin! O Bones, what have they done to you, Chalzin huj Tighe?"

He had vanished into the Ancillary Core as a child, the first of them to disappear. No older than the rest of them, his ravaged features, gaunt, starved, collapsed, were a mask of senility. His plucked flesh ran with pustules. "Abase yourselves!" cried Chalzin huj Tighe in a ghostly, foolish, imperious tone. "Cover your heads, snakes!"

Anokersh was cold, cold. His eyes were fixed in horror on the feral female. He thought of his silly, jolly pongid slavies, lively Apple, old Lazy-Legs, lewd Shrieker, always on heat, a score of the fat creatures he'd known since childhood, petted, sent ambling in their clumsy way to his bidding, and the comparison was ghastly. This female's skin was dull as the pelt of a corpse. She moved toward them, and Anokersh saw the six tiny breasts mounding her shrunken rib cage. Wild pongids massed about her as she came, cried out as she raised her arms. Beneath the armpits, two more paps jutted in the bristled fur.

"Chalzin," he shouted, "have us released! Where are your companions? Are any others alive?"

The male babbled unintelligibly and began to dance and caper in lunatic frenzy. In the swelling tide of excitement, the feral tribes moaned and swayed.

"Kersh," said a calm, sweet voice in his ear, "hold on a few more minutes."

He felt his knees buckle. "Horrible," he whispered to his spouse. "Horrible, horrible."

"We're having a little difficulty," Diitchar told him. "Some of the service tunnels have flow-welded their interface seals. When we're ready to come through, I'll let you know."

Abruptly, Chalzin huj Tighe stopped his cavorting.

A pair of powerfully muscled ferals were dragging something heavy into the clearing. They shoved it into place before the pregnant female and stood back.

Smelted raw from bulkhead metal, it was a waist-high steel egg, rust-splashed.

Anokersh felt tears leap to his eyes. It was a tortured image, in knotted unpolished metal, of *The Soul.*

The monsters crowded closer, their stink ripping at his throat, their grunting chants echoing against the deck. With an inarticulate scream of rage, T'kosh huj Nesh surged forward. In a burst of startling speed, one of the feral guards leaped after him, blunt teeth gleaming with spittle, and brought his club cracking across the artist's head. T'kosh fell. Chalzin capered to his unconscious body, gesturing in manic glee, and dragged him slowly to the altar. "Happiness and journey's end," he tittered. From each hand, the finger had been amputated. The pongids who had brought the metal egg grasped T'kosh under the arms and dragged him across the dried confusion of dead vines; Chalzin fluttered ahead, reaching down tenderly to staunch the blood oozing from the artist's scalp. They hoisted T'kosh to the altar. His limbs fell backward, dangling from the rough curving surface. His head hung, mouth wide, throat exposed. Anokersh stared, aghast. I have to wait, he told himself. I *must* wait.

With splendid dignity, the grotesque female mounted the unconscious body, her spindly legs wrapping T'kosh's shoulders, her face sinking to his groin. She hefted his unprotected genitals. A cry of pleasure rose from the ferals. Reality was a curdled, gelid wave in Anokersh's slowed brain. We have always waited, he thought. We have always been too late. Why can we never act? The Mother Goddess lowered her gaping jaws. He is sterile, the Director cried silently, absurdly. His seed is barren. It cannot advance your lust for freedom, for life.

A hissing implosion shook the air. "We're through!" Diitchar's voice cried in his ear. There were heavy thuds as plumed bodies dropped from the roof. "I'm going to detonate a flare!"

Time convulsed. *"Get down!"* Anokersh screamed to his group. "Cover your eyes! Don't look up!" He hurled himself to the deck. In the instant he buried his muzzle in dried vegetation, he saw the feral female hold high her head in fury.

Light bloomed, a silent monumental surge of blinding radiance. Even with his eyes covered, glaring crimson splashed pain. The pongids screamed in anguish, blundered heavily in blinded agony.

Anokersh felt hands at his bonds, heard the sharp whir of a power blade slicing. Then he was up, his arms around his spouse. A welding mask was thrust high on her forehead, a dark smear on gold. Flames hissed as the parched hydroponics vegetation burned.

He fell off the edge of the universe.

Instantly, the implants under his talons magnetized. A jolt went through his body as his flailing feet clanged to the deck. He gulped hard. Fire-control circuits had cut local gravity. The flames, ignited by the intense flare, smothered smokily into extinction.

Blinded, howling ferals spun slowly in the air, victims of a fail-safe system they could never have conceived of. They had never known the erotic luxury of null sleepers; weightlessness terrified them.

"Kersh, I brought you a power-gun." Diitchar thrust it into his hand, choking with loathing. The air was vile with the ferals' vomit. "Stezna has the pressure suit."

He activated his link to Control. "Leave the gravity off," he ordered the program.

T'kosh huj Nesh was still unconscious. He floated almost vertically above the metal egg, knees bent about the curve of the thing, talons clamped magnetically to its rough surface. His twisted ankles were sprained and swollen. Blood covered his groin. Stezna reached him, administered an analgesic jet, drew him carefully out of reach of the shrilling pregnant female drifting above him.

They need not die, Anokersh told himself desperately, struggling into the pressure suit. Graphs and equations blurred in his mind. They would hurtle across the interface between time and paratime, shedding their inertia into the external shields. He did not believe it.

"Back to the access shaft!" he yelled. "When you're all through into the Civilized sectors, *seal off!* Move!"

There was a greater terror. What would happen to the Ancillary Core? Like a sledgehammer blow into a naked cortex . . .

Diitchar closed the helmet over his muzzle, shot the pressure tabs. "Life-support indicators?" Her voice still came through his printed transceiver.

"All active!" he bellowed. *"Move!"*

She pressed her hands against his breast. "We've located three of the missing people," she told him softly. "Their minds are . . . damaged."

"There'll be a time for healing," he said. The horror of his duty moved in him like ice. He turned away.

When the access seal closed, he thumbed the power-setting to paralysis strength and roved through the chaos.

It was an act of mercy. The fires had died swiftly, leaving the makeshift hydroponics tanks sludgy with charred leaves, the stumps of vegetation like burned bones. Limp bodies hung about him, adults and pups. They are intelligent beings, he told himself. They are not of the Living People, but they share our consciousness. The knowledge was intolerable. He stood in silence and surveyed the work of his hands.

"Everybody's through," reported Diitchar, and for a long moment he could not comprehend her words. "Kersh," she said, a touch of panic in her voice, "we're all in. The sector locks are all sealed behind the Perimeter lines. Do you read me?"

"Yes," he said. "Close this line. I don't want *anyone* monitoring it."

"Yes, my love."

He gave the Priority code once more, told the computer to read back his program. Without hesitation it did so. His blood was liquid lead. He thought of Ghine do Lod and Thali huj Salder in equivocal bliss.

With frozen thumbs, he found the suit's safety line. He bound himself to a stanchion as far from the emergency hull lock as he could find.

He closed his eyes.

Faintly, through the thick skin of the pressure suit, there came the cry of a feral pup waking from paralysis to terror.

He screamed the activation order.

Winds roared about him. He had never known winds before. Soft, heavy thumps. There were sounds of vegetation ripping, torn in masses from their matted roots. With the crash and tinkle of breaking glass, segments of the crystal mass, the Ancillary Core, the memories of his People, sundered from the corridor walls into the high shrill keening air. The winds howled into the ultimate emptiness of paratime. His pressure suit creaked, adjusting to vacuum. Vileness clotted the outside of his faceplate.

The double doors gaped open to the gray opalescence of centuries flickering in elided passage. Lights within the empty section splashed stark on bloodstained walls. I have not killed them, he told himself. They are scattered through ages of lost time. He vomited. Vileness clotted the inside of his faceplate.

Anokersh huj Lers ordered the locks closed and sealed.

He crawled in the bowels of the Mission craft.

In the med bay, ahead, there was one last feral to dispose of.

Mistress Diitchar rhal Lers waited, with her love and forgiveness, beneath the ventilator shaft. He could not take her hand.

FIVE:

AN HABITATION OF DRAGONS

14. The Vault

Bill delFord unclipped his safety belt, climbed shakily over the side of the plastic pulley-drawn car which had brought them down from the surface. The huge cable twanged an organ note; way behind them, beyond the multiple switchbacks, the motor which drove it was taking up slack half a kilometer outside the original limits of the Vault's destructive field.

A forced draft thrust fingers into his thin hair, lifted the sweat and heat from his face. Hugh Lapp leaped athletically from the ludicrous car, so reminiscent of a carnival toy, and together they followed the gray-suited corporal down the last hundred meters of the steep tunnel.

"R&D have sent your protective suiting ahead, gentlemen," the corporal said. His voice boomed and echoed along the tunnel. "You'll change into it at this checkpoint."

Bill tried to smile an acknowledgment, knowing they might all explode into a greasy cloud of dispersed colloids at any moment. Already, thighs and belly were protesting peevishly at the unusual slope beneath his feet. There was a hollow rumbling; he looked over his shoulder. The plastic cablecar was retreating back up the boron-epoxy tube to the landing which glimmered a kilometer behind them. Even with the stiff gradient the engineers had maintained in these four-meter-diameter burrows, he and Lapp had ridden eight or nine klicks to come this deep.

"I should have insisted on phoning Selma and the boy," he said.

The astronaut glanced at him uncomfortably. "It's a son-of-a-bitch," he agreed. "Security'd never wear it. How are you feeling, Bill?"

"Same as you, I imagine. Floppy. Shitty, in fact. But feeling no pain." He started to laugh, and had to restrain himself. Ah, the whimsical bastards, he thought.

Gaslight flared white and sharp as they rounded the bend into the landing. Several troops in the gray non-national uniform of the project regarded them with dull, sullen suspicion from behind their emplacements. Bored technicians tended their makeshift instruments, conferred in murmurs. The corporal led them across the flat surface to a frail plastic box-like office, knocked, ushered them in.

General Joseph Ahearn Sawyer was a small, vigorous Texan. "Good morning, gentlemen. You're a little ahead of schedule, or I'd have met you at the terminal." He pumped their hands, directed them to curved polystyrene chairs, offered them coffee from the percolator bubbling beside his cluttered desk. "I'm delighted to meet you at last, Dr. del-Ford. Ready to make the dash to history?"

"It'll help settle my breakfast," Bill said. Less than five hundred meters from this preposterous office was the monstrous thing he and Lapp had come to challenge. He felt death snuffling for his scent. Cut the crap, he told himself sharply. Fear will keep me razor-edge alert, but not if I get morbid.

"We're all jumpy when we're waiting for action," the general said. DelFord looked away. Spare me, he groaned. But Sawyer was insisting: "Let me tell you, I came close to messing my neat new military pants the first time I— But you won't want to hear my tall combat tales. Let's go meet the gang; they're waiting in the staff room."

Enzymes swirled and clicked in Bill's brain. They seemed almost audible to him. He found himself giggling again. The goddamn stuff isn't supposed to chain-react until it's catalyzed, he thought with distant annoyance. The miracle of the age. Secret of eternal youth. But he couldn't fault the unofficial name the biochemists had chosen for the tiny peptide which the 17-Tg-M analogue was sluggishly fabricating from the beta-lipotropin proteins in his pituitary. Asinine, he reflected, chortling with merriment. If heroin is the drug of heroes, he asked himself, who will dare admit to a craving for asinine? Of course the sober souls of the Death Machine found nothing amusing in the sobriquet; they insisted that the pentapeptide be known strictly as arg-enkephalin. The amino acids danced in a chain before Bill's inward gaze, a rondo of molecules: tyrosine-glycine-glycine-phenylalanine-arginine. Religion, he thought, giggling, is indeed the opiate of the people. For what, indeed, is enkephalin, in its wholesome macrobiotic DDT-free endogenous met- and leu-varieties, but God's own pain-killer? They should have called it mysticin.

"Hugh, Hugh, my ole orbiting buddy," he said, slapping the astronaut on the back, "I'm. Truly. Feeling. No pain."

"You crazy junky," Lapp said, leading him to a couch. "You're not stoned; it's premature senility. Lie down for a moment and I'll get you a cold Coke."

"For Christ's sake," Bill said imploringly, "no artificial stimulants. We have to be pure of heart."

His head cleared as he lay there, staring up at two and a half kilometers of rock and sand. He desperately needed a cigarette. Instead, he ripped open a stick of gum. It was one of the more inconsequential side-effects of the Vault's destruction field that most of the project's nicotine addicts had switched to chewing gum. The instruments used down here all depended on jerryrigged chemical processes rather than electronic steady states—so the smokers had been obliged to leave their cigarettes on the surface, for fear of chemical explosion.

It was subtly but altogether disturbing, as he glanced around the patchwork staff room, to know that the closest electronics equipment was kilometers away. Communication with the surface was effected principally through a bulky hydraulic contraption mounted on a sturdy steel desk, its heavy tube boring up through the ceiling into rock. The input/output was a massively geared mechanical typewriter.

There was nothing in the entire area a nineteenth-century pre-electronics engineer couldn't have cobbled together . . . *if* he'd possessed the sophisticated synthetic materials, and the shop capable of turning out parts tooled to tolerances which would have staggered him.

And all this desperate ingenuity was shaped to the single appalling fact of the Vault's destructive field. It was not a gluon shield; the effect was more subtle, selective. He had seen one of its parameters altered already, when the rain stopped. Surely that was the active decision of intelligence. The central effect remained in force, however. The Vault still would not tolerate foreign electromagnetic activity an order of magnitude greater than the bioenergetic processes of a human body.

Bill sat up. His heart was hammering again. Within minutes he and Hugh would be going down to break the Vault, armed with its own key. Maybe. More probably the Vault would break them. He thought of the films of the burning man.

The astronaut joined him on the couch. Medics fussed over them. Bill said, "I'd feel happier if they'd flown Anne in." Yin and yang, he thought. There are no sexual monopoles, anymore than magnetic charges exist in isolation. The Three Musketeers face the Field Force Monster. Yet it had worked, before, at the Institute.

"Too many risks to have a woman down there," Hugh said. "I agree with them." He bunched one arm as the hypodermic was inserted into his triceps muscle, injecting the enzyme solution which would vastly accelerate his pituitary production of asinine.

Bill scowled, delivering up his own limb. "You diminish yourself, Hugh. You're maligning half the human race." He flinched. "Anne Hawthorne would have your balls for garters if she heard you agreeing with those pricks."

Harris Lowenthal leaned over them. "Time to suit up, guys." The psychologist was crisp, reassuring; the brittle cynicism of the first briefing had vanished completely. "Then we'll go down with you to the three-hundred-meter post."

"Yes," Bill said. Lowenthal was searching his face. He tried to keep his cringing fear from showing. His cheeks felt cold in the muggy air. He followed Lapp to the benches where the Russian electronics expert Komarov was waiting with the null-suits. The principal fact which had been brutally impressed upon him was that no one could enter the Vault Zone twice. The Vault permitted a single intrusion, exacting sanity as its price of admission. Second time around you were dead.

"Repeat the procedures," the psychologist demanded.

"We have one hour," Bill said tiredly. A mass of cotton was mopping its way through his brain. "You ring the bells every fifteen minutes. A series of coded klaxons counts down the last ten minutes."

The codes had been scorched into his unconscious memory by narco-hypnosis, operant conditioning, and old-fashioned fear-driven study. He would react to those bells, he thought, grimacing, if he was three days buried in hell.

"Well, General, I think that completes the review," Lowenthal said, hitching himself off the edge of the bench.

"Fine, fine." Sawyer thrust out his hand. "Dr. delFord, Captain Lapp, here's that historic moment. As soon as Komarov has you tucked into your long johns, we'll join you for a stroll down to the limit."

The specialists trooped out. My God, I wish Anne was coming with us, he thought again. His pulse accelerated. He became effectively unconscious. With dull surprise he found himself walking stiffly to the end of the landing, clad in the stifling foam-lined suit. His awareness contracted, functioning with all the effect of an integrated circuit board. Fifteen million separate metal threads were wired in a crazed tangle through the inert fabric of the suit. Lighter than chain mail, but not much more flexible, it had been poured to his specifications as exactly as a spacesuit to an astronaut's. Fedorenko believed it would damp out entirely the minute electric field generated by the human nervous system and masculature. The wiring was bonded into fibres of LI900, a Lockheed silica with a heat dissipation rate so profound that the suit could be handled with bare skin immediately after removal from a thirteen-hundred-degree Celsius kiln.

The tunnel stretched away behind them, lighted at intervals by gas mantles. Synthetic odors mingled with machine oil and human sweat. Heat poured up the tunnel, radiating from an invisible, incomprehensible skin around the Vault. Nearly three kilometers overhead, he knew, the sky was empty of clouds. The desert sun beat down, drawing a haze of a steam from the soaked summer soil.

"Won't be much more delay," Sawyer said cheerfully. Unscratchable itches raged across Bill's skin. There was a blank, foolish grin on the astronaut's face. "The research staff must have all their gear rolling as you go in, and they're still not really at home without electrons to push." A bell rang stridently. "Okay, gentlemen, that's it. I wish you luck. We'll see you at luncheon."

Bill shook his hand again and didn't feel a thing through the wired glove. Flanked by their escort of soldiers, he and Hugh walked into the final leg of the burrow.

The helmet of fine mesh surrounded his head, splintering gaslight like a prism. His left triceps was aching. Lungs burned with the fiery air fleeing up from the barrier.

This last stretch had all been dug by hand-wielded hydraulic excavators. The previous slanting kilometers of tunnel, designed to collapse as a trap for radiation or toxic gas in the event that the Vault should detonate a self-destruct, had been hammered through the raw rock strata by exquisitely fashioned shaped charges.

He smiled. The jargon, and some of the engineering concepts behind it, had wormed into his mind during the crash orientation. Suddenly, he found the Boy's Own technology refreshing, restorative. A hallucinatory vividness overcame him; he was bent over a low desk in the school library, riveted by a thick-leafed encyclopedia. It showed the brain as a small-town business, telephonists with their hair in buns, the Manager of Speech brooding on his Chamber of Commerce address, the Manager of Reflex Actions standing angrily above his ledger clerks in the Cerebellum, the Boardroom of the Cerebrum, air tubes looping from the nose to the Aerating Room. . . . The tubes of the tunnel had been lined with a space-age formula of boron fibers microscopically interlocked in tetrahedral patterns inside an epoxy bond. The adhesives had remained soft and workable until a specific catalyst was added; instantly, the epoxy set to concrete. The stressed boron-epoxy substances were incredibly light and fantastically stronger than steel. In his brain, an enzyme was reversing that process. The thought patterns of decades were melting to a spring thaw. Jesus, he told himself, the clerks have run amok. They're tearing up the records. They've taken to drink. Where are their collars? Is that a black flag they're strangling the Manager with?

"We're at the limit zone," one of the soldiers said, breaking into his anesthetic abstraction. The man flashed a signal lamp back up the tunnel.

A bell clamored. The count had begun.

"We'll be waiting for you here," the sergeant said in a low, calm tone. "Begin your return no later than the first klaxon."

"Gotcha," Hugh said. "See you, buddy."

They crossed the hot interface of the barrier and went clumsily down the ladder into the Zone.

The Vault was a dull white sphere on a perfectly flat surface. Bill had studied holograms of the shoebox cavity and the sphere it contained; now the thing itself was clearly illuminated in focused beams cast from the nest of gas mantles behind the limit.

His breath whistled through the wire grid of the null-suit helmet. His footsteps clicked and echoed. In his belly he felt a terrible, pointless betrayal.

The ball loomed, quite featureless. A refrain of doom began in Bill's mind. He glanced at the astronaut walking slowly at his side. He tried to block death from his cycling thoughts and failed. It had killed thirty-seven men. At this moment those who had not died lay strapped in hospital beds under total sedation, lest they wake up screaming, screaming . . .

Bill stopped. "Fuck it," he said. He tore off his left gauntlet. "Hugh, take your right glove off."

Alarmed, the astronaut seized his arm. "Bill, put it back on, you crazy loon. Zebrowski burned up when—"

Grappling, they fought in a mutually uncomprehending spasm of terror. Somehow the astronaut's right glove came free. Bill hurled it across the featureless surface. He gripped Hugh's hand in his bare grasp; his palm ran with perspiration. He held tight. With a spurt of shame, he felt a pulse of adolescent lust at the contact.

Suddenly the astronaut's resistance ceased. The pressure of his fingers closed on Bill's. He was leaning forward, sweat gleaming on his brow, guffawing. "DelFord," he gasped, "we can't go on meeting like this."

They waited, hands linked, until they had regained their breath. A primal contact had been closed. A current passed between them, comforting, energizing. Aristotle and Alistair Jerison would be pleased, Bill thought with dream-like detachment. And maybe Alice Langer. Hand in hand, then, like children on a strange playground, they moved again toward the Vault.

Heat from the invisible barrier was gone. Air circulated across Bill's skin, cooling him, vented from a grill under his shoulder blades. Even so, a trickle of sweat ran from his chest down his stomach.

His thoughts were in confused tatters. He awaited attack from the Vault. None came. Cautiously, according to instructions, they stopped after fifty meters. A faint dark stain marred the surface before them. No more than cinders, ashes, he thought. Hugh tugged at his hand. They edged closer, slowly circling the inert globe. They fell screaming into infinity.

—fell and fell, knees bent, arms against chest, eyes clamped shut in nausea and shock, hand locked bruisingly to hand—

I'm not falling, Bill howled furiously to himself. There's nowhere to fall. The plunging descent into hell did not abate. He knew in some realm of reason that the surface was firm beneath his booted feet. Vertigo roared in ears and guts and muscles. He forced his eyes open. They were not falling. The strain was intolerable. The astronaut was screaming something, pumping at his arm.

He did the one impossible thing: hurled himself forward, after Lapp, his arm socket jolting, directly into the endless pit which only frail rationality told him was not there.

And the rock was solid again. The illusion was cut off as abruptly as a storm at the slamming of a door.

Bill picked himself up, lurching at Hugh's shoulder, massaging his bruised knees through the heavy fabric. I can beat it, something thought. His body stood relaxing from acrophobic shock, automatically following the modified yoga sequence he'd been taught by NASA medics.

The bell rang, signaling the end of the first fifteen minutes into the Zone. They moved on again toward the Vault.

Its curved exterior seemed to hover above them like a tumbling boulder when nightmare struck.

Perspective twisted in a delirium of horror. Bill felt his body melt and stretch, a distorted caricature, arms shrinking to withered stumps, the pain of amputation, legs swollen and brittle as stilts. In the writhing ruin of Hugh's face, when he pulled the man's helmet to him, the eyes were protruding on slimy stalks from their crusted sockets. Around the dry, pitted crater of his own mouth, his tongueless, arid mouth, teeth were needle fangs of bone. He tried to conceal his face, but his hands were bulbous lumps of raw tissue flapping at his shoulders. . . .

And somehow he was giggling, with not quite the shrill madness of hysteria. Here he was with his sister Anthea, shouting in front of the big old radio, pulling ghastly faces at her; here was his grandmother with the same tiresome, stupid admonition. "I just hope," he shouted at the Vault from his ruined mouth, laughing wildly at the horrid absurdity of it, "that the wind doesn't change right now!"

The echo of his voice rang in the chamber. He caught up Hugh's hand again, shaking weakly with laughter. Swinging their arms, play soldiers, they continued circling the Vault. A tuneless song came into Billy's mind.

"Herbivores are awful bores," he sang. He reached up and took off his helmet. Jauntily, Hugh doffed his, bowled it across the blank surface.

"Obey the laws and sweep the floors," Hugh added, smirking.

Bill shook his finger for cautionary emphasis. "To shirk

their duties, tasks, and chores would not be greeted by applause."

Was a bell ringing? School's in session? Hugh skipped ahead, pretending not to hear. "They never eat with gaping jaws," he said.

"Or treat their friends to horrid roars." Who had taught him this song? Hugh put his hands on his hips and said with a rush:

"Their diet keeps them free of yaws—they buy their fruit at health-food stores and even eat their apple cores—while innate decency ensures that germs which lurk on other paws promoting noxious dermal flaws are swiftly booted out of doors."

Bill was doubled up with laughter. He dragged off his unwieldy suit, tugging the molded boots from his feet with difficulty. "When teeing off," he pointed out, "they wear plus-fours."

Lapp snorted. "At night their bedrooms ring with snores." He waited a beat, and added with a wicked grin: "They *never* patronize the whores."

Bill looked sardonically at the air force captain. "Nor do they march to foreign wars, or sponsor any foolish cause."

Hugh sneered. "They wrap their kiddies up in gauze, philosophize in gloomy saws, and when it rains, for them," he cried triumphantly, "it always pours."

"How the hell do we get in?" Bill screamed with sudden petulance at the bland, unresponsive sphere. "You want 'Open Sesame' already?"

Shock scissored his viscera. Noiselessly, without motion, an opening was there: a dark emptiness, ominous as the nest of a snake.

A voice, sweet as the tinkle of a brook, lonely as the tune of a hobo's mouth-harp at sunset, sang in his mind: YOU HAVE COME!

He could not move . . .

. . . yet he *was* moving, step after step toward the door into damnation. His mind gibbered warning, and could not heed it.

WHY ARE YOU FEARFUL? cried the beautiful voice, desolated. I HAVE AWAITED YOUR COMING FOR SO LONG. SO VERY, VERY LONG . . .

It seemed to him that a stink of putrefaction reeked in his nostrils. Snake! The stench of an ancestral enemy so vile that a million years of evolution had not expunged it from his genes. The compulsion from the Vault gripped limbs and nerves, took him against his shrieking denial into the shadows of the sphere.

"God," the astronaut said in an awed voice, "it's a computer. A wonderful computer."

Bill hardly heard him. The snake was calling him. Nobody has come this far before, some part of his mind realized. All of them had died, or crawled to the prison of madness, without reaching the Vault.

YOUR MINDS ARE BEAUTIFUL, sang the ancient voice. YOU HAVE CAST OFF THE SHACKLES.

Spittle covered his chin. Lines of light—indigo, turquoise, scarlet, flame-hot, sun-bright—leaped and shattered about him. Bill walked into the heart of the Vault.

"Geometries of light," the astronaut was saying. "The machine is showing us equations."

Bill felt an urge to worship swell within him. Stumbling, he went into the coils of light.

His mother stood before him. Her beauty was ethereal. Impossible to move, speak, swallow the saliva that ran from the corners of his mouth. He tried to clench his hands. Serpents of light swayed and wove about him, enclosing her in the darkness.

For the merest moment, the bright lights broke. His mind shuddered at the brink of devastation.

A faint, clanging, demanding cry of bells had scored ice in his brain.

Bill tried to turn, to respond to the pre-arranged signal, and as he did he saw the Serpent.

Wanambi! he screamed.

—not with indented wave prone on the ground, as since, but on his rear, circular base of rising folds, that towered fold above fold a surging Maze, his Head crested aloft, and Carbuncle his Eyes; with burnished Neck of verdant Gold, erect amidst his circling Spires, that on the grasse floated redundant: pleasing was his shape and lovely—

AH! the Serpent cried. DO NOT REJECT ME!

And in a moment of total plausibility Billy was nine years old. Autumn leaves blew wild across the old garden, caught in golden browns and reds against his mother's dress as she stood weeping, and his father's voice was grim and bitter with accusation. Billy didn't understand what was happening; he ran to his mother and she turned him aside, told him to leave them, and his father barked that he was to go inside with his big sister and prepare for dinner, and the lonely tearing in his chest burst as he ran to the house, burst to scalding tears that wracked him for hours and came again and again for weeks when he was told that she had gone and would not be coming home again. . . .

He hated her! He hoped she would die! How he hoped that a lorry would run her down, and she'd be dying, and there'd be no doctor! He hoped—

And he was weeping again, with grief and guilt, for he didn't want her hurt, didn't want her to die. But why had she gone with that man and left him here with his dull, busy father? For he loved her, Billy loved her, and wanted nothing more than to lean his tired head into her breast while she soothed his wind-torn hair, wanted only to run to her with some new creature—frog, butterfly, lizard—he'd found by the pond, or new puzzle he'd solved at school, and now she was gone and he'd never see her again . . .

. . . although he had seen her, of course, after his father had married again, married Janet, to be mother for Billy and Anthea, and mistress of the home during those long weeks when Dad's work took him back to the road, county to county. Even then she had promised to love him always . . .

. . . and now she was here, calling out to him as he turned away from her:

STAY, BILLY, WHY DO YOU REJECT ME? YOU MUST NOT FORSAKE ME NOW!

Tears filled his eyes again, and he reached out blindly for her arms, the smell of her hair and her sweet scent, reached to clasp her, passion rising in a foaming wave, reached to find her breasts golden soft, to be flesh in her flesh—

He would not look at her nakedness. Pain came sharp and terrible as teeth clamped deep into tongue. A stench vile as foaming acid. His mouth filled with the salty reek of blood.

Muscle fighting muscle, he groveled on the curving surface and prayed piteously for the bell's clamor. Her music tore him. In fury he wept, and heard the bell.

He ran past the astronaut. The harsh clangor died. In the darkness, the doorway was gone.

She waited in the Vault, with her wiles and her power, and Bill knew finally that he would never escape her.

His lips were numb. "Who are you?"

HUMAN, NEED YOU ASK? Anger and reproach filled the glorious voice. HAS YOUR SPECIES SO SOON FORGOTTEN ITS GODS?

Waves rolled and crashed from the center of the Vault, hammering his emotions. Sleep stroked his will, webbed him in a drowsy net of warmth and shadow. He was drifting from his body into the calm place. Where had Hugh gone? Far below, he saw the astronaut standing, exultant, in some psychic space of his own devising.

BELOVED HUMAN, YOU MUST ABANDON FEAR. I AM ISIS, ASTARTE, SARASVATI, CERES, THE MOTHER OF YOUR PEOPLE. COME TO MY ARMS AND TAKE NOURISHMENT, MY CHILD, MY LOVE.

Again—so soon? he thought—the bell sounded. His anguished muscles tensed against her lure, were freed.

An insight blazed through him, then, so rich and yet so clear that he was dazed by his stupidity in not having seen it from the beginning.

This is not a vault, he thought. A vault is a repository for something of inestimable value. This is a prison.

And of course the dreadful alien being which called itself a goddess was the prisoner, bound and chained eons ago by forces beyond human comprehension.

The defenses beyond the prison, the terrible distortions of reality which destroyed machines and killed men, were no more than side-effects of the Vault's primary purpose. A pang of guilt and horror went into him. It needs us, he told himself, to loose its bonds. To set it free.

He heard Hugh laughing with joy. The astronaut touched his arm. "It's come so far, Bill. It has so much to offer us!"

With loathing, Bill drew away from him. Lapp clutched at his arm. A veil of light shimmered about him. Bill delFord was gazing into a mirror, seeing his own livid face. Enormous banks of lights flickered behind him, the outward and visible signs of the transcendent computer within whose programs Hugh's consciousness floated as the merest sub-routine.

In panic, Bill-Hugh thought: This is not real. The crazy bastard is hallucinating. A cockroach, he danced a tarantella on the keyboard of a cosmic terminal. Galaxies spun, random access discs, a hundred billion chewy byte-sized stars, 2^n bits of information . . . We can simulate it for you, the computer offered.

Flow-charts branched endlessly, a hierarchy of precipitations. He conceived a cosmic pornography. Parallel loins, he thought, laughing helplessly. They met at infinity. Fusion wavered. Was it the computer, or the snake, who told him imperatively: Life is not a series of gig lamps symmetrically arranged. Life is a luminous halo surrounding us from the beginning of things to the end. This is Popper's World Three, he thought. The universe of discourse. The ontological reality within which mental objects subsist.

Horrendous wailing of the klaxons slashed the air until the very walls of the Vault seemed to reverberate. Conditioned reflexes hammered to answer them, but Hugh-Bill could not move. A faint glow filled the sphere. From the corner of his immobile eye, he saw the shape of a Teleport grid brighten until its metal bars shined like polished brass. Colors danced within it: violet, blue, green, yellow. Golden radiance flared to clear white. Beyond the grid was a place so strange he could not comprehend it. Machines were there, and luminescence, and things too strange to name. The alien's voice spoke sharply, commandingly. It was his mother's voice.

This is not happening, Bill told himself again. It is a children's cartoon. It is a Jungian projection of archetypes. His head filled at once with a scream of fury.

Through the detonations of his retinas, Bill saw a centaur enter the Sphere. Lightly it stepped and with enormous majesty, across the lowest bar, hooves clashing musically upon the metal floor. A wave of charismatic power surged from the being. Bill stared in wondering confusion. Symbols, symbols only.

THE DREAMING IS DONE, ULURU, the centaur said. THE BATTLE IN HEAVEN IS OVER.

Frenzied flicker of display lights flashed like a neon advertisement, an electric delusion. Through it, the snake reared and plunged, golden plumes rippling to a winter's gale.

Gracefully, the centaur trod back through the grid, touched a series of engraved controls on its own machines. A dome of absolute black locked around the nauseating thing crouched in the center of the Sphere. A vibration of intolerable power shook the Vault. The imprisoning dome rose, black as polished ebony. It passed weightlessly through the grid.

The centaur paused, gazing down at the humans. Bill felt no fear at all; he was suffused with tremendous awe at the strength and tenderness with which it regarded him. When it held out its huge hands, Bill reached up, wonderingly, and took them. Its grasp was firm. He felt the fatherly love which flowed from the creature.

YOUR FEARE IT SELF OF DEATH REMOVES THE FEAR, it told him, with his father's voice. But his father was dead. WHY, THEN, WAS THIS FORBID? WHY BUT TO AWE, WHY BUT TO KEEP YE LOW AND IGNORANT, HIS WORSHIPPERS; HE KNOWS THAT IN THE DAY YE EATE THEREOF, YOUR EYES THAT SEEM SO CLEAR, YET ARE BUT DIM, SHALL PERFECTLY BE THEN OPEND AND CLEAR'D, AND YE SHALL BE AS GODS, KNOWING BOTH GOOD AND EVIL AS THEY KNOW.

It's the Wanambi, Bill thought, astonished. *This* is the Wanambi. Transfigured to a god, taking Milton's words by right. He glanced at the astronaut. Reflected lights danced on Hugh's face, in the darkness; on the curved mirrors of his eyes, a huge console flared with pattern.

THAT YE SHOULD BE AS GODS, SINCE I AS MAN, INTERNAL MAN, IS BUT PROPORTION MEET, the Computer said, I OF IRON HUMAN, YEE OF HUMAN GODS. SO YE SHALL DIE, PERHAPS, BY PUTTING OFF HUMAN, TO PUT ON GODS, DEATH TO BE WISHT, THOUGH THREATENED, WHICH NO WORSE THAN THIS CAN BRING? AND WHAT ARE GODS THAT MAN MAY NOT BECOME AS THEY?

The centaur was telling him, he realized, the advantages of death.

But it's so much to give up, he thought with a bitter pang.

Bill hung above his exhausted body like a cloud of light. Hugh Lapp's discarded flesh—like his own, temporarily abandoned—lay in the darkness beside him. They were alone, as from the start they had been alone. It had not been necessary to escape the Vault Sphere, for they had never been inside it, not literally. There was no centaur, no Snake, no superlative alien computer; there never had been. The immense curve of the unbreached Vault soared like an ideal cliff above their bodies, eclipsing the tunnel and its gas mantles. We thought we were inside the Vault, Bill told himself, considering with a certain amusement the metaphors which had been drawn out from his own unconscious. In fact, the Vault was within us. Now, finally, all the childish symbols of hallucination were gone.

He caught himself. Hardly fair, old son. Intellect, as always, yearned to trivialize that which was more profound and solidly rooted than intellect. The Vault consciousness had revealed itself to him in symbols dense with meaning and grandeur, even as he had struggled within it like a salmon breasting a foaming torrent. Now, lightly, he allowed his awareness to caress the surface of that emblematic communication, to perceive what it had offered without imposing too brutally his own limiting interpretations. Phallic Snake? Yet the Serpent had also been Mother, nurturant, beguiling, exquisite. If the Vault entity had borrowed Milton's tropes from *Paradise Lost,* borrowed Satan's challenge to Adam, it had meant to convey by that allusion no simple single thing. For the centaur, too, had spoken them, and had entered to protect Bill and Hugh, in allegory, from that archetypal Bad Mother which every child dreads in nightmare and fairytale. The wicked witch is dead. . . .

Yet the centaur (and Bill found himself curiously warmed by a memory, from his own childhood, of reading by a winter fire a heavy blue-covered illustrated Homer, while a thrumming cat stretched beneath his stroking hand) was no less an ancient, powerful symbol for the beast in humanity, the wild, rutting, cruel fusion of animal force and sublime intellect. Why, then, had he chosen the centaur for his guardian? Bill brooded, and understanding remained locked away. Mentally, then, he shrugged . . . and a wash of recognition came to him, from the Vault intelligence which even now awaited his decision:

Chiron, it reminded him, was a centaur, and from the strong herb-scented hands of Chiron had first been passed the secrets of medicine into the possession of humanity. Hunter, yes, and prophet, too, Chiron had been beyond all else the source of healing, mentor of the Father of Medicine, teacher of Aesculapius himself. Little wonder, Bill thought with delight at his own vanity and sentimentality, that the Vault consciousness had located that lost image, drawn it out from his soul and given it illusory flesh in order to soothe the frightening ambiguities of its own more complex reality.

Now, Bill saw, he was at last purified of that need, beyond the necessity for parables, for dialectic. Out-of-the-body, he floated aloft, almost free of his own chrysalis flesh, and his apprehension of humanity's condition expanded dizzyingly, like a blow, like a powerful scent smashing with sweet force into the cavities of his skull. Spread all beyond him he saw the world, with its billion malnourished children and its hospitals and flowering gardens, its toxins and its wheat fields blowing golden in the sun, its missiles buried in concrete and drifting like sharks, its scientific attainments and distortions, its glories of art, the touch of a gentle hand, the brutal rape, the gleeful, hysterical murder: the immense lack of knowing, the isolation . . .

"Of course," he said, with abrupt, luminous understanding. "I see."

And yet he knew, with a tightening of his throat, that there would be pain for Selma and Ben, for Anne, his hundred friends. Could he inflict grief on those he loved best, loved truly? Like an arrow of pale fire he passed to their home, to the crumpled bed where Selma lay sleeping. The digital clock showed that by her time it lacked a quarter-hour of midnight. Without stirring, she knew his presence. Willy, she told him, you should have phoned ahead. I'd have— Oh. He took her hand and she came up out of her body into his arms, pressing her face against his chest. Must you, Willy? We shall weep for you. He told her: This will be a dream to comfort you. Remember it. Soon we'll be together again. She snorted, as she had always snorted at the humbug of mediums and spiritualists and priests; there were tears in her eyes. Somehow he had supposed that she would come out of the flesh with the lithe, youthful beauty of the first years of their marriage. Instead, he found her ample body unchanged; all the lines of experience and woe and laughter remained in her face. You are a wonderfully centered person, Selma, he told her with genuine admiration. I love you so much. Together, hand in hand, they passed into the boy's room and gazed down on the unfinished face. A nimbus flowed about Ben, a flux of inchoate longings and first beginnings, tentative, promising strength and endurance and joy. I'll keep an eye on you both, Bill said. He kissed Selma gently and then, as he turned to go, with a wink he tweaked her heavy backside.

Hovering, he considered his pulsing heart, atria and ventricles, relaxing in diastole, contracting fiercely in systole, the striated muscles of interdigitated actin and myosin filaments, the resting membrane potential at eighty-four millivolts and its reverse potential convulsion to one hundred three millivolts. He observed the twin syncytiums, and the impulses surging across the A-V bundle. He waited for the depolarization plateau, watched the calcium ions diffusing inward through the cardiac membrane, its permeability to potassium ions falling. The depleted tissues outside the membrane sucked hungrily at the calcium suspended in the enclosing extracellular fluids. He reached down calmly, then, and shooed the ions away. Potassium conductance plummeted. The dynamic of his heart sagged, faltered, ceased. He died.

15. The Vault

As he voids himself into death it is, of course, the rushing of a great wind, yet it's from behind that the hot gusts buffet him, seizing out his breath into the vacuum of their going, a wind heedless as the life-denying gales of oxygen sucked past the asphyxiating mouth into the ignited furnace of a city at ground-zero, in firestorm, it smites him, and yes, he is thunderstruck, for all his preparations and expectancy; indeed, as his breath is torn out without a cry, he is suspended in timeless astonishment until he recalls that he is not the dead man, not Bill delFord, but as always merely Mouse, conduit to the world's clamor, that diapason of the many living and the numberless dead, Mouse the misbegotten son of light-struck delirious Eleanor, with the voice of the dead man separating now from his central focus and telling him in his dream Son you will wake up soon, get dressed without waking your uncle and come to the Vault, and he nods in his sleep, knowing the guards will not hinder his passage, that they will not see him; he awakens, staring into the darkness, listening to Alf snoring in the other bed, the vague hiss of the air conditioner but no voice, the dead man waiting for him in confident silence as he rubs his eyes, pushes back the bedcovers, takes his clothes from the dresser and slips into them, leaving off his shoes as he creeps on tiptoes to the door, finds no one in the corridor and makes his way through the complex byways to the main tunnel sloping to the Vault, and the voice which spoke to him in dream is correct, he alone moves in this quietness despite the three shifts of the project, the scientific and military staff who usually throng the burrows without regard to surface time; even so, as he comes to the final stretch of the tube he drops on his belly and peers around the corner, sees the two guards lounging against the dull tetrahedral tiles swapping gossip in laconic Russian, and something extraordinary happens: one man clutches his stomach in midsentence, sags slowly, falls full length to the ground while the other stands for a moment in shock, crouches, speaks urgently to the unconscious guard, checks his pulse, pulls back one of his eyelids, stands again in agitation, glancing at the big spring-powered warning bell which is reserved for extreme emergencies, drags his eyes away from it with swift, anguished decision and runs up the tunnel, Mouse freezing as the guard pelts around the corner, past him in the direction of the military staff room, running, impossibly, as though he hasn't seen Mouse crouched on the ground, and with no hesitation Mouse scrambles to his feet, swings around the corner, and sprints for the final landing and its heat barrier, the gusts lifting his hair and flapping his loose shirt tails, and in the dimness the huge white globe he saw once before at the top of the steps from the Teleport Gate glimmers in the center of the chamber like the unhatched egg of a gigantic reptile, the source and repository for the multitudinous clamoring tempest of voices, echoed in the hard anger of the shouts behind him at the landing, the doctor and the men in gray uniforms running to the fallen man and seeing him as he swings over the edge, legs dangling above the pile of rubble, letting go and tumbling into the lethal zone of the Vault.

"Sarge, it's the kid again! Omigod he's gone into the Zone! We gotta get the crazy little bastard out before—"

"The *kid?* But he's up on the surface."

"Listen, Ramon, I'm not fuckin' blind. I don't give a shit where he's *supposed* to be; he's just gone over the edge into the goddamn *Vault.*"

"I saw him, too, Sarge." Boots pounding. "Jesus, he's still alive. He's just standing there. Hey, you damned fool kid, get back up here! Herrick, gimme a hand with this ladder."

"He *can't* be alive. He's been in there once before—the Vault kills repeaters. It smears them all over the—"

Good boy, Mouse, the dead man tells him, and his friends Helen and Annie are standing there behind Bill, nodding in encouragement; just wait there a bit longer, Bill says, while they get the rope ladder down to you and then you can go back to bed.

"He doesn't look dead to me," one of the guards is saying in Russian. "I tell ya, Titov, the lad's weird, a zombie. From what I heard, he nearly had the Yanks pushing the big button."

"You're full of crap, Leonov. Where'd you hear that? He's just a baby. Got a special hot-line to old Sevastyianov, eh?" Guffaws.

Mouse nimbly mounts the mass of broken stone again, grasps the rope ladder, climbs to the edge of the tunnel.

"Are you all right, boy? What in heaven's name— Here, give me your wrist. Hmm, pulse is a little fast, probably the exertion. Okay, Sergeant Ramon, let's get him to sick-bay."

"Hey, Leonov, if you know everything, why the hell are we still farting around with rope ladders?"

"Don't you know anything, Titov? Nah, that's right, you came in after us Stakhanovite heroes dug the tunnel. Well, comrade, first they tried an aluminum staircase. Flash! Lots of poison in the air. Plastic steps. Poof! I tell ya, the place is weird, the kid's weird, the whole—"

Mouse slides into the coma of release, ascending to light, to radiance, passing beyond words. After a timeless time Helen comes to him again, leads him out of the body to the room where his uncle sits across a desk from the American general. Joseph Ahern Sawyer looks old and wan, coming around the desk to sit next to Alf, a small, worn-covered volume closed in his hands.

"Dr. Dean—Alf—I know you didn't fully approve of us bringing young Hieronymus down again into such proximity to the Vault."

"General, you know damned well it was against my explicit plea. There can be no possible purpose served by having him here. It's immoral and probably illegal. You killed two fine men yesterday, Sawyer, and now you're exposing a sick fourteen-year-old boy to psychological stresses that a normal adolescent couldn't—"

"The boy is a walking bomb." Sawyer leaves the words hanging for a long moment in the air. "For you, Alf, this situation is entirely a personal tragedy. I understand perfectly, and I would think less of you if your response was otherwise. Alf, I'm a father, and a grandfather. I *know* the pain you're suffering."

"Then send us back to the surface. For Christ's sake, General, send Mouse home. I'm prepared to stay here, if need be—"

"Alf," the general says quietly, "you still don't understand. At this moment, the boy is precisely as important as the aliens' Vault. When he produced that document, that diary from the Russian Kukushkin, he came close to precipitating a nuclear holocaust."

"I don't believe that," Alf says flatly. "You have espionage agents, and so do they. You have viral experiments that must have produced horrors just as repulsive as 17-Tg-M."

"We are teetering on a knife-edge," the general says. He goes to a percolator, pours steaming coffee into two china cups. "Nuclear deterrence is about to join chain mail and castle walls. *Any* edge might tip the balance." He says abruptly, "Do you remember the *Foxbat* incident in the mid-seventies?"

"The Soviet fighter-bomber that ended up in Japan?"

"We had its avionics stripped within days. When our own *Tomcat* went off the flat top into the wide blue sea, we spent a small fortune raising it before the Russkies could pay us back in kind. If either bloc had had a Mouse, it could have learned as much as it wished without the risk of diplomatic incident, just by asking him."

The anthropologist is shocked into immobility. Slowly, his coffee spills into the saucer. "My God!" he says. "You want to use him as a spy. Is that all you see?"

"No!" Sawyer's left hand cracks down on the front of the desk. "I want desperately to prevent him from ever being used as a spy. We are not ready for absolute access to all the dirty little secrets in the world. Obligatory honesty is the one virtue the world could not tolerate. Not one stone standing on another, our fields sown with salt . . ." He takes a deep breath between clenched teeth. "Alf, this is hardly the best circumstance to talk about such a dismal topic as the state of my soul, but what I have to say concerns you and Mouse and a decision I have to take very soon."

He picks up the small volume once more from the desk. "Alf, are you a religious man?"

"I— Uh, I imagine I might be classed as a humanist agnostic—that is, I worship at no church and enter 'No Religion' on the Census form, but I guess when it comes down to it, I believe in the god who puts the Big Bangs in the cyclic universe."

Sawyer smiles faintly. "Son, your theology is a little out of date. You should talk to Fedorenko and his pal Lennox Harrington. Gluon theory has made a small alteration to cosmology: the hypothesis they're running this year is the Big Bag theory." He opens the book. "Alf, this Bible came to me from my grandfather. My father scorned the old man's belief, thinking ridicule a fashionable attitude to adopt, and his life was a sad, empty thing to behold, as sad and empty as the lives of the children today. Are you familiar with the story of Abraham and Isaac?"

Mouse gazes down on his uncle, sees Alf's annoyance and growing fear.

"I'm more familiar with the myths of the Murinbata and Ngularrnga Aboriginals than those of the Jews." When the general looks at him in silence, he adds with hostility, "I've heard the Leonard Cohen track."

"Bear with me, Alf. Chapter Twenty-two of Genesis records that God said to Abraham: 'Take thy only son, thy beloved son Isaac, with thee to the land of Moria, and there offer him to me in burned sacrifice on a mountain I will show you.' And they rode off with their servants, stopping at the foot of the mountain, and Abraham took his son up the slope. 'They went on together,' the Old Testament tells us, 'till they reached the place God had shown him—' "

"For Christ's sake, Sawyer," Alf says angrily, "I don't want to hear this bloodthirsty, simpleminded—"

"Dr. Dean, indulge me for a moment." The general lowers his eyes once more to the book. " 'And here he built an altar, and set the wood in order on it; then he bound his son Isaac and laid him down there on the altar, above the pile of wood. And he reached out, and took up the knife, to slay his son.' "

Alf is on his feet, his hands on Sawyer's collar. "You bastard," he says in a high, impassioned voice. "You sanctimonious bastard. A walking bomb? And you've decided to defuse him, have you? Turn him off. What technique do you have in mind for the operation? A formal bullet in the head for potential treason? Or a nice clean injection from a veterinarian?"

At last the general's restraint wears thin; with an incisive, savage upward chop of both hands he frees himself from the wild man's grip and pushes him back heavily into his chair. Breathing hard, he says, "Dr. Dean, I'll let your grotesque performance pass just this once. Try anything like that again and I'll have you in solitary confinement so fast you won't have time to puke." More calmly he regains his own seat. "I pray to God that Mouse will *not* come to harm, that you and he can be returned to the outside world speedily, sound in body and spirit. Alf, this morning at three o'clock your ward left the room where you were both sleeping, made his way undetected to the Vault, and entered the Zone."

The color leaves Alf's face; he sags. "The Vault? You say he's in the Vault?"

"No. He came out immediately, unharmed. Do you understand what this implies?" The general picks up his book again. "Isaac, too, was spared in the moment of his father's test. And when it was done, an angel of the Lord said to Abraham: 'I know now that thou fearest God; for my sake thou wast ready to give up thy only son.' Listen, Alf. God told that righteous man: 'I have taken an oath by my own Name to reward thee for this act of thine, when thou wast ready to give up thy only son for my sake. More and more will I bless thee, more and more will I give increase to thy posterity, till they are countless as the stars in heaven.' Do you see, Alf? As the stars in heaven! 'Thy children shall storm the gates of their enemies.' " Reverently, he closes the book.

Cringing, shaking violently, Alf says, "You intend to send Mouse back into the Vault. My God, you really do. You're insane."

Sawyer is not offended. "Alf, we must have those bodies retrieved. The need is imperative. We have pathologists standing by for post-mortems, neurologists who can determine the degree of effectiveness of the arg-enkephalin defense. I have already told you that this decision has harrowed my soul. Now I realize that God has directed me to the answer. He alone is the giver of life, and He will take it back in any manner He chooses." Sawyer's hand lingers on the book. "This may be His final test for us, and He shall reward obedience to His divine Will by blessing the nation whose sons do His bidding."

Mouse, hovering, sees his uncle lean forward, sees in the tension of his muscles and the constricting flares of his aura the unbearable anguish of the man.

"You're going to kill the child because you want him dead. He frightens you, and your canting hypocrisy gives you a convenient set of skirts to cower behind. You're *not* doing it after instruction from God. I don't know," he says, hands gripped trembling on the arms of his chair, "if even a direct command from the voice of God would be sufficient justification for the murder of a child, but the fact is you're going to do it for *your* reasons, for patriotism and knowledge and power and greed. It's the way the old men have always acted. You lust after death, you send your children off to die in the wars you've made in your guile and voracity—" He is close to hysteria. "Isn't it time to stop, now, while we're still just a part of human history? Don't you understand that the thing down there is a gate into something bigger than your pathetic, bloody-minded God?"

"That's enough!" In white-faced fury, the general rises to his feet. "I will not listen to this puerile blasphemy. You sicken me, Dean. You represent everything vile and ignoble in this disintegrating culture." Shouting, he summons his aide. "Get this black son-of-a-bitch out of my sight!" He glances at the clock on the wall. "And get the Vault technicians on their toes. The boy goes in at midday. That gives them a little over ninety minutes to have their instruments ready."

So you see, the dead tell Mouse, it is always the same: those who love are always too late and too weak; power is the domain of the blind and deaf; we have shown you a judgment wrought not in this moment, not on these principals, but in all the history of a living species, so that now you know who you are and what you must do: Yes, Mouse says, going to his insensible body, sinking once more into the demarcations of mortality, and he opens his eyes to the dim gaslight of the sickbay, the rage of his maturity like the rushing of a great wind within his breast, the dormant spark of his consciousness rising out of the embers of two million years of waiting humanity, the hot gusts of its sudden brilliant incandescence buffeting him, drawing in his breath to cry from the depths of his single identity, "It is begun!"

He rises from the bed and walks unnoticed through the midst of the medical staff, the soldiers in the corridors, technicians cursing at their balky mechanisms, and enters the general's office. "Come with me," he tells the startled man, and turns without another word to find his uncle. "Alf, we're going down to the Vault," he explains to the sick man, helping him get to his feet. An aureole of power brings them without protest in his wake, autumn leaves tumbling obediently to the change of time, Sawyer's teeth bared, his eyes wide and staring, Alf numbed in shock, and they make their way down the steep slope to the wall of invisible fire and through it, to the lip of the echoing cavern.

"Follow me," says the young man. "The Soul Core will not harm you."

They enter the ten circles of light which guard the Resting Place.

"The realities of metaphysics can only be approached," Mouse explains, "through the intermediaries of symbols. Here is the domain of humanity, the tribunal of the dead and living, the image of your heritage from the earliest brutes who found fire and stone and projected from their desperation the first flickerings of consciousness."

From deepest bloody jasper they advance to jacinth, the orange pall of a moon moving into the world's shadow.

"Pi-Ioh rules this realm of Angels, the damaged ones who came before humanity and suffered exile. You share their seed, though they abandoned your world before the second coming of consciousness. It is their base you found on the moon, their point of departure for the stars."

At the third circle, a topaz glow touches their faces.

"Here are the Archangels, the custodians of genetic advance to perception and memory; their liege is Thoth, Pi-Hermes."

A tremble of generative power comes with the brightening of sardonyx.

"Surth commands the Principalities, who capture the sun's

energy in living cells and bring forth the oxygen which fuels all consciousness."

In the gold of chrysolite they find the sun itself, fusing the light breath of space to the spinning, heavy building blocks of matter.

"Here is supreme beauty, the great Virtues whose head is Pi-Rhe."

They lift their hands against the swelling glory, the golden-green effulgence of chrysoprase.

"The sixth circle is the reign of justice, of those noble Powers who bend the knee to Ertosi, whose arms wield the sword."

Now the light is sheerest emerald, spirit and matter brought together in life knowing itself.

"True knowledge is love," Mouse says. "Pi-Zeus is father of life, and his servants are the Dominations."

Sawyer falls to his knees, clutching his heart, in the cascade of beryl radiance. The boy lifts him, leads him through the eighth circle.

"The dead pass backward through the mystery of Time to the center of reality. These are the Thrones, commanded by Rempha, lord of the dimensions beyond space."

At the ninth circle, they blaze in the searing blue of sapphire, the purest glory of the star Canopus.

"We approach our destination. Here is a profound mystery, the deepest archetypal ideas of this world's consciousness. They are the Cherubim, lances of light in their hands, under the guidance of Intelligence."

"Mouse, please, no," begs Alf, palms pressed into his eyes, and: "I—*can't* . . ." shrieks Sawyer.

"The tenth circle," the young man says inexorably, thrusting them forward into the violet, the incomprehensible ultraviolet of absolute amethyst, "is the realm of the Seraphim, the veil of eternity, the Cloud of Unknowing, the edge of the expanding universe where *tau* becomes infinite."

Screaming in the intolerable cosmic splendor, they lurch through the tenth circle. Darkness enfolds them. The flesh has not peeled from their bones, stripped by the lashing X rays at the perimeter of the universal singularity. Tears cover their wet cheeks, blur their slowly restored sight. Above them, immense and enduring, hangs the white curve of the Vault's central Sphere. In his resonant, unbroken voice, with the mien of a Druid, Hieronymus Dean tells the two adults: "Bow your heads. You stand in the Presence of the Tabernacle."

And the dead man hoots with silent laughter; Jesus, Mouse, he says chidingly, throttle back a bit on the bass pedal, you'll have Sawyer throwing a psychotic episode; here, permit me to borrow your larynx for a moment.

Mouse releases his body, and when he speaks his voice has deepened, taken on completely the tone of Bill delFord.

"You'll have to forgive the boy, gentlemen; he's just discovered the joys and excesses of Wagnerian adolescence and it's gone to his head."

The general reels away, his right hand twitching in a cruciform gesture. Alf merely sways, blinking slowly.

"For Christ's sake," says Bill's voice, irascibly, from the young man's mouth, "is there anybody there? One knock for yes, two knocks for no."

"You utter the Name?" Sawyer shrieks. "Foul, unclean creature." He blunders into a transparent, charged barrier; all his scant hair lifts, in a parody of fright, from his scalp.

"If you'd prefer to talk to the Man Himself," Bill's voice says with peppery scorn, "I could arrange it, but we'd have to patch the conversation through a translator unless you speak fluent Aramaic."

"Antichrist!"

"Pull yourself together, man, or I'll have you dismantled under the provisions of the Shoddy Constructions Act of 4004 B.C. Oh, good grief, Hugh, he was right about his combat nerves—he's just shat himself again. Sawyer, it's a good thing we're a Rogerian, empathic, non-judgmental God. Though I confess my fund of positive regard for you is becoming increasingly conditional."

"Mouse," Alf says, seizing the young man's broad shoulders, "stop it. Stop it. This is sheer sadism."

Calm eyes meet his accusing, fearful gaze. Mouse says in his own tones, from the center of his newly found identity, "I'm sorry, you're right. They don't realize their own force. It's only a few hours since they died, you see. In many ways they're wiser than I am, but they're like men drunk for the first time." He stoops beside the general, who lies curled in his own filth, the four fingers of his right hand jammed in his mouth. "I am not the Antichrist, Joseph. Stand up. I have no intention of punishing you further. Believe me, General, I'm sorry we humiliated you." With a sweet, wry smile he adds, "I'm only human."

"I wish I could believe that, Mouse," Alf says. He steadies Sawyer as the man gets totteringly to his feet. "Why have you brought us into this terrible place?"

"I'll show you." Mouse touches the pink-gray folds of their cortical rinds, bypassing sense with a complex pulse of long-frequency radiation.

They stand, it seems, under the smoky brilliance of tropical noon, hot swamps stretching torpid before them. There is a thrashing; a huge fin-spined reptile, long-tailed and narrow-shouldered, but the size of a fully grown lion, is tearing at the slow, blundering beast it has dragged from the fetid water. Somehow they know that they are displaced in time as well as space, that the equatorial sun glares down not on some distant planet, but on Southwest America, as it was two hundred seventy million years in the past. Blood pours from the opened side of the massive Diadectes; it dies without complaint as the spined Dimetrodon lunches on its flesh.

"This is Permian Earth," Mouse tells them, bringing their knowledge into precise focus. "All the continents are welded into a single gigantic ecology. Glaciers cover India, southern Africa, Antarctica, Australia, while life thrives in Western Europe and America. Half the world is locked into winter, empty of living creatures, for these reptiles take their heat from the sun. In the long nights of the glacial latitudes, only the smallest of them can find sanctuary in hibernation, buried in insulating mud. But twenty million years later—"

Snow is melting to a filthy slush, crystals of ice chiming as the wind breaks them from low, dead branches. They huddle from the chill, rays of reflected light spearing their eyes. A small, hairy creature scurries across the snow, a Moschorhind, more mammal than reptile in its trotting gait.

"The therapsids have evolved endothermy," Mouse tells them. "No mammals exist yet on the Earth, but these reptiles have catapulted in a genetic explosion to the beginnings of warm-blooded dominance."

"Take us back!" Sawyer screams. "I don't believe—*What are you doing to me?*"

"I am showing you the history of consciousness," the young man tells him gravely. "There's no reason for alarm; we're safe from the animals. This is a—call it a reconstruction." For an instant, they are back in the cavern of the

Vault, the Sphere's enormous curve looming over them. Then they seem to be standing on the fine white sand of a Jurassic shore. Blue ocean surges gently; the long necks of plesiosaurs lift gracefully from the buoyant water, snap down to scoop fish from the shallows.

"We have moved forward almost a hundred million years," Mouse says. "The polar ice has long diminished. All the world is mild. It'll be eons before such a paradise comes again. Now the dinosaurs truly rule the world, though the first mammals have found their modest homes in the ecology." They flash into snows once more, under the purple sky of southern spring. On the horizon, citadels of ice tower to the sky. At their feet, though, the light covering of snow is crossed with the deep tracks of heavy reptiles. "Now that the breakthrough to endothermy has been consolidated, deep Gondwana has been thoroughly colonized by the descendants of the early warm-blooded therapsids and thecodonts."

"Mouse," Alf says incredulously, "are you saying that the dinosaurs were not cold-blooded? Why did they die out when the glaciers returned?"

"That was not the reason," Mouse says. "The temperature of the ocean dropped only slightly between the Cretaceous and the Cenozoic. The difference could *not* affect the dinosaurs, since most of them possessed homeostatic temperature regulation."

Again, he strokes their brains; awareness expands convulsively. The ectothermic animals, they understand, are those which depend for the stability of their metabolism on the vagaries of weather as much as on the energy released from the food they consume. With the leap to "warm-bloodedness," high basal metabolism replaces this utter dependence upon the benevolence of climate. Chemical activity in the cells soars by four times; heart, lungs, muscles surge in endurance. The cost is defrayed to the supporting ecology—endotherms are greedy, of necessity, gulping down twenty or thirty times the mass of food required to sustain their slower cousins. Thermal loss becomes a larger threat, to be countered by the selection of genes for insulation—feathers, hair.

"My God," Alf breathes, with abrupt, acute insight. "The Plumed Serpent. The feathered dragon in my dream."

"Yes," says Mouse.

Eighty million years flicker in a gray haze; they look

out across a late Cretaceous vista of howling blizzard, darkened sky. A troop of small, drenched figures moves bent against the frozen wind. Stone knives are clenched in their three-fingered hands. Rude garments cover their heads and shoulders. The figures at the rear of the group drag several slaughtered animals through the snow. Sawyer gasps, strangling; the man in the lead has turned, and in the failed light the lips of his muzzle peel back from long, sharp teeth in a bark of command; it is suddenly, mind-wrenchingly evident that he is not a man at all.

"But this is—the Earth?" Alf cries.

"It is," Mouse says. "Pangaea has long since broken up; the continents are slowly drifting apart into their present locations. India is moving on its plate toward collision with Asia. There are lemurs in the tropics, but their kin will never develop into human beings. We are standing near the northern extremities of Antarctica. Australia has still not fully fractured away. You are looking at the first intelligent beings brought forth from the loins of our world."

The dinosaurs stump through the snow with the stolid patience of all primitive hunters. Even the tallest of them stand only as high as the general's shoulder.

Sawyer whirls on the young man in triumph. "Lies!" he says, his eyes dilated in the gloom. "A fabrication to tempt my faith! I am not deceived, evil one. Look at their skulls. They can't possibly be intelligent; their cranial capacity doesn't exceed five hundred cc's. I am not an ignoramus, Father of Lies!" Incredibly, he smirks. "Try to be consistent."

"Even in your own terms," Mouse says wearily, "you damn yourself in your pride. Look now."

He transduces their perception to the astral spectrum. The icy landscape is whipped away. Pale lights glow where the dinosaurs trudge, plasmoid globes of red and violet. Streamers of luminance web the aura, linking them in a shuttling loom of shared awareness. Beyond the group, the sky is hazy with a dome of shimmering filaments.

"These creatures," Mouse explains, "are roughly equivalent to Homo erectus. They make simple tools, they know the use of fire when they can find wood in this appalling territory, they share a rudimentary language. But far more profoundly, they have taken the step to collective identity."

Alf whispers, in astonishment, "A true social *gestalt?* They share a single consciousness?"

"They constitute a collective unconscious," Mouse corrects him. "Individually, they are less intelligent than chimpanzees. But their brains are sufficiently complex to perform the crucial duties of an organ for intelligence: the transduction of percepts to the collective biocomputer, and the return interface of concepts and will to their expression in individual behavior."

Day returns. Now they view a warm valley cut through stupendous glaciers. From the icy hill where they stand, a panorama of clustered stone structures is visible in the midst of huge-leafed trees and fat, browsing reptiles, floating artifacts moving with purposeful grace above the boughs, brightly plumed bipedal reptiles taking their ease in civic clearings, a faint skirl of alien pipes reaching up in snatches to the hill. Stooped, furry, ape-like creatures scurry among the intelligent dragons.

"We are at thirty million years. This is no longer entirely a reconstruction. The scene we view is the enhanced trace memory of an Ancestor who lingered for a moment upon this spot."

"Those apes—"

"Archaic pongids. They are the root stock of Homo sapiens as we know it; today, their principal non-hominid representatives are the orangs, the gorillas, and the chimps. Hylobatids—today, the gibbons and siamangs—diverged from the primary monkey lineage at about this time."

Sawyer says, "This is insane. The map on the moon is only five millions later than this, and there's not the slightest trace of a reptile civilization."

"Wait," Mouse says. He shifts to the astral spectrum. Radiance is a lacework of ineffable energies, the arterial map of an entire culture, each individual the synapse of a thousand contacts. They behold a hierarchy of connection which brings tears to their eyes.

"It's—lovely," Alf says. The general is silent; his fingers close, and relax, and grip once more, nails pressing deep into palms.

"We are close to the center of the mystery. What you see is a symbolic transformation of a ceaseless ebb and flow of information, an exchange of information from brain to brain mediated by low frequency fields of about five hundred cycles per second and a millionth of a watt in strength. For Saurus sapiens at this point of cultural evolution, each living nervous system is a single integrated circuit in a vast biocomputer running millions of shared-time programs. Joseph, you have had experience with electronics—do you see the cultural implications which shaped the evolution of this species?"

"Noise," the general says, his eyes glazed. "Intensity reduction. Impossible. Impossible. If these beasts were a hive with a single compound intelligence, they would be penned into a niche ten or twenty kilometers across."

"Just so," Mouse says. "For the dinosaurs, there was no Magellan. At a distance of ten thousand kilometers from the center of their community, their channel to the collective repository of functioning intelligence would be slashed by ninety-nine percent. They would be reduced to the status of animals—worse, for in their evolution, their specialized instincts had been abandoned. The Saurians had a saying as old as language itself: 'The Resting Place and the Nesting Place are one.' It was not piety alone; the principle was a recognition of their absolute mutual dependence, the imperative of their territorial confinement."

"Telepathy . . ." Sawyer says softly. "What tacticians they must have been."

"No," says Mouse sharply. "War would have been an abhorrence to them, had they been capable of conceiving such a thing. Do you amputate part of your own brain? More: the Saurians were pure carnivores. As Homo sapiens developed an incest taboo to contain the terrible possibilities of perennial sexuality, Saurus sapiens evolved a virtually infrangible prohibition on intraspecific killing." He glances at them carefully. "To cement this taboo, they extended their carnivore habits in a striking, paradoxical ritual." He pauses. Alf looks at him, aghast.

"They ate their dead," the anthropologist guesses. He turns away, revulsion in his face.

"By consuming those they had lost," Mouse declares with passion, "they affirmed the sacred dignity of each individual's life. No flesh is so sweet as the meat of one's own kind. When a species is obliged by instinct to eat of its dead, it is faced time without number with the final test of its own morality."

"Satan," Sawyer says joyously, "you convict yourself out of your own mouth. No crime is so foul, so unspeakable as cannibalism—no, not even incest. And you praise these loathesome beasts!"

Mouse regards him. "Do you recall the greatest Sacrament of your faith, Joseph? 'Take, eat, for this is My Body. Drink, for this is My Blood.' "

Sawyer's face becomes a mask of rage. "Filth!" he screams, lunging at the young man. Impalpable hands seem to turn him aside, leave him crouched amid ice and ancient stone. "The Eucharist is a mystery of God's incarnation, a symbol of the sacrifice—"

"It is a recollection at a hundred removes," Mouse tells him with magisterial authority, "of the sacred ceremony of Saurus sapiens."

The sun leaps to a new position in the sky. Snow is gone; long emerald grasses toss in a warm breeze, dotted with gold, with crimson, with violet blooms. A huge throng gather in the meadows, falling lightly as leaves from the bright blue of the sky. Within the immense, mountainous translucent pyramid which soars above them into lacy clouds, the Sphere of the Vault hovers like a pearl.

"We are ten thousand years in the future," Mouse says, and even his clear young voice is hushed.

"It's *not* our world," Alf says. He looks at his nephew in perplexity, his features drawn and lined in the clarity of sunlit morning.

"It is our planet Earth," Mouse says cryptically. "It is the world of Saurus sapiens, immortal, triumphant, a species poised at the culmination of thirty million years of peaceful civilization. They await the Parousia."

Fragrance billows on the breeze, and the sweet musk of the fearful descending throng. Alf stumbles forward into the tall, blowing waves of grass; daffodils open their golden throats to the sun; his hand brushes the thorns of a rose bush, and a droplet of his blood sinks into the red velvet of its petals; yellow marigolds lie before him in drunken profusion, violets and hyacinths reflect the sky, poppies sway on their furry stems in a vivid delirium of crimsons and saffron. His chest heaves; he labors under some insupportable emotion. Mouse touches his torn hand.

"This is their glory and their tragedy, Alf. They have come to this place on this day to die, every one of them, and in dying to share the gift of consciousness and immortality with the lost dead who went before them."

"I don't understand," the man whimpers. At his side, the general is rocking, rocking, oblivious.

"Look upon the living brain," Mouse says. Without departing from the meadow, they stand somehow in a hazy glory of neural processes, a vast fluorescent veil nebula, magnified beyond comprehension. "You've been taught," says the young man, "that the brain is the seat of consciousness, that memory and thought and will are functions of these ten billion cortical neurons, each of them linked to ten or a hundred thousand others, a biocomputer of 10^{14} bits of storage capacity. Yet your neurologists also know that great sections of the cortex can be excised without impairing mental function. They have already discovered the proteins and peptides which activate synaptic junctions, and they have calculated correctly that to store the memories of a lifetime would require more than one hundred kilograms of these minute amino-acid chains."

"Lashley," Sawyer mumbles in the dull tone of a somnambulist. Slowly he raises his head. "Karl Lashley said that memory was simply not possible."

Mouse nods. "And that was thirty years ago. Today, the fact is indisputable. What the theorists have neglected is the connection *between* human beings, the constant flux of data we transmit and receive in the ultra-low frequency band. The brain and nervous system," he tells them, expanding the glowing display into a gigantic web of light, "is an indexing system, a file of coding procedures, a folded aerial a million meters in length. The deep structures of thought and language are a common property, spread with massive redundancy through the brains of every human alive on the planet. We are one another."

Their attention returns to the bright meadow. It is dense with the hues of feathered beings. A strange music flows and lifts: the dinosaurs are singing. Waves pass through the throng, crossing and recrossing, like interference bands in a spectrum: the beautiful creatures are dancing. Above them, crystalline and glorious, the pyramid cups its shining jewel.

"Why, this is hell," the general says wonderingly, "and these are the dead. I had not thought hell would be so pretty."

"These are the living," Mouse corrects him. "Those are the dead, the immortal dead, in the Soul Core." He lifts his hand toward the Sphere. "Your priests had an intuition of it, and called it the Kingdom of Heaven. The Hindus were closer to the truth. They termed it the Akasic Records."

Sawyer flinches, but refuses to speak. Alf says, with growing excitement, "Of course. Of course. For every neuron, every synaptic connection, they've built a permanent record in non-biological archives. The Sphere is an additional redundancy, a one-to-one map of the central identity of every individual. But surely at death—"

"Death is the release of individual consciousness from the constraints of the body. It is the extension of life into a realm of absolute connectedness, of collective consciousness, governed by the laws of liberated imagination."

Swirling to a song like wind, the plumed serpents dance like dervishes. The grass is crushed and muddy beneath their taloned feet. There are no children among them.

"Do you see," Mouse asks, "why they held their beloved Ancestors in such reverence? It was a respect for their sources which human beings cannot yet begin to appreciate. So finally, when their technology advanced to the point when the manufacture of the Soul Core was feasible, the aspiration was born to share this potential eternity of life with those who had perished."

"Not from the stars," Alf breathes. He stares at the reptiles as they still their dance and press forward to the stupendous perimeter of the translucent pyramid. "It's from the future. From a—different—future."

"Yes," Mouse says. The air is brightening about them, filling with enormous energies. Streamers of violet light leap from the crystalline faces of the pyramid, lashing the sky. Moaning, the dragons are taking one another's hands. A lance of blinding radiance hurls from the sky. Shimmering like a new sun, the Sphere, the Soul Core, pulses in its cage. In the absolute hush, they look down as the multitude falls slowly in a massive spill of unresisting muscle, bone, flesh. The Sphere blinks and is gone. They stand beneath its great curve in the cavern under the Australian desert.

"They all—died?" Sawyer says, his voice peaking to a paralysis of horror.

"They live," Mouse tells him. "They are all around us. We know them in our dreams. Your faith calls them Cherubim and Seraphim."

A shudder passes through Alf's body. "Something went wrong, didn't it, Mouse? Instead of saving their ancestors, they—aborted them. And left us here instead."

"It was a star," the young man tells them. "A super nova. The time machine was accelerating into its history, with the Soul Core locked under an inpenetrable gluon shield. A rudimentary Ancillary Core was on board, programmed with minimal consciousness, to enable emergency crews to function. Those crews were governed more by ritual than by true intelligence."

And standing in the shadow of the Vault, he shows them the poignant history of disaster: of the generation hatched to set right the tragedy—Anokersh huj Lers and Mistress Diitchar, maimed Riona, vengeful, baffled T'kosh huj Nesh. The devastating exile of the feral pongids.

"But even then the dragons failed," Alf says. "They destroyed themselves."

A melancholy beyond grief sweeps over Mouse. "The crew were excluded by the gluon shield from participation in the full consciousness of the species. The supernova pulse ruined the control system of their craft, and they lacked the understanding to repair it. So the damaged craft stopped too late. It overshot its destination by half a million years."

"The *Vault* caused the extinction of the dinosaurs?"

"And of Saurus erectus, the dragons' primeval ancestors. The species had only just begun to emerge. The presence of the Vault consciousness was as searing and destructive to that primitive *gestalt* mind as the glare of the sun on an eye forced open to it." Mouse's formal diction cannot disguise his anguish. "Their tentative intelligence shriveled under a radiance it could not blink from. The evolutionary option closed to them. They perished still-born, with the rest of their kind, and the small stupid mammals took their kingdom by default."

Sawyer is crouching, and his mouth is bloody where teeth have sunk into the flesh of his lips. "No," he says, with terrible, threatening intensity. "No, no. We are not descended from those feral beasts. We are formed in His likeness, not from the garbage of a mutant slave race. I will not." He pauses. Red spittle foams at the corners of his mouth. "Believe." Tensed to leap, to murder, to avenge the pitiful mythology of his life, he falls instead and weeps, convulsively, in bursting sobs.

Mouse crouches beside him and cradles the man's head in his lap.

"We are not the ferals' children," he says gently. "We are the sons and daughters of the Soul Core. The pongids were scattered into real-time like chaff, spread across a thousand years. They emerged into a different history, twenty-five million years ago, long before humankind had evolved. They had known only *The Soul,* after all. They were strangers in a strange land and they used the consciousness of the Soul Core to help them escape it forever. That installation on the moon was the pongids' work, Joseph, the machine they built to catapult them to the stars."

"We've never found any trace of them on Earth, Mouse. Surely a species capable of star travel would leave evidence of their presence behind."

"How much of Antarctica's ice have you dug up, Alf?"

"I do not believe it," Sawyer says. "Why would they abandon the Earth? It was an empty paradise."

"Yes, the reptiles were gone, for the crew were sterile. But the minds of the dragons remained in the Core, like gods who had driven the ferals from the garden. They felt as you do. They would not serve. Perhaps their children are waiting for us out there. In the world they left, our own hominid ancestors evolved to take the dragons' place."

Mouse ascends from himself to the balm of the hundred billion minds abstracted in the mirror of the Soul Core. His role as Intercessor is almost done. Soon he will submit to the temptation which took Bill and Hugh too early from the flesh to the soaring freedoms of eternity. Distantly, he is aware that Alf kneels before him, searching his passive face.

"How did the hominids do it? By slow adaptation to the Vault intelligence? But Mouse, Homo sapiens evolved in Africa, on the other side of the world, and was *never* restricted by such limitations on movement.

"Nor were the Saurians, after the Soul Core was built. It's a sublimely sensitive amplifying device, Alf, a gluon lattice denser than neutronium, with the properties of a single perfect crystal. At the lowest biological frequencies, especially the 7.8 and 14.1 cycles of the brain, atmosphere and ground act as a wave-guide, a resonator, which carries the output of each brain around the world with hardly any attenuation. Each of us, from before birth, embeds a characteristic 'fingerprint' signal in the Vault, and for the rest of our lives each cortical impulse is stored in a specific, identifiable matrix. When all transmission and reception of signals is cut off," he adds, "as it was for Bill and Hugh and Anne under Kukushkin's gluon shield, the brain is reduced to a babbling parody of intelligence, a half-witted indexing system just barely capable of puns as its highest level of accomplishment."

The anthropologist struggles for objections. "The lunar astronauts, Mouse. Why weren't their mental functions impaired?"

Mouse grins impishly. "Would anyone have noticed?"

"Come off it." The man's self-possession is a frayed string. "There'd be at least a three-second lag due to the to-and-fro time for radiation to—"

Mouse sighs. "Alf, you can't expect to grasp the workings of a biotechnology thousands of years in advance of human science. The Soul Core is *not* restricted to electromagnetic modes. A full spectrum of faster-than-light tachyon radiation is available to it, and humans have evolved to take advantage of the fact. Telepathy and precognition are not solely the result of leakage from mind to mind within the Core—some paranormal phenomena are purely tachyonic. Eventually, when you have learned to communicate with the dead in the Core, all these things will be made clear."

"You smug little bastard." Alf draws back with abrupt aversion. "When your thousand-year Reich dawns? With Hieronymus Dean as its Messiah?" He stumbles, shocked by his own words. "It sent you, didn't it?" he says. "It decided the time was ripe for its revelation, and it caused your mother to overdose herself with LSD. My God. My God."

Dreamily, scarcely audibly, Mouse says, "The Rainbow Serpent, Alf. The Road-maker, the Opener of Wombs."

The man's mouth tightens; he pushes himself to his feet. "Is there no end to it, Mouse? Do we have *any* freedom? Did it make me an anthropologist so I'd fetch you to it twenty years later? Did it turn Bill delFord on to auras and mysticism, then discard him when he'd done his job? Jesus, Mouse, did it put the structure for 17-Tg-M in somebody's mind, at the risk of nuclear war and worse, just for the benefit of its belated self-disclosure?" The anger of his aura beats in Mouse's vision like tongues of ruddy flame.

"Alf," the strange child says at last, "the Core is not demonic, it is not divine. It's *us*—you, Joseph here, me, Bill, Hugh, Victor, my mother. It's humanity, and the Saurians. We are larger than you've ever conceived, Alf; at our profoundest depths, we are a unity of consciousness which at last is ready to find its identity."

He bends over the unconscious general, tenderly cleaning the bloody mucus from the man's face. When he looks up to Alf once more, he finds himself filled with a tranquil exultation. "Alf, Alf, it won't all come at once. You'll lose nothing of yourself, I promise you. But what lies ahead for us . . ."

Mouse closes his eyes, and opens himself to the intuitions of eternity. Galaxies glow in veils of fire to the farthest dark, aflame with knowledge and awareness and love. It is a vision of an almost unimaginably distant future. He knows, with a joyous satisfaction, that he will live to join it.

For the present, there are immediate tasks. To his uncle he says, "Give me a hand with Joseph, Alf, and we'll get him to the doctor."

Behind them, as they lug Sawyer to the brilliant lights at the tunnel's mouth, the pale immense sphere of the Soul Core hovers, patiently attuned to the clamor, the emotions, the restless dreams of a world warming to the sun of its second spring.